THE LAND SOUTH
OF THE CLOUDS

The Land South of the Clouds

of the Clouds

Genaro Kỳ Lý Smith

2016
University of Louisiana at Lafayette Press

ISBN 13 (paper): 978-1-935754-80-0

http://ulpress.org
University of Louisiana at Lafayette Press
P.O. Box 40831
Lafayette, LA 70504-0831

Printed on acid-free paper in Canada

Library of Congress Cataloging-in-Publication Data
Names: Smith, Genaro Kỳ Lý, 1968- author.
Title: The land south of the clouds / by Genaro Kỳ Lý Smith.
Description: Lafayette, LA : University of Louisiana at
Lafayette Press, 2016.
Identifiers: LCCN 2016014457 | ISBN 9781935754800 (paper :
alk. paper)
Classification: LCC PS3619.M5859 L37 2016 | DDC 813/.6--
dc23
LC record available at https://lccn.loc.gov/2016014457

For my mother Ngoc Thi Smith
and in memory of my grandfather Lý Loĉ

Asia Minor, Los Angeles,
June 1979

I am ten when Mother teaches me to lie. For the past couple of weeks, Mother told me to tell anyone who calls—except for Aunt Pham Thi and her family—that she doesn't live here anymore.

"You can even tell them I'm dead," she said one evening while I watched her pack pantaloons, Capri pants, and *áo dàis* she had not worn since the day she came to America. She went through and emptied dresser drawers and shoe boxes kept atop closet shelves for Polaroids of family picnics at Griffith Park, and jade figurines to fill the large black Samsonite suitcase she had lying open on the bed. Between the long-sleeved white gowns, she tucked away a bundle of her father's letters she had saved over the years, letters with blue stripes lining the edges, and stamps of tanks and the wavering red Communist flag still intact.

"Yes," she nodded as she closed the suitcase and snapped shut the locks. "Tell them I'm dead. Tell them anything you want to. Now," she set the Samsonite on the floor, "put this in your room. Somewhere where I can find it."

I haven't told anyone yet, but now that she is waiting out on the front patio for a taxi to take her to the airport, everything from car accidents to cancer to murder crosses my mind. From the front door, I practice the lies I will tell people while watching Mother as she stands between the potted *mai* trees; every inch of their branches is covered with tiny yellow-blossomed flowers. Beside her is the Samsonite with the red, white, and blue tag tied to the handle. She is on her way to the airport to board a plane for Vietnam, and all I can do is stand here. I can't even bring myself to wake up Dad, who'd probably stare at me through half-shut eyes, mumble something I can't understand, and throw the covers over his head because it is his only day off. Besides, I promised Mother I wouldn't say anything until after she leaves, or until Dad wakes up.

"She died of…cancer," I whisper, though I don't know what it means even after I had asked Mother a couple days ago. She told me it was something small and black and it lived inside of us and grew.

"And as it grows," she said, "it eats you up inside 'til there is nothing left of you."

The sun has already risen, and from our home atop a hill overlooking downtown Los Angeles, the black and silver skyscrapers look small. Mother turns her head to the side, and I get a glimpse of her profile before she faces downtown, which is barely aroused with traffic. Earlier I had tried calling her several times but she wouldn't answer me, or even tell me to go back inside. So I stare at her long black hair uncut since the day she was born. It hangs straight down her back just below the waist.

"She died in…a car accident," I say.

This time she doesn't turn her head. She remains still with arms crossed in front of her. Whatever excuse I practice doesn't fit, and whenever I come up with the truth I think for one moment that it sounds better. But what do I tell them when they ask why?

"She doesn't live here anymore," I say, and when I open my mouth to explain, nothing comes out.

Mother begins humming quietly to herself, and then stops. When she starts up again, she goes into a song she used to sing back home in Vinh-Long or Pleiku or Saigon or wherever Dad was stationed at the time. She stretches and turns words in her throat until she shapes the right sounds, then releases them. Her voice grows louder and I keep looking behind me for Dad. Still her voice rises, extending vowels into the next word so that I can't hear where one word ends and the other begins. Just to make sure Dad doesn't wake up, I go back inside the house, through the living room, and stand in the hallway. From the hallway I can still watch Mother while keeping an eye out for Dad. The door to the bedroom is partly opened, and Dad's snoring fills the room. Only when he breathes out in broken whistles can I hear Mother singing. I want to go back to the front door. Instead, I stay where I am between them, listening to their sounds and how they don't go together: one sound drowning out the other.

Mother sings louder and her body begins to sway from her efforts, so much so that she begins to bend her knees. When she straightens up, she has the suitcase in her hand but continues singing as she comes away from the patio and stands at the steps. I assume the taxi has just pulled up along the curb.

Mother steps down and nearly falls over from the weight of the suitcase. Before taking another step, she holds the handle with both hands and leans to one side for balance. Her thick-soled sandals and ankles disappear.

Then her knees and thighs and the suitcase, and from the waist up there is only her long hair. The way she leans to one side seems like she is fighting whatever is pulling her down. Her shoulders and head stay afloat for a moment before the right shoulder dips from view, and then she is gone.

I run to the front door and stop. I can't see the taxi down below because of the second level patios on both sides of the steps, only the rooftops of homes across the unseen street and downtown L.A. I do not even yell out good-bye. She never turned around to say anything. She keeps singing.

I turn to scream for Dad. But I promised her. Afraid to miss even the sound of her taxi leaving, I stay by the door and continue to ball up my pajama pants. And then I hear it. The taxi pulls away from the curb and halts at the corner stop sign before taking off down Montana Avenue, and I want to go after her. I think that if I am fast enough and rely on the hill to carry me down, I can catch her at the light. But I am afraid she may see me in the rearview mirror when she sits forward in her seat to talk to the driver. I am afraid of seeing the taxi pull farther way.

"She is dead," I say. "How?" *Something black ate her up from the inside.* "I don't know. She's dead."

Mother is on her way to the airport, and I wonder if I will ever hear from her. Or if Dad will go after her, but I doubt that he will ever speak her name again. I go back inside and walk through the living room until I am in the hallway. The door is still partially opened, and Dad's snoring sounds louder now that Mother is gone. I never doubted Mother when she said she was leaving, but I didn't think it would be this soon.

I walk down the hallway to the bedroom and look inside. Though the curtains are drawn, the room is still sunny, and Dad is underneath the white comforters, which rise and fall. His big black feet hang over the edge of the bed, and his legs are tangled up in the sheet. I open the door just a little and it creaks, and I am ready to jump back in case he wakes up. But his snoring hasn't changed and I stand there for a moment before poking my head inside.

"Dad?" I say. The comforters rise and fall. "Dad," I whisper harshly. "Dad," I say a little louder.

I open the door a little wider and step inside the bedroom to make my way to Dad. Before I am even there, someone from behind me says, "Get out of there Long-Vanh."

I jump and in turning around to look behind me, I hit the door with my arm. Mother is at the end of the hallway, suitcase in hands. She sets it down and says, "Come here."

I look at Dad beneath all the covers. I make my way down the hallway to Mother, and as she waits my ears burn, my legs become wobbly, and I can hardly breathe. I stand in front of her and she stares right at me, and I have to open my mouth to breathe. Her small lips are pressed together, and it doesn't seem like she is going to speak.

"I…uh," I say, pointing my thumb over my shoulder. "I, I."

Mother points a finger at me and says, "Don't tell your Dad." She punctuates each word with a jab of her finger.

"Yes. But, I—" I turn halfway around to face their bedroom with my thumb pointed.

"I mean *anyone*," she continues jabbing. "You hear me?"

I nod. She lowers her hand, taps the suitcase and says, "Now, keep this in your room. Somewhere where I can find it."

She straightens up, walks around me, heads to the bedroom and closes the door behind her.

Monday

"I thought I was back in Saigon," Uncle Ngô says as he brings one end of the bamboo shoot to his mouth and blows. A belch of whistles sounds from the holes he just finished drilling. He blows again getting cleaner whistles. Uncle Ngô takes the switchblade and begins to clear away the splinters from around the holes. "You sure you not hear singing yes-ter-day morning?"

He looks up at me, and there is a thin bone-white cut through the thick black hairs of his right brow.

"I didn't hear any singing," I say. "I was asleep."

I turn to look at the pile of bamboo shoots beside him and pretend I am interested. Their thickness is that of a man's thumb, but they are all different in length. They look like flutes and piccolos. When I notice he is still staring at me, I take up the shortest one and fit my fingers over the holes.

"I swear I hear singing in sleep," he insists. "You sure, Long-Vanh?"

I stare him in the eyes long enough to say, "I didn't hear a thing. I was asleep."

This is what Mother went through yesterday when she spoke to Dad. Luckily for her, Dad was busy all day studying accounting and going over notes. He just sat there with his long legs stretched underneath the dinner table, hunched over his work with a pencil in hand and a calculator that sputtered every time he punched in numbers. When he did ask her a question, Mother looked at him long enough to hear it, but before she answered him, she looked away.

The Samsonite is still in my closet. It is tucked among the boxed and broken toys and the clutter of tennis shoes. All day yesterday whenever Mother's eyes met mine, I expected her to bring it up. I wanted her to ask for it back, unpack her clothes, her father's letters, the Polaroids, and other contents. At times I wanted to remind her of the thing she told me to keep, but I was afraid she might go into my bedroom, grab the Samsonite, and leave whether or not Dad was awake.

But Mother went about the house sweeping and vacuuming floors and cooking meals. All day she looked out the living room window to check the sun's progress, and I knew what she wanted out of the day: to pass quickly so that Dad could go to sleep only to wake up Monday morning, because with school and work, with studying and sleeping, it meant none of us would hardly see him for the next six days.

I put the bamboo shoot back with the rest and sit on the ledge. Below, a mailman wearing one of those safari hats, only blue, and mirrored sunglasses, makes his way in our direction. He enters the Casa de Maria Apartments, stands in front of a row of mailboxes, and begins to sort through the letters, bills, and small packages. Over in downtown, the streets and freeways are packed with people driving to lunch.

"It sound like your mother. Then, it sound like somebo-dy not your mother."

"Who was the other person?" I ask.

"I not know who," he shakes his head. "The singing

sound real," he goes on. "I want to wake up, but I tell myself, 'No! Dream is good. Wake up and song will go away.'"

Uncle Ngô smiles up at me. He is sitting among the
basil and spearmint plants, tomato vines, stalks of lemon grass, and Serrano pepper bushes grown in coffee tins,
wooden troughs, plastic milk jugs, and two-liter Pepsi
bottles with the tops cut off. He returns to his work, and
only when he leans forward does the bone-white cut in
his right eyebrow disappear, and he is whole again. Aside
from the cut in his brow, there are no other scars. His
hands and arms are even absent of nicks and burns. The
only other blemish is the black grit underneath his fingernails he can't seem to wash clean after working ten-hour
days at the auto shop.

"Do you know the song?" I ask.

"Yes. I know song. Very old song."

Uncle Ngô sets the bamboo shoot along with the others and rests the switchblade on the ground. He rubs his
fingers together, blows on them, and then wipes his hands
on his jeans. He stands up and stretches his hands over his
head. Uncle Ngô unrolls the soft pack of Marlboro Reds
from the sleeve of his T-shirt, frees a cigarette with a quick
jerk of his wrist, places the cigarette between his lips, and
digs into his pocket for the Zippo, the one he brought over
from Vietnam. The one with the word *Cowboy* engraved
on one side, the *y* underlining the whole word in a looping
pattern like a rope. Uncle Ngô pockets the Zippo and joins
me at the ledge. He takes a drag and holds it for a while before he forces smoke between his teeth. When the smoke
rises and brushes his face, he squints.

"She sing about her father," he says. "She appear to

him in dream. She say she return to him. One day he wake up and she is there. She is not a dream. She is real."

I want Uncle Ngô to sing the song, or at least say the words so that I know what Mother has been singing about all these years. But he has said enough. The moment Uncle Ngô's eyes move, I know he isn't thinking about the song but mentally measuring Mother's makeshift garden, and how he will construct the bamboo shoots.

He is making a drip-irrigation system. Ever since the garden grew and Mother got a job at Hernandez's Sew Yourself making dresses alongside Aunt Pham Thi, Mother hasn't had time to tend to the garden, much less water it. She doesn't use a hose. She fills a bucket with water and scoops a handful for every vine, bush, sapling, stalk, shoot, and seed. With the drip-irrigation system, all she or anyone has to do is turn on the faucet.

"Will you get it done today?"

"I need to. I work at shop to-mor-row," he says.

The mailman leaves the entryway of the Casa de Maria Apartments and heads in our direction. He takes one of the many rubber bands from around his wrist, wraps a bundle of mail together, and deposits it into the neighbor's mailbox. He looks up and sees us sitting on the ledge before he slowly takes the stairs one at a time. I stand up to meet him at the top of the steps.

"How's it going?" I ask.

"Hot," he says and hands me the mail without stepping onto the walkway. He turns around, and before he walks back down he adjusts the bag over his shoulder for balance.

I sift through the mail: power bill, phone bill, coupons

for Ralph's Supermarket, a booklet advertising sale items at Thrifty's Drugstore, flyers for grand openings to Chinese and Mexican restaurants—EAT IN or TAKE OUT—and a letter with blue stripes bordering the edges.

Uncle Ngô squints at the letter. He brings his hand up and traces the thin scar with his finger. He keeps at it and after a while it seems he's trying to cover up the scar.

········

I know Mother will want to read the letter as soon as possible. So I head to Hernandez's Sew Yourself knowing that the possibility of her being there is slim since it is lunchtime, and the shop may be empty for the hour they are allowed. The sweatshop is located on Hoover Street, which means I have to walk down Montana Avenue and go by Aunt Pham Thi and Handsome Harlemite's apartment on Silver Lake Avenue, over the hill past rows and rows of houses owned by Japanese, Chinese, Koreans, and Vietnamese who turned their front lawns into vegetable and herb gardens and extended the eaves of the roofs to make their homes look like temples; past duplexes crammed with too many people, and finally leave our neighborhood of Asia Minor and enter an area called *La Olla*, Spanish for the stew.

When I get to Aunt Pham Thi and Handsome Harlemite's apartment, I walk upstairs and knock on the door. Phượng opens the door, chewing gum. I look past her and see no one sitting at the dinner table.

"They're not here," she says, and blows a pink bubble. When it pops she sucks it back inside her mouth and continues chewing.

"Are they having lunch at the shop?" I ask and realize if they're not here, it means they are having lunch at the shop.

"Yeah, I guess. Why are you looking for your mom?"

I show her the letter and make sure she can read the address: Vinh-Long, Vietnam. Phượng moves the gum around in her mouth. She takes her thick wavy hair in both hands, swirls it into a tight bun, and tucks in the tail end.

"Well, Mia isn't home. I might as well help you find her." Phượng reaches for the key hanging behind the door and locks it before pocketing the key.

We walk up the hill. Houses lean into the steep slope to stay upright, and when we come over the hill we immediately see Tú Đức bent double inside a trash can. Strewn all over the lawn are empty beer and soda bottles and cans. Resting on its kickstand is his bicycle with a bell and a steel basket fastened to the front of the handlebars. Tú Đức's hands come up, dumping cans and bottles on the ground.

"No wonder he smells like piss and shit," I say.

Phượng clucks her tongue, gives me a dirty look and says, "Dick."

We pick up our pace, nearly jogging, but Tú Đức straightens up.

"*Hiii*," he wails. His eyes widen for a brief moment before they begin to blink continuously. "Where you go?" he asks.

"I'm trying to find my mom," I say.

"Your mother, your mother, your mother—" he chants barely loud enough for us to hear.

His eyes blink faster, and Phượng has to look down

at the bottles and cans on the ground. Tú Đức's shirt is dirty with black and brown lines crisscrossing the areas beneath his arms and stomach. His hands are coated and sticky, the knuckles scraped, and the lines are black from sweet syrup. His gray slacks are spotted from shaking all the cans and bottles of leftover fluids. He is losing his hair at seventeen, but what's left is matted against his forehead. Lines of sweat have dried along his neck from hours in the sun, and dangling from a gold necklace is the laughing Buddha made of jade. It is not the whole Buddha, just his face, full and round. A piece has been chipped at the corner of his face so that it seems he is not laughing but screaming in pain.

"—your mother, your mother, your mother—" he keeps going, eyes blinking.

"Look, when you see her, Tú Đức, tell her I'm looking for her." I walk away.

"See her, who?" he says.

I don't bother to turn around. I keep walking.

"See her, who?" he begins to whine.

I keep walking, and from behind me I hear Phượng encouraging Tú Đức to pick up the bottles and cans. She catches up with me and I hear the *clink-clink-clank* of bottles and cans being tossed into the metal basket.

"God, he gets on my nerves," I say.

"You know he can't help it. You *know* he's retarded."

I remember I asked Uncle Ngô if Tú Đức would ever grow out of being retarded, like kids growing into their clothes, or losing the baby fat.

"Im-pos-si-ble. As im-pos-si-ble as man grow back leg or arm when blown off," he said.

We cross Hoover Street and enter Hernandez's Sew
Yourself. Two Mexican women are the only ones in the
shop; the humming from their machines barely makes
noise.

The older and biggest one looks up from her work and
says, "You mama not here. She go to lunch."

"Where'd she go?" I ask.

"She go home," she says, roughly sounding out the *h*.

I know she doesn't know what she's talking about, but
I don't say anything. I leave them to their work and go
outside with Phượng. We sit with our backs against the
wall. Hoover Street is filled with brown-skinned people;
they enter and exit the Mexican liquor store across the
street. Shoeless, unwashed, and shirtless children run into
the store and walk out licking lollipops, sucking on col-
orful Popsicles and drinking Coca-Colas. The streets and
sidewalks are growing heavier with traffic as people make
their way back to work.

I stare at the envelope, at each individual letter and
the accent marks each one has: curved tails hang off vowels and consonants, and straight, slanted, or roof-shaped
lines float over them. They look like they've been dressed
up, suited for the long journey halfway across the world.
I don't know how to read them. Mother never taught me
the language.

"The accent marks not only change the way a word
sounds," Phượng once explained, "but they also change a
word's meaning many times." I nodded my head like I understood perfectly well what she was saying.

I raise the letter up to the sun to see if I can read anything, maybe have Phượng translate what she can, but

though the sun shines brightly I can't see a thing. I give up trying and place the letter on my lap, and I think to myself, *Why bother?* In the next couple of days, maybe even later on today, I will know what is going on with my grandfather Lý Loĉ. Phượng will listen to Mother and Aunt Pham Thi talk about the letter over dinner or on their daily walks.

Whenever Mother receives a letter she'll leave it on the dinner table for days, sometimes weeks. Folded into three sections with the ends facing up, I've gone through her letters when Mother wasn't around. I've tried to find words that looked like the ones Phượng used when speaking of Lý Loĉ, but nothing ever came close in appearance to *captured, starved, beaten.*

Once I even tried reading the words without the accent marks, pretended they were not hanging off letters or over them in different angles, but it was no use. The sounds I came up with were just sounds. I couldn't say, "That sounds like *rain*." Or, "This sounds like *blood*."

Only when Mother returned to the letters on the dinner table did I sense some things were wrong. She'd whisper aloud when reading and I'd listen to the way the tone of her voice rose and fell, imagine her tongue stress over the accent marks as she spoke each word slowly. The emphasis on sound made her throat go so dry at times that she had to stop and swallow. She'd swallow again before continuing, but her voice would tremble, and I'd listen for the word that proved too much for her throat, the moment in which the next syllable suddenly dropped right out from under her or made her throat close up from straining to form the right sound. Sometimes when she read, she'd scratch the corner of her forehead and make her way down past her temple until she was at her throat. And sometimes she'd cry halfway through that she had to set aside the letter for a later time.

I never knew what she did with the letters until I watched her pack two nights ago.

"Long-Vanh," Phượng taps my leg. "Our mothers are coming."

Mother and Aunt Pham Thi are crossing Hoover Street while looking down at their feet, heads heavy from the weight of their conversation. They both have their hair in a bun. They've rolled up the bottom of their Jordache jeans to keep from stepping on the hem with their thick-soled sandals. Their T-shirts with the single breast pocket are untucked. They don't look up until Phượng and I stand on our feet. And when they do, Mother stops in the middle of the sidewalk and stares at the letter in my hand. People walk around her to get by.

Night: Lessons in Translation

The sun is setting behind the mountains, and the skyscrapers are rust-colored silhouettes. Uncle Ngô is out on the patio with fists on his hips and a cigarette between his lips as he surveys the bamboo shoots he finished whittling for the irrigation system he is building for Mother. Each time he changes his stance he deflects some of the glare off the living room window.

"Your grandfather is not doing well," Phượng says.

Phượng and I are up against the hallway wall, listening to our mothers talk about the letter in Vietnamese. Phượng translates.

"They think he has pneumonia again. Maybe," she adds. "He has fluids in his lungs. *That,* they know for sure."

Uncle Ngô changes his stance so that he leans heavily on one leg. His fists remain on his hips.

"Some of his ribs are broken. They're not...mending as well as they should." Phượng leans forward. "He doesn't know how much longer he can stand this. After four years he is not used to this life. How can he be? How can anyone? The uncertainty from one day to the next is enough to kill him."

Uncle Ngô takes a last drag off his cigarette before tossing it on the ground. He sits on the ledge and leans forward to rest his elbows and forearms on his knees.

"Is that all?" I whisper.

"*Shhh,*" Phượng brings a finger to her lips. Her shoulders drop, but the lines on her forehead deepen. Phượng leans forward a little more. Uncle Ngô stands up only to take up two bamboo shoots. "He wants to die." Phượng moves back. "He wants to go to sleep and never wake up."

For a long time Phượng leans forward, mouth open, ready to speak. Uncle Ngô joins the two bamboo shoots together, fitting them into a plastic elbow joint used for pipes. Because of the glare coming off the window, because he is screwing the pieces together, it looks like Uncle Ngô is attaching the bamboo to the end of his finger. Phượng's eyes widen all of a sudden.

From the kitchen we hear a chair scraping the floor. Phượng suddenly hisses, "*Oh shit!*" and slaps me on the arm as she runs past me and I run as quickly but as quietly as possible back to my room. I try to close the door, but the fear of taking too long to do so and having Mother open it into me makes me leave it ajar. I sit on the bed next to Phượng.

"*Shit, shit, shit,*" she mutters.

We watch the door and hear the sound of approaching footsteps. Mother sticks her head in, and Phượng sits up straight, hands in her lap. Mother opens the door all the way.

"What are you two doing?" she asks.

"Nothing," I say. "Waiting for dinner. Do you want us to help you?"

She shakes her head. Her eyes are moist, and rather than use her hand to wipe them dry, she blinks repeatedly. Her bottom lip trembles, and I expect her to say something, but she only manages to shake her head again before leaving.

Phượng and I watch Mother walk down the hallway

back to the kitchen.

"Lý Loc may not live," Phượng says. "Your grandfather is very sick."

"Anything else?"

Phượng turns to me, "Isn't that enough?"

I get up from off the bed and go to the closet. I open the door and look inside.

"What are you doing?" Phượng asks.

I don't answer her. The Samsonite is in the back of the small dark closet. I hold the door open wide enough to let in light. The suitcase stands among the tennis shoes, the Superman and Captain Marvel dolls with capes missing, and the board games with the corners of the lids taped several times. I keep my hand on the doorknob and just stare at what the suitcase holds. Tucked between my mother's long-sleeved gowns are her father's letters bound together by a rubber band. And I wonder if Mother will come into my room later on tonight and add today's letter to the bundle, or start another collection in her dresser drawer where she keeps her bras and panties.

Then there are the photographs in an envelope. They are pictures of a picnic we had at Griffith Park on Labor Day with Aunt Pham Thi, Uncle Handsome Harlemite, Mia, and Phượng. There is a picture Dad took of Mother and me. We were sitting at the picnic table fixing our burgers with ketchup and onions when Uncle Handsome Harlemite said something that made Dad take up the camera. He looked through the lens and turned it until he got it in focus and said, "Smile." Mother and I barely looked up in time before Dad pushed the button because we were still surprised not only by what Uncle Handsome Harlemite had said, but by the way he laughed afterwards.

Mother set her bun and bottle of ketchup on the bench. She moved closer to me, wrapped an arm around my shoulder, and drew me nearer. Dad snapped another picture. Her small, straight, white teeth showed when she smiled; my shirt wrinkled from her tight grasp. I stared straight ahead at the camera with shoulders hunched, eyebrows arched, mouth opened. I still held the bun in my hand. That was the last time Mother smiled.

I continue to stare at the suitcase. Although the red, white, and blue tag is still tied to the handle and hangs the way I remember it, a thought occurs to me. What if Mother came in here, switched all the contents of the suitcase into another one, and set this one here to make it seem like the idea of leaving hadn't crossed her mind? Maybe she decided she was going to do this the moment she saw me in her bedroom trying to wake up Dad.

I reach in and grab the handle and lift; its weight relieves me.

"What are you looking for?" Phượng asks.

I stoop down and rattle some of the board games and throw the dolls around before straightening up. I grab the doorknob and turn it a couple of times and without looking at her, say, "I don't know. I thought we could play a game or something after dinner." I close the door. "But I don't feel like playing."

••••••••

It's a routine I've learned ever since Mother first received news that Lý Lôc was placed in a reeducation camp. From the day she gets the letter it may take her a week to put it away in the drawer. But the day she receives it, she spends a part of the evening with Aunt Pham Thi. They immediately go on their evening walk, something they do after dinner. Their walks take them down the hill to Silver Lake Avenue toward *La Olla*, Spanish for The Stew, but once they get to Hoover Street, they turn around and head back, fearful of the men who linger in the doorways of pool halls and bars with bottles in their hands. Because of today's letter, Mother and Aunt Pham Thi won't be back for some time. Most likely they've just started walking the same route for the second time to exhaust the contents of the letter and what she will do.

When Mother gets back, she will turn on the television in the living room and watch *The Bob Newhart Show, The Jeffersons,* or *M*A*S*H*. She'll sit there, but as soon as the first commercial comes on, she'll get off the sofa, go to the dinner table, and unfold the letter, leaving me to watch TV alone. Tonight, none of the sitcoms are on because every station is covering the Iran Hostage Crisis, which has been going on for nearly two hundred days now. They show the same images every night: President Carter walking from the White House to the helicopter on the front lawn; newsmen in two-piece suits reporting the situation with blank expressions; and the hostages waving from windows. We never see their faces, only their hands, waving. The hostage situation is the same every night, and it doesn't matter how much they cover, how much footage they show, the stories are all the same—the Americans are hostages.

It's too depressing to stay up and listen to Mother change a word's pitch so that she gets a different meaning, and by doing so she gets a different story. Sometimes the stories don't make sense and she's stuck with the news she doesn't want: Lý Loc is not doing well. Lý Loc is sick. Lý Loc has been beaten. Again. His bones are not mending properly. So after Mother and Aunt Pham Thi head out for their evening walk, Phượng goes home, and Uncle Ngô is downstairs in his garage-bedroom to sleep so that he can rise for an early morning at the auto shop. I immediately go to my room and lie in bed without bothering to undress or even brush my teeth.

I just lie there with the lights off and watch the night get dark enough to where the moon shines through the only window in my room. But long before this happens, the geckos are already clinging to the window screen. They began coming after Mother built the garden. Uncle Ngô said they were our ancestors who came to protect us, and to make our lives in Los Angeles kind. They crowded my window because they recognized a room where nightmares visited often, so they were there to keep the bad dreams away. I didn't take after them with my tennis shoes whenever I saw them clinging to the stucco walls during the day, nor did I slap the window. Uncle Ngô had one in his room, a fat one that slept on his bed during the day. He claimed it was his father, who was a glutton, who drank too much, gambled, and slept with many, many women, and lost a good portion of his wealth because of this.

Tonight, there are about thirty of them waiting for mosquitoes and gnats to land. They move with such quickness that their darting motions startle me. I try not to blink as I wait for them to move, to hear the scratching sounds their tiny claws make against the screen when they rush to snatch up the insects that barely land. The geckos dart all at once, feeding off the screen. They go at it for quite some time, and then they stop all of a sudden because the window rattles from the front door being slammed shut. The geckos scramble and all I'm left with is the moonlight through the window and I know Mother has just come home.

She tosses a set of keys on the dinner table. In a moment, the television comes on, the knob clicks several times, and in between are voices and static, voices and static, until the click settles on a station and there is laughter. I listen to the laughter in the living room and know that as soon as it stops, and there is a moment of silence before voices and jingles, she will be at the dinner table, reading.

The geckos have come back. They crowd only the edges of the screen, and they don't dart around as much. A chair scrapes the floor, a long, drawn-out rising scratch. Even though the television is on, I can hear Mother reading aloud over the volume. Her language sounds like the language of birds: the constant chatter without any pauses; the repetition of sounds that change with every rise and fall of a syllable. The words she speaks are just sounds to me. Nothing comes close to "bones mending," "pneumonia," or "water in the lungs." The further along she reads, the lower her voice gets until she is whispering, and it sounds like prayer.

My closet door is closed. Mother hasn't mentioned the suitcase. She knows it's in there. That is where she found it Sunday morning when she came into my room. I was asleep when I heard the soft pacing of footsteps, the door creaking open on its hinges, the sound of something heavy being budged from its place, and the shortness of breath. That was when I woke up in time to see Mother closing the closet door. She turned and stared at me as if daring me to say something.

"I'm leaving now. If you're going to wake up your dad, at least wait until I am gone. You understand," she pointed at me.

It wasn't until I nodded that she let her hand drop. She took the Samsonite by the handle with both hands, lifted the suitcase, and walked out. I waited until I heard the front door open before I got out of bed. I went down the hallway and saw that their bedroom door wasn't closed all the way. I could hear Dad snoring; the noise filled the room and escaped and traveled down the hallway. Mother had left the front door open, and I assumed she had expected me to come and at least stand at the door. At least to watch her for the last time. At least that.

Now Mother has a reason to leave. What's to stop her now? I sit up in bed and listen. Mother's voice is rising again, and I get out of bed and head toward the closet. My heart beats in my throat and my ears grow hot. I open the door and see the suitcase. I tug the handle, but its weight only makes my heart beat faster, and I'm beginning to doubt myself. My ears are clogged up by my heart beating in my throat and I can't hear anything, not the television, not Mother's reading. I swallow but it gets worse. Now it feels like there is a heart thumping in each ear.

I grab the handle of the Samsonite with both hands, hoping this will stop my shaking, but it's no use. Without setting it down to rest my arms, I carry it across the bedroom, and as I make my way to the window, I watch the light underneath the door, watch for her shadow if she should come. However, the light seeping in from the living room isn't disturbed or broken.

We do not have a big backyard. It is more a side yard than anything, with a heavy growth of ivy. The neighbor's fence, which is about four feet from my window, is overgrown with ivy that comes down to cover the ground. When I raise the window, the geckos scurry off. The screen is held in place with a single hook to the windowsill, and when I undo it, the screen falls off and into the ivy. It stands up on its own for a moment before leaning against the wall. I reach down and bring the screen inside.

I squat down and take hold of the suitcase from the bottom and lift it onto the windowsill. The Samsonite slips out of my hands and falls onto the ground and I don't know whether it is because it's too dark or if the ivy is thicker than I thought, but I can't see the Samsonite. I turn and check the light underneath my door. Nothing.

Just to make sure, I lift myself up on the windowsill and sit there before jumping and landing on the ivy-covered ground. It takes me a while to find my footing because the ivy is so thick that I have a hard time feeling the ground. My feet keep slipping through the pockets of leaves and the vines tangle around my ankles every time I take a step. I find the suitcase, and just as I figured, it is above the ivy. At first I pull the vines over it, but they are too thick to stay in place. So I tear at the vines hanging off the fence to cover the Samsonite, feel each strand stretch and cut into my hands from pulling until they snap. I keep pulling and yanking at them, hear them break clean, and twice I am thrown against the wall when strands finally give. I pull and yank, stretch and tear until my fingers scrape the wooden fence. When I think I have enough, I throw everything into one big pile—a mound of vines covers the suitcase.

I have to hold onto the sill, hop up and down in one spot to lift myself up and climb back inside my bedroom. The light underneath the door is bright. I take up the screen, and this is more difficult than I imagined it would be. There isn't a hook for the top half. Instead the top half has to stay inside a metal slat, but as soon as I slip the top half into it, the screen stays snug long enough for me to set the hook in place. I reach up, take hold of the window, and shut it.

I'm still shaking. What if Mother comes in tonight to get it? What will I tell her? Lie and say Dad took it? Or tell her if she wants it she should climb out the window and dig it out from underneath the ivy?

I get back into bed. All I can hear is the sound of my own breathing, and it scares me because I believe Mother can hear me over her own voice and the television. My breathing settles. My fingers ache and my fingertips throb, and I realize they're filled with tiny splinters. Welts rise and take shape and harden the more I rub my fingers and hands. I watch the window, but it is bare of geckos. They'll come back, I tell myself. They'll come back and cover the window screen, and hide what I have done, but I am asleep before I can see them return.

The Bone Orchard

Lý Lôc is lying on a cot in only his pajama pants. His ribs arch like a bridge of rainbows and he cannot see over his chest and belly. He stares up at the ceiling made of palm fronds and every time he breathes, his body balloons and the skin around his ribs become taut like tents imprisoning wind. When he tries to move, the water sloshes against the wall of his skin, the cave of his cavity.

There are other patients in the bamboo hospital. The young man sitting cross-legged in a cot beside Lý Lôc has no arms.

"They won't grow," he says when he notices Lý Lôc staring at his shoulders clean of stumps. "I pray to Buddha, talk to the places where my arms should be, but they will not grow."

There are no walls in the hospital, so the patients stare out over the rice fields where people wearing torn black pajamas wade knee-high in water and stoop over to plant baby rice stalks. They plunge stalks into the muddy waters, twist roots into the soil. They travel in a straight line like cranes, standing up to move only to stoop over to plant. Soldiers wearing pith helmets watch over the workers. Their gun belts are slung over their shoulders as they cradle M16s. They smoke cigarettes, which remain the same in length. Crows and Magpies roam the fields, plucking seeds from the mud.

"They will grow. If you water them daily, they will grow," the man says.

Lý Lôc tucks his arm underneath his head as a pillow,

27

and his stomach jiggles; the water rushes from the pit of his stomach up to his chest and back down again. Just as the water in his body settles, soldiers surround him and point the barrel of their M16s at his head. Lý Loc turns to the man with no arms.

"If you water them daily, they will grow," he tells Lý Loc.

The soldiers yell at Lý Loc to stand up. They motion with their rifles, up, up. Lý Loc puts out his arms to grab a hold of something to help himself up, but there is nothing for him to grasp. He rolls out of his cot with knees bent and arms stretched in front of him so that he falls to the floor on all fours. The water in his body sloshes about, hitting ribs and lungs, and moving the heart.

Still, the soldiers surround him with weapons aimed, the barrels indicating up, up. They lead him outside, past the men and women bent over planting rice, past the mocking blackbirds. Lý Loc moves as fast as he can, shuffling his feet as he holds his belly in both hands. They trudge along the dikes separating the mature rice fields from the young shoots. They come over a mound and Lý Loc stops.

Uncle Ngô is moving from one bamboo shoot to the next, connecting the ends. He stands in a field of milk-white bones stacked in rows and rows. They stretch as far as the horizon. Crows clutch bones between their beaks, fly up high enough and let them drop and crack open upon rocks and other bones. They swoop down and peck at the marrow.

Uncle Ngô looks up from his work and shields his eyes from the sun with one hand. He continues connecting the ends of the bamboo shoots.

One soldier leans in and says to Lý Loc, "They will grow if you water on a daily basis. This you at least owe the communists, if not for Uncle Hồ."

Lý Lôc goes forward until he is before Uncle Ngô. Uncle Ngô takes up the last bamboo shoot and plugs it into Lý Lôc's navel.

"No good. Not work well," Uncle Ngô says.

He takes out his switchblade and whittles the end of the bamboo shoot so that it is pointed. He tries again, shoving the bamboo into Lý Lôc's navel. Uncle Ngô has to whittle the end, and he keeps whittling until bamboo shavings coat his boots. He plugs the shoot into Lý Lôc and there is a rumbling from within. The bamboo shoot trembles in Uncle Ngô's hands, and soon the others vibrate. Water sprouts from the holes Uncle Ngô bore into them. Thin streams of water arch and wet the rows of piled bones.

The soldiers watch in silence. The rumbling continues, and the bamboo shoots vibrate so much that Uncle Ngô tightens his hold. The violent trembling goes on, and Uncle Ngô's whole body shakes. Water gushes forth from Lý Lôc's navel, knocking Uncle Ngô to the ground. The soldiers rush forth and plug their hands over Lý Lôc's navel, but the force of the water bats their hands away.

Lý Lôc holds his belly; the swelling does not go down. Uncle Ngô crawls on hands and knees beneath inches of water as the fields flood and the rows of bones begin to stir. They uproot from the soil, and they float in place. The water floods the fields of bones, and soldiers watch the water washing clean the earth.

From the horizon, men and women wade through the fields, their faces shielded by the conal sun hats they wear. They weave through the watery graves in a crooked line. Each person throws out his arms, and fishing nets spin away *from them and sift the water like dust. The men and women pull in their nets; caught in the mesh are bones, hundreds of bones, thousands of bones. The boys and girls in tiny junks untangle the bones from the nets their parents hand them. The adults cast fresher nets. Lý Loĉ continues to gush. The soldiers lay down their weapons and slump to their knees and chant for things to grow, things that can fill their emptiness, fill what is missing and make them whole again. The fishermen and women drag in nets and bones, nothing but bones.*

Tuesday: Kill the Children

Mother has told me several times she will kill me herself one day. No kidding. And no one will ever ask where I am because people will understand. She tells me this from time to time, and I've kept this in mind ever since we came to America when I was five years old. She said that in America children got off easy. They cause harm to someone, they get a spanking. They lie and cheat, they get a spanking. They fail their classes and swear at their teachers, they get a spanking. They get caught fooling around, spanking.

"In Vietnam, we just kill the kids," she'd say while chopping up a catfish into sections, cutting clean the head from the body. "That way," she'd continue, "there is no room for argument, no time wasted in trying to discipline what cannot be straightened."

I'm surprised she didn't say it when she went in that first morning to get her packed suitcase out of my closet and warned me not to wake up Dad, or when she caught me in her bedroom trying to wake him up. This told me she didn't really mean it. But she used to tell me this often enough that I kept quiet at home. When she said this in front of Aunt Pham Thi, Uncle Ngô, Phượng, or Mia, they all had their heads down, and I believed Mother.

"And when we kill them," Mother would say some other time for no reason, "no one ever questions where they are, because they know."

I asked Phượng once whether or not this was true. She

didn't know.

"I don't think it's true," she said. "Besides, if it were, Mia'd be dead by now. Vietnam or America, Dad would have killed her."

To be safe, I keep to myself and never ask any questions or act out while I am with her, especially in public. Even though it is summer, I still have to wake up at 6:30 in the morning to go to Hernandez's Sew Yourself with Mother. The moment we step outside our home, that's when it begins; that's when I am careful of what I do. On our way down Montana Avenue, we pick up Aunt Pham Thi and the three of us walk through Asia Minor. On mornings such as this one, I feel like an adult because they all leave their houses at the same time to catch the early bus for downtown to work as cooks and busboys, baggers and stock clerks; for a dime extra they get transfers that take them into Chinatown where some work in Chinese, Korean, and Vietnamese restaurants, markets, and jewelry shops. Some wear sun hats; they are the gardeners who tend the lawns and pools of white people in the neighboring cities of Los Feliz and Hollywood.

I walk behind Mother and Aunt Pham Thi as they speak to each other in Vietnamese. I keep my head up like I understand what they're saying, but also to show everyone that I am the obedient son. But people don't take notice. They keep their eyes to themselves and they hold their tongues because they know what I am. And what I am is something small and black, one of several burdens in Mother's life. It's why Mother wants me to behave—because I am at a disadvantage, she once told me. So why ruin it even more for Mother, much less for myself?

"It gives them another reason to hate you. They point and say, 'typical.' And then they'll point at me with pity," she said.

So I behave and stay behind Mother and Aunt Pham Thi, and I don't say a word. This way, I figure I'm not something black like a cancer slowing Mother down, but a smudge she can't get rid of but at least live with.

Ahead, two Korean women walk toward us. Mother and Aunt Pham Thi look up in time, and Mother says, "Excuse me," before she and Aunt Pham Thi step onto the grass to let them pass. I do the same, and I watch my feet so as not to step in dog shit. The Korean women walk on by with their heads up, eyes straight ahead, and lips closed. Mother and Aunt Pham Thi walk a while on the grass before getting back onto the sidewalk. Every morning for the past two summers I've joined them for work, it has been the same. They step aside for the Korean women, and I've never once heard them say "thank you" or "hello." They just keep walking through us, but I keep quiet.

Mother and Aunt Pham Thi don't waste any time when they get to the shop. They pick up immediately where they left off yesterday. They always make sure their machines are threaded with a new spool, that the patterns to be sewn are not only cut and pinned, but stacked beside their machines. They have all of this done the day before, unlike the Mexican women who spend a good hour in the morning preparing their patterns before making one stitch. This always bothers José, the sweatshop owner. He'd stand outside his office and mutter curses in Spanish before going back inside his office.

Mother and Aunt Pham Thi sit forward in their seats

and watch the fabric they feed through the rapidly pounding needle. It has been an hour since we arrived and already the sweatshop is whirring with the constant motion
of needles stitching patterns. Mother and Aunt Pham Thi
are up front, closest to the door where the two best Singers
are while the Mexican women all take up the back end of
the shop. They fill the small place with fast-spoken Spanish, and their constant laughter is thick and heavy. Some
of their children are sitting at the women's feet playing
with dolls and Mattel cars and trucks. Mother can't stand
the children. The noise level around noon is unbearable
at times, and Mother and Aunt Pham Thi have to hum to
tune them out. It's not so bad now; the children are still
woozy from sleep, and I sit by the front door where I read
books to stay out of Mother's way. Dad always has me
reading books during the summer. Told me once that just
because school is out doesn't mean I stop learning.

Because I don't have a watch, I've learned to tell time
by the telephone pole's shadow: 9:00 a.m. When the shadow sweeps out over the street and falls across José's blue
Mustang, cutting it in two, I know it is noon and it is time
for lunch back at Aunt Pham Thi's apartment where I'll
stay for the rest of the day with Phượng.

I am reading when someone's shadow darkens the
page. I look up and it is Aunt Pham Thi drinking a Coke.
Her hair is pulled back into a bun and her skin gleams
from perspiration.

"Ten o'clock and already I tired from work," she says
staring out across the street and squinting from the sun.

The Mexican children who run around in front of the
liquor store wear the same clothes. They chase each other

with sticks around scraggly guava trees and parked cars.

"You're tired because you walked for a long time last night," I say.

Aunt Pham Thi shakes the can of Coke and I can hear what's left of it splash against the sides. She tilts her head back and sucks. She taps the lip of the can against her teeth to shake out the remaining drops.

"Is Mother OK?" I ask.

"What are you reading?" she asks.

"*The Invisible Man.*"

"Why don't you watch movie?" she smiles. "It come on late night."

"I did. That's why Dad is making me read it."

"It's like the film?"

"Yes."

"Really?" Aunt Pham Thi straightens up as she lowers the empty can at her side. "What part you on?"

"Right now the invisible man is angry because it's getting old: the whole trick of appearing and disappearing, and having fun by scaring people. Now he wants to be seen again, especially by the woman he loves. He doesn't want her to forget what he looks like, afraid she won't love him anymore."

Aunt Pham Thi's smile closes until her lips are together. She stares at the can in her hand and begins to flex her fingers; the aluminum crinkles.

"Keep reading. We be home soon for lunch."

She goes back inside and sits at her Singer. Mother finishes a knee-length green dress with a simple belt cut from the same cloth. She fits the shoulders around the plastic curves of the hanger so that the dress falls right. After that she stoops down and inserts a blue safety pin at the bottom of the dress. Each woman has a different colored marker. It is José's way of knowing how many dresses each woman made in order to pay them. Ten o'clock and there are three yellows, three blues. Aunt Pham Thi is yellow.

Còn Lại

Phượng has lunch made by the time the three of us leave the shop and come home. The hour Mother and Aunt Pham Thi have for lunch goes slow because no one says a word. We just keep our heads down and eat, knowing Mother is thinking about the letter. During the whole hour I expect Mother to stare off at some corner of the room like she did last night during dinner when her attention went to the letter left on the counter. The flap to the envelope was untucked, and we knew she wanted to get up from the table and reread the letter. At least she is eating more than last night.

There is only the sound of the electric fan set on ME-DIUM. It sits on the counter turning its head from side to side. Aside from that and the sound of our chopsticks hitting the sides and bottoms of the bowls, there is the traffic down below.

Mother and Aunt Pham Thi return to work, and Phượng and I are trying to take our naps in the back bedroom on the twin bed, the only bed in the apartment. No one uses this bed at night. Her family sleeps on the living room floor in descending order from father to the youngest daughter. The only time this bed is ever used is for us to take naps, or when Uncle Handsome Harlemite and Aunt Pham Thi have sex late at night. I've spent the night many times, slept on the living room floor next to Phượng, and we would be awakened by drawn-out grunts and moans like two people struggling. Phượng and I would lie there

37

facing the hallway that leads to the back bedroom, and
listen.

Traffic is gone. Everyone has driven back to work, but
Phượng and I can't sleep. There is always too much sunlight even with the curtains closed. So we lie there with our
shoulders and arms touching as we stare up at the ceiling.

"She was normal today," I say.

Phượng says *um-hm* and keeps her eyes focused on
the ceiling and I know she doesn't want to look at me,
afraid I'd ask her to come to our house to translate the
letter. And always I've had to beg her, and she'd give in. But
I already know all there is to know. And besides, Mother
will have to find the buried suitcase out back if she plans
on leaving.

When I awoke this morning to get ready to join Mother for work, I noticed the window was bare of geckos.
There are usually a couple of them most mornings, but
today they never came back, and I remember the dream
I had of Lý Loâc. They always come every time a letter arrives. The first time I had one I told Mother. I thought she
would smile and hug me, encourage me to have more, and
even sit down with me while I tell them to her. I thought
that she'd see that I was, after all, a part of her and what she
had left behind, that I, too, am an extension of Lý Loâc, of
our country, though I am only half.

But she only stopped scrubbing the skillet with the
Brillo pad and looked at me.

"Don't dream about him," she said. "You were too
young to remember him. So don't dream about him. You
hear me?"

I actually answered OK, as if it were possible to control

what I dreamed. She continued scrubbing the skillet with fast, rough motions until black flecks fell into the sudsy dishwater. But I wanted to tell her that in some dreams he was doing well. He was fully clothed and his feet were never bare, his broken bones mended themselves, and blood flowed within rather than without.

"So what do you want to do today?" I ask.

Before Phượng can say anything, we hear the front door open and close. Whispered voices fill the living room, and then *shush*. Footsteps make their way to the back bedroom, and it's Mia. She leans against the doorway with arms crossed just below her breasts. She places one leg behind the other. The navy blue T-shirt she wears is so tight I can see the outline of her bra. I stare at her white legs, from the ankles to the muscular, round calves, the smoothness of her thighs up to where they disappear into her cut off, white shorts. Her hair is long like Mother's, and out of everyone in the family, she is the palest.

"Are you two love birds done taking a nap?" she asks.

Phượng props herself up on her elbows and asks, "Why? Do you and Kenneth want to screw?" she giggles.

"*José!*" she says harshly and looks behind her. "And what business is it of yours what we do?"

"You're only fourteen. And dad is going to kill you if he finds out. He'll kill you, then kick your ass," Phượng laughs.

"Dad won't find out." Mia leans forward. "Now are you done taking a nap?" She stands up straight with fists on her hips.

"No. Why don't you and . . . *José* go to the laundry room? Take him where you took *Kenneth*. Besides, Long-

Vanh and I want to do it."

"Huh?" I snap my head at Phượng.

Mia throws her head back and laughs. "Long-Vanh wouldn't know what to do with his little prick," she says.

"It's not little," I stammer. "You want to see?"

"You little shit. Both of you can go to hell."

Mia leaves and we hear her whisper to José. Soon, the front door opens, and she slams it so hard that the curtains move. Phượng falls back on the bed and laughs. When the laughter settles I ask, "So what do you want to do?"

·········

Phượng attends Hoover Street Elementary School in *La Olla*. Across the street is the park with only two baseball fields, a playground with swings, slides and seesaws, and an indoor basketball court. When Phượng and I round the corner, we immediately see a group of older kids we don't like and stop. China Dog is in the parking lot sitting on the hood of his Mustang. He's surrounded by his friends and his little brother Fat Chan, a boy who's thirteen and was in my fifth grade class. A boy who gives me and Phượng trouble because we're *còn lại*, half-breeds.

"What do you want to do?" Phượng asks.

"Go to the gym. Come on."

We cross the street and steer clear of the parking lot. As we make our way past the playground filled with mothers watching over their kids sliding down the metal chutes or pushing their children on swings from behind, I turn my head in China Dog's direction and catch Fat Chan smiling at me.

I grow weak all of a sudden and my legs stiffen with

each step. We go inside the gym and there are older boys playing five-on-five basketball, most of them blacks and Mexicans, and I know we're safe in here in case Fat Chan decides to come and bother us. In here, he can't call me a yellow nigger, not unless he wants half the people in the gym beating the crap out of him.

The players hustle back and forth; their high-top Converse tennis shoes squeak when they drive down the lane, post up, or set picks. It's shirts versus skins, and those without shirts are wet with sweat. The waistbands of their shorts and sweat pants are soaked. We walk along the edge of the court, past the stage where the gym manager on duty is a tall boy with a whistle dangling from his neck. He sits on the stage with some girl in shorts and a terry cloth halter-top leaning against him and between his legs. Her arms hook his legs; her hands cup his hairy calves.

Phượng and I sit on the bleachers close to a group of black girls who sit forward watching their boyfriends play. No sooner do we sit, than Fat Chan enters with another boy. It isn't China Dog, but it's someone older, maybe fifteen or sixteen. They linger at the doors. There are the other double doors at the opposite end, but they are closed. No one can enter from the outside, and I wonder if China Dog and his friends are waiting on the other side for us.

"Damn," I whisper. "Why didn't we just turn back?"

"Because they'd follow us," Phượng says.

She's thinking about the last school term when she walked home one day. Fat Chan saw her walking by his house and he stayed right behind her calling her gook, yellow nigger, half-breed, and anything else he could think of. And as he ran off each name, he laughed in a way that added weight to his words: head back, eyes shut tight, mouth opened wide to allow the laugh to carry. He snorted when his laughter faded, and the rolls of fat bounced underneath his tight fitting shirt. She told him to leave her alone, but this only made him shove her from behind. He didn't hit her, but she started to cry, and she was embarrassed. She told me she had rather been hit. That way it would have been understandable that she cried. The crying started not when he shoved her, but when he called her a *còn lại*, a half-breed, and the shove was the exclamation point. To Phượng and me, the word had always sounded like what it is: a lie, a con. Like our existence isn't really true because we are half of one thing and half of another, but never whole. And because we are never whole, it is a con, a way of tricking people into thinking we are something complete. Mother once told me that in Vietnam, half-breeds are considered nothing.

Aside from Phượng, Fat Chan had bothered me in class the last school term. He sat two seats behind me, and he'd spit spitballs into my afro or lean forward to mark up my shirt with a marker. In the afternoons when Mother picked me up from school, I had to walk beside her or slightly behind so she didn't question who had made those marks. I never told the teacher or turned around in my seat to tell him to stop for a couple of reasons: he was bigger than me, and I was afraid if the teacher made him sit in the corner or send him to the principal's office, then I'd get it. Not from him necessarily, but most likely from his older brother China Dog, who'd been expelled from several high schools for fighting. Once, he even slapped his teacher. I heard she was about thirty-five or -six.

Everyone in the neighborhood knows their parents can't control them. They barely speak English. People say they've seen China Dog and Fat Chan yell back at them, yell with such anger that the elders who went on their evening walks slowed down to watch the parents shrink and lean away from the words that spat from the sons' mouths.

Some say they do not respect their father in particular because he was a South Vietnamese Army officer. Because the South Vietnamese Army could not defeat the communists, this embarrassed Fat Chan and China Dog. They were the product of their father's failure, of his fall from grace, and living in the U.S. was disgraceful, for they, too, could not defeat the communists. They turned tail and ran was what the sons have said. At least that's what I've heard. I've also heard that one day the boys plan to save grace, and everyone will know what they did. One day.

"We'll just stay here for a while," Phượng says.

I nod my head, and together we watch the game. The players pound the hardwood floor, bringing all their weight down so that their steps echo inside the gym. And as they take positions, they swing their elbows high and catch opponents on the chests and arms, or they brace their opponents' backs with forearms. At times, we glance at the door. Fat Chan and the other boy are still standing there, smiling. At this moment I wish Uncle Ngô were here. I wish we had turned back when we came around the corner and saw them in the parking lot.

When the players run to the end of the court nearest the open doors, this gives me the chance to watch Fat Chan through the constant ball passing and hands waving, and he's staring right at me. Fat Chan rubs the backs of his shapeless knuckles before shaking his hands and wiggling each thick finger. He does all of this while grinning. I think he knows that I was the one who got him suspended with only a week left of school. I wrote a letter to Miss Rice and left it on her desk during recess: *Chan was the one who wrote on your board.* I didn't sign it.

Miss Rice had a tendency to accuse without questioning. She went and stood over Fat Chan.

"Cross-eyed nigger am I?" she said.

She grabbed him by the arm and yanked him out of his chair. For someone who was shorter and weighed less, she managed to pull Fat Chan to his feet and drag him down the aisle. She walked so fast that Fat Chan kept stumbling, and as they passed me, he looked back. But I kept my head down, and that was my mistake. Everyone looked but me. He had been suspended the final week of school, and every day when I left class I stood by the building and scanned the playground and the streets beyond the chain-linked fence for any sign of him. But he never waited at some street corner or behind the bushes and trees or on the playground for me.

Fat Chan and the other boy leave the gym, and that makes me just as nervous.

"Fat asshole is still outside," Phượng says. "We'll wait. We'll wait for a long time."

········

The number of people thinned as the hours passed. The guys are still pushing up and down the court with the same level of energy as before. In the past two hours we saw Fat Chan only once. He stuck his head in, then left.

The manager on duty checks his watch, reaches for the whistle and blows.

"Five more minutes," he yells.

The girl, who has been leaning between his legs all this time, puts her head far back until the skin stretches so tight around her throat that I can see the bones of her neck. She puckers her lips and the park manager kisses her.

"We leave with everyone else."

"OK," Phượng agrees.

When five minutes are up the manager blows the whistle and yells, "OK. Time's up."

The girl comes away from between the boy's legs and scoots over to allow him to jump down from the stage. The basketball players shake and slap each other's hands as they make their way to us where they sit on the bottom row and towel themselves off from all the sweat, uncap bottles of fruit punch and sodas and take deep gulps. After replacing the caps, they throw their wet shirts and towels into nylon duffel bags and put on clean dry ones.

As they make their way across the court, Phượng and I step down from the bleachers and follow them. We get outside and we are close behind them as most head to their cars and bicycles.

Phượng looks around. There are only empty baseball fields, the tall eucalyptus trees in the far end hiding the freeway and the sound of traffic, and the playground filled with children and their mothers.

"I don't see him," Phượng says.

We continue to follow the players to the parking lot. Some get into cars while others walk across the street. We maintain a good distance behind them, but it only lasts a block. They head for the tunnel, which takes them underneath the freeway, and Phượng and I are alone. We look about us and we feel exposed among the houses with neatly mown lawns, the near-empty streets of parked cars, the trash cans set by the curbs for pickup, a different smell of *La Olla* rich with fried marinated beef and chicken, tortillas warmed over stoves, and beans boiled to a mush.

We keep walking, making sure to look behind us every so often. But there is no one. When we round the corner, we both sigh. Tú Đức is bent over on a narrow strip of grass near the curb, picking up bottles and cans he found in the trashcan and throwing them inside a plastic bag. He's wearing the same pants he had on yesterday, and I can't tell if they've gotten dirtier since then. His bicycle is in the middle of the sidewalk. He straightens up when he sees us coming.

"Hiii," he sings. "Where you go?"

"We're going home," Phượng answers him before looking away.

Tú Đức's eyes blink repeatedly. "I collect cans and bottles."

"Yeah, we know."

Tú Đức has done this for so long that he knows what days to enter a neighborhood. Our trash pick up is on Mondays, *La Olla*'s on Tuesdays, and Los Feliz's on Wednesdays. His older sister, Yên, has told us that Tú Đức has even gone as far as Baldwin Park on Thursdays, a good ten miles one way. But he knows where all the recycling centers are, so he unloads and collects his money before moving on.

"You want to walk home with us?" I ask.

"No." His eyes stop blinking all of a sudden as he flinches. Just before speaking, his eyes continue to blink. "No. I collect cans and bottles. I buy radio. See," he points at his bike. "I collect cans and bottles and buy bike. *Three* months," he holds up two fingers. The third is halfway up. "Three months I walk. Now," he smiles, showing all of his green teeth, "I ride and collect cans and bottles."

Phượng still looks up and down the street for any sign of Fat Chan. She shuffles from one foot to the other as she clenches her fists. Tú Đức bends over and continues picking up the cans and bottles from off the lawn. He shakes some of them and liquid splatters against his pant legs. The laughing Buddha he wears dangles and taps against his chin as he moves about the lawn.

"OK Tú Đức. We're going to go."

He stands halfway up, hand ready to pick up a Coke can.

"Where you go?"

"Home, Tú Đức. We're going home, remember?"

"Oh." He stays stooped over blinking up at us. He looks past us and sings, "Heeyyy. Chan. Look, Chan." He points.

We look behind us and take off running. I glance over my shoulder to see Fat Chan running: his eyes are nearly shut as he concentrates on pumping his arms and kicking his knees so high that it makes his stomach bounce around. Tú Đức shouts, "Where you go? Where you go?"

We keep running. When we get to the corner Phượng runs on, but I stop and turn around. Fat Chan finally reaches Tú Đức. I become still the moment Fat Chan grabs hold of the handlebars and starts running with the bike. He runs past Tú Đức, and for a brief moment Tú Đức watches Fat Chan trying to straddle the bike but doing a poor job of it. Tú Đức lets go of the plastic bag and runs after Fat Chan. He catches him by the shirttail and takes a hold of his arm so that the bike wobbles. Fat Chan puts his feet down to steady himself but he falls. When he gets up, he swings at Tú Đức and catches him on the right eye.

Tú Đức covers his eye as he spins around and stays bent over, and Fat Chan jumps Tú Đức from behind and they fall on the lawn. When he has Tú Đức pinned beneath him, he begins pounding on his head and chest. Tú Đức squirms as he tries to cover himself with one hand and waves up at Fat Chan with the other in hopes of blocking the blows. But they keep coming.

"Long-Vanh, come on."

Phượng stands at the far corner. Behind her is Hoover Street; cars pass back and forth. I turn back to Fat Chan and Tú Đức on the grass.

"Hey fatso," I yell. "Fatso," I yell louder.

He looks in my direction.

I start to walk in their direction and yell, "Get off him you fat fuck. Get off him you fat sonofabitch."

The moment he stands up, I stop, and as soon as he picks up the bike, straddles it and begins pedaling, I turn and run. As I turn the corner, I catch sight of Phượng making her way to the sweatshop on Hoover Street, so I run faster. I take one last look behind me and Fat Chan just gets to the corner where I stood watching him beat up on Tú Đức. I run down Hoover Street and jog into the shop where Phượng is waiting.

"Where you two come from?" Aunt Pham Thi asks. "And why you breathe so heavy?"

"We just came from the park," Phượng says in between breaths. "You lose," she says to me and manages a shaky giggle.

"What?" Mother asks as she turns the wheel to lift up the needle from the dress.

"I bet Long-Vanh I can beat him in a running race," Phượng explains. "From the park all the way here."

I sit on one of the chairs in the corner where they keep all the unused fabric in one big bin. My legs ache and begin to stiffen. I let my arms dangle at my sides to loosen them so they'll stop shaking. My heart thumps in my throat and I can hardly hear the hum of machines.

Phượng and I stare at one another, and we both know not to mention to Mother what just happened. Even though we did nothing to cause trouble, that is not the way our mothers see it. They believe if one behaves, then trouble should not come. If it does, then we did something wrong to bring it upon ourselves.

"Long-Vanh," Aunt Pham Thi says. "Beaten by a girl." She laughs. "Shame on you. What kind of a man are you?"

Wednesday

We don't talk about what happened yesterday. Today after we took our sleepless nap, Phượng and I decide to stay home and watch television. Just like yesterday, Mia comes home with José. The moment she walks in she acts surprised to find us home. She stops from walking in any further as though making up her mind whether or not to come in. But José makes that decision for her by closing the door behind him.

"You must be José." Phượng grins.

José jerks his head, pointing with his chin in a way that means "hello" and "yes" at the same time. One of his arms is covered with a tattoo of a woman in a long flowing dress. Her feet are bare, a part of her shoulder is exposed, and strands of her hair, though kept in a bun, whips in the wind as does her dress. I don't know exactly who she is. It could be Mary or some other woman from the Bible I'm not familiar with, or some made up goddess. It could be his mother for all I know, or his last girlfriend.

"Mia talks about you quite a bit," Phượng goes on.

Mia glares at Phượng. José doesn't say a word. He only leans back, setting the long silver chain dangling from his pocket to sway. The way he stands, the way his hair is greased back makes it seem like there is wind in the living room.

"José and I want to be alone," Mia says leaning forward.

"You don't need the whole apartment. All you need is

51

the bedroom."

One corner of José's lips perks up into a smile as he nods his head slowly.

"We're watching *All My Children*," I say. "You won't be disturbing us."

Mia narrows her eyes and shakes her head before uncrossing her arms, and I can barely see her nipples beneath the white shirt she wears without a bra. She stomps off to the bedroom. José follows her, walking with what looks like a limp. Every guy I've seen Mia with were boys Uncle Handsome Harlemite disliked, and not for the only reason that they are all older—though it is the only reason he shouts at her—but that they don't act responsibly or they aren't acceptable because of their appearances. Most of them don't have jobs, they're in a gang, they drink beer, they don't say "hello," "good afternoon," "good evening," or even "good-bye, it was nice to meet you."

To Uncle Handsome Harlemite, no one is good enough for his daughters no matter the boy's race. This became clear one day when all of us went to Griffith Park for a picnic last year on Labor Day. Uncle Handsome Harlemite served burgers straight from the grill. Dad put a new roll of film in the camera and wound it. Mia was moody as always because she couldn't bring Jim, her boyfriend at the time. Uncle Handsome Harlemite had it out with her earlier that day just before we went by the apartment to follow them to the park. And when he called her over to get her burger, she got up and walked over and held out her plate, buns opened to receive the charred patty. She returned to the bench without saying thank you.

Rather than yell at her, Uncle Handsome Harlemite

teased her about the boys she liked. Said they were ugly, and what made them so were their lack of manners. And if they couldn't respect the girl's parents, then they would never be allowed past the front door. He kept laughing at the idea: opening the door only to slam it in their faces upon seeing them dressed in tank tops, and jeans or khakis two sizes too big.

"What about me and Long-Vanh? You wouldn't mind us getting married would you, Dad?" Phượng smiled.

Uncle Handsome Harlemite chuckled. "No, no. We've got enough mixed nuts. Don't need to breed pistachios with cashews."

I had just lifted my bun to pour ketchup on my patty when I froze and thought, *What had I done to be compared to Mia's boyfriends?* That was when Dad said, "Smile," and Mother put her arm around me. She gripped my shoulder as if to say, *You've done nothing wrong.*

When Dad lowered the camera, I saw the look on his face. He tucked in his lips and I knew he was biting his bottom lip, knew he wanted to speak. But the only thing he could do was take pictures. So he stayed behind the camera, made sure his large hands hid most of his face. I knew Phượng was embarrassed by what her father had said. She ate her hamburger in silence and never looked up from her paper plate. Dad took his seat across from me at the bench and began putting together his burger. Mother took my plate.

"Here," she said, and began fixing my burger with onions, pickles, and lettuce. She even filled my Dixie cup with ice and poured Coke. Halfway through the meal she asked me how was my burger. Uncle Handsome Harlemite

ate and talked and laughed, about what I don't remember,
but it wasn't about Mia and her choice of boys or half-
breeds.

Phượng gets up from off the couch, walks over to the
television, and turns up the volume. "Come on," she whispers.

We make our way down the hallway on tiptoes so the
floor doesn't creak. Before we even get to the door, we can
hear smacking, the rustling of sheets, heavy breathing,
and the bed moaning from their movements.

Phượng takes a hold of the knob and turns it all the
way before pushing the door open just a crack. She peaks
in and I have to go down on my knees to look. They are
both dressed, and I can see Mia underneath José. All I can
see of her is her face, her lips mashed against José's, her
long black hair covering the pillows, and her pale white
legs bent at the knees. José has one hand underneath Mia's
shirt, and my heart beats faster until I am near deaf and I
have to open my mouth to breathe. Phượng shifts her feet,
tapping me in the back.

José massages Mia's breast and he pinches the nipple
and makes Mia fight for air. And I wish he'd move his hand
away for a moment so I can see her whole breast, see how
big they really are, see the roundness of her nipples and
how much they perk up. But his hand is large, and the
shirt is not pulled up all the way.

Then he does something which makes me suck in air,
and I think I made a sound because Phượng taps me twice
on the back with her knee. José pulls away long enough
to lift Mia's shirt, exposing one breast. Without hesitat-
ing, he kisses her nipple, then licks it with only the tip of

his tongue. He circles her nipple and Mia arches her back
and moans; her head buries deeper into the pillows with
eyes shut tight. And she rubs her legs against his, and I
see the muscles in her thigh tighten and loosen. José licks
hungrily, then locks his mouth around her whole breast.
He sucks and sucks until I think he's going to swallow her
whole. Phượng grabs the knob and closes the door shut.
She begins walking back into the living room and I get up
off my knees and follow her, and I want to ask her if she
wanted to try something like that.

But I am reminded of the picnic, and how we avoid-
ed each other's eyes like we're doing now as we watch *All
My Children*, and even during the commercials. After the
picnic that day we packed everything and headed for the
car. Aunt Pham Thi's family had already left because Uncle
Handsome Harlemite had to work soon. We loaded the ice
chest, blankets, and brown bag filled with chips and nap-
kins, paper plates, and brownies into the trunk and Dad
handed Mother the keys.

"What are you doing?" she asked.

"Just around the parking lot Vu-An. Just drive around
the parking lot. Get in Long-Vanh," Dad told me. "Get in,"
he said again when he saw me standing there looking at
the car.

I got in and Dad sat in the passenger seat. Mother
stared at the keys in her hand.

"Right there," he pointed at the ignition, and Mother
had to lean down to where it looked as though she were
putting her eye near a peephole. Dad talked her through
it, told her how the car operated, what each letter meant,
and how if she were going forward the shift should always

be on "D." And since she had never driven a car before, he said it was best never to be put in a situation where she would have to reverse. He said that reverse was hard for those who didn't know how to drive because they were always afraid of what was behind them.

She sat forward in her seat, staring at the Firebird's hood to see where it ended. Finally, she shifted the gear to "D" and pressed the gas all the way down and all of us slammed back into our seats. She immediately stepped on the brakes, throwing us forward.

"Put your seat belt on son," Dad said. "It'll keep you alive." We all laughed. "Slowly," he said. "Very slowly."

The car lurched forward, but she kept from stepping on the brakes. She drove straight across the lot, heading for the concrete slats smeared with black streaks.

"You can steer, you know. Turn."

Mother turned the wheel, and she kept it turned. We drove in a big, slow circle in the empty parking lot. She pressed a little harder on the gas, and still we moved in a circle. Dad started laughing at Mother who was hunched over the wheel, staring at the front end of the car.

"Stop laughing at me Wil. You make me nervous," she stammered, but the stuttering turned into giggles. They laughed as we circled the parking lot. Mother drove us in loose circles, following the front end of the car, laughing and circling until she stopped from dizziness. Still she laughed as she held her head in her hands, laughed until it hurt.

········

At home, just before the sun went down, I went outside after noticing the wide open front door and found Dad sitting in one of the wicker chairs smoking a cigarette. He stared at the sun setting over Downtown L.A. He caught sight of me from the corner of his eyes and told me to sit by him.

Even after I took my seat he remained quiet. He just kept smoking and staring at the sun and I just watched the tall avocado, banana, and mango trees towering over the houses across the street. The trees were abundant with underdeveloped fruits grown too late in the season to harvest. They would only purple and blacken before reaching their full size and color and rot on the limbs.

Dad leaned forward in his chair to snuff out the cigarette in the ashtray on the ground.

"Sometimes Harlemite says things and never thinks about who's around. You're going to hear a lot of that, and not just from him. The thing is: how are you going to handle it?—what are you going to do or say in return? That is the problem—what do you do in return?"

Dad sat back and wedged his fingers inside the soft pack for another cigarette. I waited for him to speak again, but he only lit the cigarette and smoked and we sat there until it was nearly dark and he went inside. I guess I was waiting for him to tell the story I've only heard once, of how Lý Lôc didn't accept Dad. Lý Lôc even went so far as to disown Mother as his daughter when she married Dad. I guess I wanted to hear his side, about what it was like to have the door slammed in his face, and why, even after that, he continued to meet Mother in secret at the marketplaces or in some restaurant before they got married.

That night while watching the geckos feed off the win-

dow screen for bugs, I heard Dad singing Smokey Robinson and the Miracles' "Ooh Baby Baby." Mother said he
used to sing Smokey Robinson songs to her when they
were dating in Vietnam. He even sounded like Smokey, a
voice so thin and soft that I expected it to crack, to give out
in the middle of a word.

Thursday

Depending on what day it is, and the classes they are taking, and whether or not they are both in the same classes; or if the schedule at Forest Lawn Mortuary changed all of a sudden because the new man got spooked when patrolling the graveyards at night, and Uncle Handsome Harlemite has to pull a double shift making sure no teenagers do anything to the tombstones; or a test is coming up and Dad wants to stay at school and study because he sees no point in going home for several hours knowing he'll have to be back for work, and then classes soon after his shift is over; or that it has been several days since Uncle Handsome Harlemite last slept with his wife, and rather than get the few hours of needed sleep, he goes to the back bedroom with Pham Thi while their daughters—Mia and Phượng—sleep on the living room floor and listen to their parents' grunting coming from the back bedroom; depending on whether or not Dad brings dinner with him to school, or if he catches the roach-coach in time to buy a beef burrito with a side order of rice and a Coca-Cola; or he knows that after his last class it will take a lot out of him to drive home, eat dinner, sleep a couple of hours, and come back that he decides he will eat a meal from what the vending machines on campus have to offer; or if Dad and Uncle Handsome Harlemite decide if they want to chance waiting in a long line of cars just to fill up their tanks, a problem everyone faces for nearly seven months since the Americans were taken hostage in Iran,

59

only when all these factors are set aside do Dad and Uncle Harlemite decide at whose place they will have dinner when they get home around eight.

I am in the living room watching a rerun of *All in the Family*, and Mother is at the dinner table reading the letter again when Dad and Uncle Handsome Harlemite walk in. They fill the house with the sound of their steel-toed boots thudding on the hardwood floor. They sigh as they bend over to loosen the laces. Uncle Handsome Harlemite is wearing his uniform. Although the tie is knotted at the collar, his shirt is untucked, but I can see the butt of his gun pressing against the shirttail as he unties the other shoelace.

Dad removes the navy-blue beanie from his head before straightening up and he begins to pull at his afro. Dad walks over and kisses Mother on the cheek before heading into the kitchen.

"Hi Vu-An," Uncle Handsome Harlemite says to Mother and kisses her on the cheek. Mother looks up with a frown set from reading and says hello.

"Hey there little man," he calls to me.

"Hi Uncle Handsome."

While Dad lifts the lids off pots and pans and rearranges them on the burners before turning them on, Mother folds the letter and slips it inside the envelope. She drags the chair back to stand up, and Dad's eyes immediately go to the four dull scratches in the hardwood he spent hours on hands and knees polishing. I keep watching Archie Bunker calling Michael "meathead" and "Pollack" and wait for Dad to holler at Mother like he has done every time, but Dad sees the letter in her hand and keeps quiet.

Mother goes to the bedroom, and the lights flood the hallway for a moment before she closes the door. While the pork chops and red beans and white rice are warming up, Dad sits at the dinner table with Uncle Handsome Harlemite to smoke and drink a Schlitz beer.

"When are we going to study?" Uncle Handsome Harlemite asks. His voice is not soft as usual, and he's slurring his words rather than pronouncing every syllable.

"Good question," Dad says. "Studied all day Sunday. Didn't do much good. I had no idea what accumulative meant until I opened my notebook."

There is a long pause before Uncle Handsome Harlemite speaks, and though it is in a low voice, he muscles the words from his mouth.

"When the *hell* do we get to study?"

Dad shakes his head. For someone whose skin appears smooth and soft, it surprises me to see Uncle Handsome Harlemite lean forward in his chair, frowning. He is as youthful looking as a boy, but to hear him curse ages him into an adult. It's rare to see him get angry, or raise his voice. Uncle Handsome Harlemite doesn't even raise his voice with his daughters. Sometimes all he has to do is look at them when they've said something out of line or done something wrong in public.

Like the time we had lunch at a Vietnamese restaurant in Chinatown. At one point, Mia said something about not wanting to use chopsticks because whenever she ate at a friend's house they never used them. Aunt Pham Thi stopped chewing all of a sudden and her body slumped in the chair as though someone had hit her. Dad and Mother kept their heads down and ate. Everyone at the nearby

tables stared at Mia, their faces close to the bowls, their
eyes bulging out of their sockets like animals drinking
from a watering hole, suddenly startled by noise. Uncle
Handsome Harlemite stared at Mia from across the table.
He chewed his food, teeth grinding the piece of beef to a
soft pulp. I could see the muscles in his jaws work to grind
the food, but it seemed no matter how much he chewed, it
wasn't going to make it go down any easier.

Mia forced herself to eat; she barely opened her
mouth to take in the food, and her hand shook so much
that she even dropped the chopsticks once and immediately picked them off the table. I asked Phượng the next
day what Uncle Handsome Harlemite did to Mia.

"Nothing," Phượng said. "She just kept her mouth
shut the rest of the day."

After finishing his cigarette, Dad goes back into the
kitchen to fix their plates and to get two more cans of
Schlitz from the refrigerator. They begin eating when Uncle Handsome Harlemite says he should come over more
often. "I'm not kidding. This is *damn* good," he says.

They eat without stopping. The moment they swallow they shove a fork full of red beans and rice into their
mouths. Even before swallowing their food they take long
gulps of beer. Their forks continually scratch the plates
when mixing beans and rice; they cut into the tough pork
chops, which finally give in at the last thread, and the
knives hit the plates hard enough that the ringing sounds
hurt my ears. They pause with fork and knife in hands
while chewing the soft beans and hard meat. And then
they are at it again with forks and knives, cutting and stirring their food.

When they are through with the pork chops, they gnaw on the bones, stripping them of the hard grizzle and cartilage. Bones drop onto the plates, and they reach inside the bag of Wonder Bread and finger several slices they use to sop up the gravy until their plates are clean. When they are through, they sit back in their chairs, suck at their teeth, and free up the wedged pieces of meat with their fingernails.

••••••••

They go outside and sit in wicker chairs on the left side patio to smoke cigarettes and drink more Schlitz. Since it is finals week, they talk about what might be on the tests, scared over what they might have missed, admit each other's fears so that they find comfort in the fact that the other is just as doubtful. They were in the war together. Although they were cooks, they had seen it all, heard severed limbs and flying bodies stories, saw the helicopters bringing in the dead from off the fields. Dad and Uncle Handsome Harlemite heard the ongoing shootings and bombings at night when sleeping in their barracks and they had to take up their M16s and fire at the night. Now, several years have passed since the end of the war and they worry over formulas and calculations and what goes into the debit slots, net and gross columns the way soldiers worry about the uncertainty of the next moment in the fields. Their talks can go on until they have to go work the graveyard shift, or they can last the duration of a cigarette. In which case, they'll go their separate ways and sleep for a couple of hours.

I am not allowed to be outside with them. Dad doesn't

want me to listen to what they have to say. Most nights they have the front door open, and sometimes pieces of their conversations with the occasional outburst of laughter drifts inside. I turn off the television and head to my bedroom. On the way there, I stop in the hallway. From behind their partially closed door I can hear the faint rustling of paper. Outside, far away, comes the steady rumbling of a loud engine; the car makes its way into Asia Minor, rattling windows and shelves and nerves, and I wonder how Mia gets so lucky, how she knows what time to come home? The rumbling settles in one place, and Handsome is most likely griping over the same noise he has complained about for the past couple of months, a noise he doesn't know his daughter is responsible for bringing into Asia Minor.

I go to my room, and before I close the door behind me, the car speeds away, the rumbling fades, and Mother's voice takes shape and fills the house. I stare at her door. When her voice begins to lower, I close my door and turn off the lights as if darkness can somehow shut off her voice.

Nursing

"Long-Vanh."

It only takes him to say my name once to wake me. That and the air in my bedroom seems to thin whenever Dad enters. I prop myself up on my elbows and squint at him standing over me. Dressed in jeans, a gray sweat shirt, and a navy-blue beanie over his head, Dad grips a pair of gray gloves.

"You want to go to work with me?"

I look at the clock on my nightstand, and it is 10:30. Though my eyes are tearing from the bright light and my head swims with sleep, I tell him OK.

"Hurry up and get ready," he says and walks out.

The air returns. I didn't bother to undress before I fell asleep, so I lie back down and take deep breaths to clear my head and wait for the tears to dry up before getting out of bed. I can hear him pacing about the kitchen, no doubt fixing a thermos of coffee. He bangs the cabinet doors shut after taking down Saran wrap and a brown paper bag to pack his meal.

I sit up in bed and begin putting on my shoes, anxious to leave this house, leave Mother by herself. And as I tie the laces I wonder if she'll be here when we get back, suitcase or not.

· · · · · · · ·

Dad ripped baseboards, knocked down whole walls,

65

wrenched shutters and doors from their hinges, pried rot-
ted hardwood to uproot foundations, and hauled debris
to dumpsters. The electric saws, sanders, and drills he was
not allowed to touch. They were for the white men who
were properly schooled or had taken up the trade of car-
pentry since their fathers had done it and their fathers before them; or they were hired because they were friends of
a friend who knew friends.

Dad brought us over to New Orleans in February
of 1972, a year and two months before every American
climbed over fences and into helicopters to leave Saigon.
For the next four years, Dad woke up at five in the morning
and caught the bus, trolley car, or ferry boat—depending
on the job site—and took apart old Victorian houses in the
Garden District, Metairie, Algiers, and other suburbs of
New Orleans for a construction company whose specialty
was to restore them. Dad called the job a back breaker.
Five years old and I'd stare at his broad back whenever he
came home from work to see if there was anything wrong.
But his back was always straight, muscular.

Mother and I used to ride the trolley car down St.
Charles to one of the sites to bring him lunch, but after
a while he forbade us from coming. Dad said he couldn't
stand the way the other men, especially the black men,
stared at his wife, the way their eyes traveled up and down
her body. He hated how they bowed to her, called her
mama san, and showed their white teeth when grinning.
But it didn't stop there at the job sites. It happened everywhere we went. People constantly did double-takes.
Dad never glared at them, nor said a word or stared them
down, but their incessant need to stop what they were do-

ing to look at us got to him at times so that he'd take Mother's hand in his.

Tired of New Orleans and the South in general, Dad moved us to the section of Silver Lake in Los Angeles known as Asia Minor, where people were a little more tolerable of such marriages. He enrolled himself in the same college he worked as a janitor. Dad said a janitor's job was easier for two reasons: less strain on the back, and there were no white men standing over him to make sure he was doing the job right, or keeping him from doing it.

Dad steers the lime-green Firebird into the parking lot across the street from Los Angeles Community College. People lean in the doorways of a pizza shop and pool hall next to the lot, smoking cigarettes. Dad and I walk across North Vermont Avenue and enter through the tall, double iron-wrought gates.

Although it is eleven o'clock, there are still students with book sacks slung over their shoulders. They linger in the poorly lit outdoor hallways discussing classes that had ended an hour ago. We walk down most hallways with vending machines offering candy bars, peanuts, chips, and even apples and oranges. And I imagine the nights Dad doesn't come home that he's standing in front of these machines, counting and depositing change until he fills his hunger.

We enter the Liberal Arts building, a three-story brick building with all the lights on and the blinds open. Dad immediately goes to the door marked CUSTODIAN and wheels out the pushcart filled with spray bottles, Ajax, squeegees, dusters, rolls of paper towels, a sweeper and broom.

"Fill the bucket with hot water and bring it to where I am," he says.

After filling it with hot water from the sink inside the CUSTODIAN room, I roll it out and follow the clatter of chairs in the classroom down the hall.

"Start erasing the boards and wipe them down with a wet cloth." He continues moving chairs about with one hand and sweeps the floor with the other.

I do as he says and as I am erasing the board, I read what's on it: "Dr. Frankenstein as parent" is on one side, and underneath this is a list of words: "nurturer, provider, disciplinarian."

I turn around to mention to Dad what the class is reading, but he's busy sweeping balled-up papers, candy wrappers, and paper clips. So I don't say anything because he'll start lecturing me on education and how it was a good thing he made me read *Frankenstein* last summer when he saw Phượng and me watching a Frankenstein marathon on television.

"That's nothing like the book," he said when he passed in front of us to take a book down from off the shelf. "Here," he handed me the book. "Read this rather than watch that bullshit," he said before going about his way and getting a can of Schlitz and returning to the patio.

I take the wet cloth and wipe the chalkboard. It becomes black and shiny, almost new. But after it dries I can still see faint traces of words on the board:

"Frankenstein as God"
creator, inventor
resurrects what is dead—Lazarus?

goes against natural order
wrathful

"OK, I'm done."

Dad has just finished sweeping everything into a pile. He looks up at the board.

"That's good. Now go to all the other rooms and do the same."

Something different is on the chalkboard in every classroom. Spanish words are written on every inch of the chalkboard in one room, and though I do not speak a word of it, I can tell because of the squiggly lines atop n's and vowels attached at the end of words similar to those in English. Their accent marks, all two of them, aren't as dressy, much less numerous, as the ones in the letters Mother receives. And I wonder if Mother is up at this hour of the night, rereading the letter as she sometimes has in the past. Not to disturb Dad's sleep in the times he has actually come home, she'd read at the dinner table. Her lips would move: each syllable she uttered undressed the words' meanings. If she is up, at least she'll have the letter, not the Samsonite filled with her things.

Dad moves around the room down the hall. I hear the sweeping of straw against linoleum, the wadded-up papers rolling across the floor, and I think of the geckos scrambling across the window screen for insects, and Mother's Samsonite buried in the ivy of our backyard.

········

By the time Dad is done with all the rooms, I have already swept the hallway floor. I sit on the floor at the end of the hallway and watch Dad wring the mop. He leans all his weight on the lever of the washboard to drain all the excess water. He holds the mop up high with one hand and walks to the end of the hallway. With legs apart and both hands on the handle, Dad drags the mop back and forth, back and forth, touching the floorboards on both sides. He sways side to side, his arms move in a rhythm. From this distance, it looks like Dad has taken a thin person with hair, curly and thick as ropes, and turned the person upside down.

Dad continues to sway side to side, and slowly he steps backwards though it seems he is swaying in place. Though he is watching the floor he mops, and though his back is to me, he tucks his chin in as if to keep his head from hitting the fluorescent lights. I keep watching him as he sways from floorboard to floorboard until his rhythm calms me.

········

"Long-Vanh. Wake up."

Dad stands over me. He wiggles his hands free of the gray cotton gloves. He holds them by the wrists in one hand and turns away. I get to my feet and follow him outside. The air is still and warm. Dad and I walk next door to the INFIRMARY. The double glass doors slide open automatically. Dad walks right up to the counter where a young woman sits. Her blonde hair is done up in a bun. When Dad rests his elbows on the counter and leans forward, the woman's round blue eyes widen. She smiles, showing no teeth until her lips part to speak.

"Hi Wil," she sits up in her chair, and already I don't

like the way she calls Dad by his first name like she has said it many times when no one is around. I don't like the way Dad leans on the counter, one leg back, his head thrust over the counter. Rather than lean back in her chair, she sits forward, and in that moment I know. I know she is the woman whose name Mother always demanded those nights he'd come home late. Just watching them upsets me because I am now aware of something I didn't want to know. It's like Dad has entrusted me to keep this secret without my permission and now I am forced to keep quiet, keep this secret for him. It bothers me because Dad didn't ask me to keep a promise.

The nurse looks past Dad and says, "This is your son, Long-Vanh."

She leans forward in her seat a little more, and Dad twists around in my direction. Only now he has one elbow on the counter.

"Yes, that's him."

"What's wrong?" She pouts. "Are we sleepy tonight?"

"I'm afraid he's had it for the night," Dad says. "Do you mind, Sharon, if he sleeps in one of the beds?"

"Sure," Sharon stretches the word. "Sure he can." She stands up and comes from around the counter. "Come on Long-Vanh," she motions to the back room with the lights off.

I go to her, to her white blouse, pants, shoes, and teeth. Sharon places a hand on my shoulder and leads me inside the room.

"Which bed would you like to sleep in, the one by the window?" She asks. Before I can answer she walks me over to the bed by the window.

Sharon draws the thin blue blanket back and says, "OK, take off your shoes and hop in."

"I'll be back after my shift to get him."

"OK," Sharon says. "He'll be alright." She turns to me and smiles.

I look past her, and Dad is gone. I hear the double glass doors automatically slide open and shut. Sharon draws up a chair next to the bed and sits, crossing one leg over the other at the knees. Because she is leaned forward in her chair, the gold crucifix dangles on a necklace, and I stare at it hanging where her breasts join together. I must have stared at the top part of her breasts too long because Sharon looks down, and I thought she was going to snap at me. Instead, she holds the crucifix between two fingers. She smiles as she slides it back and forth on the thin gold necklace.

"The one I really want," she tugs on the crucifix, "is the one with Jesus on the cross. But that's expensive."

I only hum and nod once, wondering why she would want a man nailed to a cross. Dad told me the man was God's son, and the only thing I understand about Him is that He once made many miracles. That He was once powerful. But anyone powerful must crumble; anyone strong will weaken and give was how Dad explained it. And when I asked him if He was so powerful, why did He die, Dad said He had a duty to fulfill.

"Your father talks about you a lot."

I keep quiet, smile and wait to hear what she has to say next, but she doesn't say anything else. She just smiles and plays with the crucifix, and I'm pretending to stare at it like I'm interested. All I want is to see her breasts.

Sharon suddenly sits up in her chair and says, "There he is." I follow her gaze out the window and in the building next to us—the LIBERAL ARTS building—on the second floor is Dad, sweeping in one of the classrooms. He moves chairs and desks to get at the trash. Sharon watches Dad; her hand absently moves the crucifix back and forth. Dad leans forward with one hand on the table pushing it back, sweeping, then dragging it back to its original place. At the same time he works the broom with the other hand, I imagine Dad mopping up Sharon in bed—maybe even this bed—as he holds one of her legs around his shoulder with one arm as he pushes into her hips, and the upper part of her shoulders dig into the bed. I picture Dad doing this to Sharon as I once saw Dad do to Mother one night when I was awakened by a sudden scream. Because Dad is bigger and taller than Mother, I thought he was hurting her. But she didn't tell Dad to stop, and I imagine Sharon telling Dad not to stop. She moans and fights to breathe, and she's sweating—her whole body wet with sweat. She doesn't mind so long as Dad is pushing into her, so long as he holds her leg in place around his shoulder and neck with one arm wrapped around her thighs. All I know of sex is groaning, pain, and sweat, and I picture Dad mopping up the bed sheets with Sharon's wet body, her long, blond hair a mess around her neck and face, her bottom lip clenched between her teeth.

Sharon moves the crucifix back and forth so fast that it makes noise. Her eyes are on Dad and I'm waiting for her to sit forward again. Hopefully, she'll forget how far forward she sat the last time and she'll hunch over so that I can finally see more of her round, full breasts. But as long as Dad is holding her attention, she'll remain sitting up in her chair.

The crucifix suddenly stops, and Sharon's shoulders drop. Dad has turned off the lights and left the room. Sharon sighs and lets the crucifix go and it bounces off her chest before settling between them. Still, I continue to wait for her to sit forward, and the way she stares into the darkness of the next building tells me she's allowed Dad to look at her breasts uncovered by blouse and bra. And I'm sure by the way she continues to stare into the darkness that her breasts have given into Dad's hands as he wiped sweat from their soft curves.

Friday Morning

Even though it is 6:30, Art's Deli is crowded. We're seated at a booth by the window, and I wish we were sitting at the counter with the turning stools, our backs to the early morning sun, for I can hardly keep my eyes open. I have to bring one hand to the side of my face, elbow resting on the tabletop. Dad takes the container of sugar and pours some into his cup of coffee and stirs before taking a sip. I take the container from him and add milk until it reaches a light brown.

"Did Sharon go home early?" I ask.

Dad frowns at me. Sharon wasn't there when Dad came to get me. I expected to see her behind the counter, her golden hair swirled into a bun, the gold crucifix resting between her breasts, and her smile. Instead there was another lady scribbling in folders. She was a heavy woman, the buttons of her top struggled to stay closed, and the fabric stretched from the rolls around her stomach and ribs.

"She wasn't there when we left," I say. "She's nice."

Dad's face relaxes as he stares out the window, and only now do I see just how tired he is. The edges of his black pupils are red, and they bleed into the white. There are lines beneath his eyes, and they look bruised and bluish. Without the gloves, his nails are scuffed and scratched, the skin around them white and dried and cut. In some places the skin has parted from the nails, and his knuckles are so ashy and cracked that the lines are deep. The deep lines part his skin, mapping the years of his labor, and I want to pour coffee over the backs of his hands to darken them again, give Dad back his color. But one hand suddenly moves away to reach into the coat pocket for the pack of cigarettes.

"Yeah, she's nice. She goes to school during the day."

"Why? She's a nurse."

"Intern."

"What's that?"

"It's when they work for little or no money. She's not a nurse yet. After a while, after completing their school work, they have to work a job . . . either on campus or at a hospital—" Dad slips a cigarette from the pack and puts it in his mouth "—to gain experience, gain the number of required hours." He finally lights his cigarette and inhales. After he exhales, keeping in mind to blow the smoke against the window, he says, "If she doesn't have enough hours, she's not qualified." Dad raises a hand to his mouth as if to take another drag, but he bites on the corner of his thumbnail instead while staring out the window. "And if she's not qualified, she won't graduate."

I take a sip of coffee and wonder if Dad is having an affair with Sharon, then I'm disappointed. She's an intern, not even a real nurse, but someone who falls short of being complete. Mother only sews dresses and blouses, but at least she takes fabric, cuts patterns, stitches hem lines, attaches collars, cuffs, buttons, and clasps to make something whole.

We sit and drink our coffees, but I take small sips to make the one cup I'm allowed last.

"When are you going to be done with school?" I ask.

"One more year," he says.

One more year, I think to myself, of seeing Sharon. Dad rubs one side of his face, and before bringing his hand away, he scrapes at the dirt in the inside corners of his eyes. As tall as he is, as broad as his back and as wide as his shoulders are, I see him as breakable. There were many nights and afternoons—depending on his schedule—in which I watched him study at the dinner table, the hardcover books as thick as dictionaries spread out before him, his eyes moving over the pages, and when he mumbled, it was more to the hand holding the pencil than to hear himself. The longer he studied the more stooped he became, until I thought he would touch the table with his chest. And in those rare moments I got to see him study, I thought of him as someone getting smaller in size, small to where he is open to harm and he can't even protect himself.

I think that if he wasn't going to school and he only had the job, then he could stay home more often and be there for us, for Mother especially. Give her more attention than he's giving her now, and she will want to stay, perhaps forget about Lý Lôc altogether. But a year? She could leave within a year. I want to tell Dad to quit his job. I want to tell him in a year he won't have a wife and that all that work and studying was all for nothing.

And I wonder what he would have done that morning had he woken up: blink his eyes, roll over and pull the covers over his head? Or maybe he'd swing his legs out of bed and plant his feet on the floor and sit for a while before crying into his hands.

"Did you ever want to go back . . . to Vietnam?" I ask.

Although I have my head down as I prepare to take a
sip, I can feel him frowning at me by the way he sits still,
the cigarette resting between his fingers.

"Say what?"

"You know, see where you worked and lived? You
think one day we can go back?" I take a sip of my coffee.
"See Lý Loc."

The wrinkles on his forehead ease as he draws the cigarette to his lips, but just before taking a drag, he pulls it
away.

"You can, I guess. With Uncle Ngô, with your mother.
I don't want to go back." He draws on his cigarette. "Besides, you can't go there now."

"How come? I just want to visit?"

"No. No one can go back."

"How about for a week or a couple of days?"

"No one can go back."

"How about if they really wanted to?—because of a
sick relative? Then?

"*Long*," he raises his voice, and a few people turn their
heads in our direction. "No one can go back even if they
wanted to. No one. We don't have an embassy there anymore. Nothing can protect us, and besides, they won't take
you back."

"Even if they *want* to go back to live there?"

Dad sits back against the stuffed vinyl seat and sighs.

"*Shit*, boy, what did I *just* say?"

I stare at my cup of coffee. Dad sighs one more time
before sitting forward in his seat. A milky film has risen to
the surface of the coffee, coiling within itself, and I begin
to stir it to make the pale film disappear. When I stop, the

pale film rises to the surface, and I realize it won't go away.

Mother won't be going anywhere, even if she asks, even if she begs them to let her in. I can imagine her getting off the plane, climbing down the roll-away steps with the Samsonite in both hands. And as she steps onto the runway, she sets the suitcase down to rest her arms. Before she can take it up again, however, her own people are surrounding her and pointing up the roll-away steps, telling her to board the plane. Lý Loĉ is there as well, wrists bound by ropes, and he's telling Mother, "You left once. What makes you think we want you back?"

Tuesday Revisited

I'm in the living room replacing burnt incense sticks and wiping dust off the framed photographs of Lý Loc when I hear a woman's voice. I look out the window and see Yên, Tú Đức's older sister, take her final step onto the patio. Uncle Ngô stands up to meet her. Her hands move wildly as she speaks. Uncle Ngô nods and I know she's talking about Tú Đức and the bicycle. I run the dust rag over the windowsill.

Uncle Ngô puts his hands out as though signaling a car to slow down, but her mouth keeps moving, arms flailing. Finally, Uncle Ngô grabs Yên by the shoulders and shakes her until she falls against him, crying. He holds her away from him and he has to bend down, body curved like the letter "C" to look her in the eyes. He puts one arm around her and together they walk down the steps.

I open the door and step outside and wait until I hear Uncle Ngô's car start and take off down the street before I head for Phượng's apartment. I get to the bottom of Montana Avenue and I see them: Tú Đức, Phượng, Uncle Ngô, and Yên standing in a circle. I am about to walk back up the hill, but Phượng's glance in my direction makes everyone turn to look, so I make my way over. Before I even get there I can see the bruises blacken Tú Đức's eyes and cheeks. His right eye is nearly swollen shut, and Yên is trying to hold his face still so she can look over the bruises and cuts. Phượng looks down at the ground and shuffles from one foot to the other.

"Hey. You OK?" I ask.

Tú Đức opens his mouth and only his left eye blinks repeatedly. His right eye twitches, failing to close completely.

"You not help me." He points. Tú Đức shakes his head from between Yên's hands and moves away. His bottom lip begins to quiver. "You not help me."

"I tried. I tried to help. I called him. Told him to get off you."

"You not help me." He says harshly, and spit forms at the corners of his mouth.

I shrug with palms out, shake my head, and try to say something.

"Get in the car Tú," Uncle Ngô demands. "We go get your bicycle."

"Yes, get in the car," Tú Đức repeats, and as he walks to the car, he keeps tracing the bumps on his face.

"I tried Uncle Ngô. Really I did."

"It okay. Go home."

"You won't tell Mother, will you? She doesn't have to know."

"We talk later. Now go home. Go," he jerks his head in the direction of home, and he and Yên get in the car and drive off.

"It's okay," Phượng says.

"I tried."

"What could we have done? At least you did something. At least you got him to stop hitting him so that he could chase us."

I feel a little better, for what would be the point of getting my ass whooped? But her reasoning only makes me feel good for a moment before feeling terrible again. I feel awful because the beating was meant for me. Those big fists coming down on Tú Đức, even when Fat Chan wasn't aiming, resulted in a bruised and swollen face, split and broken in places that seem will never heal.

And I think of my face. I want to take my hands out of my pockets and feel my own face, imagine knuckles breaking bone and teeth being loosened from their roots. And to feel something as soft as lips tear and split and run with so much blood that it is all I taste in my mouth. The warmth of it fills my mouth and catches in my throat where I can't swallow because I'm too stunned, too numb from the blows.

"Don't think about it," Phượng says.

I mutter okay and just then loud rumbling approaches, and we turn toward the hill. A black Mercury Cougar with a raised rear comes over the hill and it slows down to make a turn into the dirt lot and we wince from the engine's loud rumbling. Mia is cuddling with the driver, head on his shoulder. When he stops the car and lets it idle, she lifts her head up and kisses him. Even with the car idling, the engine is still loud. Mia climbs out of the car and watches the guy back out into the street and take off in the opposite direction.

Mia turns to walk to the apartment and stops when she sees us. She parts her bangs to the sides, then tucks the loose strand of hair behind her ears, wets her lips, and tugs at the hem of her frayed cut off shorts. Her nipples stand out from underneath her T-shirt made thin from constant washing; she's like a spring roll wrapped tight in moist rice paper, paper thin enough to see the things it holds together.

"What the hell are you two staring at?" she says and makes her way up the steps.

Handsome

It's Uncle Handsome Harlemite's day off, and like Dad, he sits at the dinner table going over notes he wrote in the margins of his textbooks. He bends over his opened books with a frown that takes in everything, and glides a pencil across graphing paper—numbers he calculates as proof of his understanding of gains and losses. Mia sits on the couch flipping through an old issue of *McCall's* her mother brought home from the shop. She divides her time looking up from the pages to watch her father studying and glancing at the open windows listening to the sounds of cars passing.

Mother is in the kitchen cooking. She slices celery, chops cilantro, and cuts tomatoes in quarters for the sweet and sour soup. Dad is home sleeping, and he has me reading H.G. Wells' *The Time Machine*. I sit at the dinner table with the book resting on the edge so that I can give Uncle Handsome Harlemite room to work.

"Shit!" Uncle Handsome Harlemite whispers sharply.

He pecks at the pad of paper with the pencil, then scratches out the numbers. He mouths each number he jots down, stares hard at it before writing the next number. And when he is done, he straightens up before bending over the figures and going through the calculations.

Aunt Pham Thi and Phượng come home with bags in each hand. Their hair is coming loose from the tightly wrapped buns, and their necks and faces glisten with sweat.

"*Buddha*, it's hot. Next time I go morning when it's not so hot," Aunt Pham Thi says as she makes her way into the kitchen.

They set the bags on the counter and begin unpacking what they bought: fish sauce, lemons, vinegar, more tomatoes, a bunch of Thai basil, salt, and whole catfish. "Aren't they beautiful?" Aunt Pham Thi unwraps the papers to show Mother the catfish.

"Set them on the counter and I'll take care of them," Mother says, and Phượng unpacks the other two tightly wrapped in white paper.

Uncle Handsome Harlemite makes a sound and sits back in his seat as he spears his pencil through his afro he hasn't bothered to comb. He crosses his arms and nods his head and makes the sound again. He reaches for the pencil and begins the next problem.

Mia continues to glance over at the window and at her father. She flips through a couple of pages without looking at the pictures. And I wonder who she's waiting for?— José? Kenneth?—someone new? She closes the magazine and throws it on the coffee table and takes up the next one. She sighs and sits back in the couch. "God, these things are big," I hear Mother mutter as she places one on the chopping board.

She grabs the whetstone from the drawer and begins to sharpen the large knife. The gritty sandy-sounding rhythm increases with each passing of the knife's edge across the thick gray block. Uncle Handsome Harlemite puts a hand to his forehead to hide the frown that hardens with each passing of the knife. He sighs, but he doesn't say anything. He traces over the numbers he has written, darkening them.

Mother puts the whetstone back in the drawer and inserts the tip of the knife into the belly deep enough to slice it clean open. Mother reaches two fingers inside and rips out the intestines and puts them on the white wrapping paper. She feels around the inside to make sure she got it all.

From afar there comes a loud rumbling. Mia stares at Uncle Handsome Harlemite from above the magazine. She closes the magazine, tosses it on the coffee table and says, "I'm going to hang outside for a while."

Just as she stands up from the couch, Uncle Handsome Harlemite orders her to sit down, that dinner is almost done and she should help in the kitchen.

"Mia," Mother calls out, "come on. You can cut the rest of the tomatoes."

Mia's shoulders slouch as she sighs and gives a disgusted look that Uncle Handsome Harlemite doesn't see. She stomps across the living room on her way to the kitchen.

"Don't stomp!" Uncle Handsome Harlemite hollers. "Can't you see I'm trying to study?" He goes back to his work and Mia lightens her steps. "Jesus Christ! Car is making so much damn noise."

The rumbling grows louder. It feels like it's underneath us, coming through the floor, through the carpet.

"Jesus Christ!" Uncle Handsome Harlemite throws his pencil down, jumps up out of his chair and goes to all the windows and slams them shut. The noise still comes through, rattling the windows, jiggling the photographs and clay figurines on the shelves. Uncle Handsome Harlemite glares at the car down below. He turns away from the window, angry and muttering, and because of the noise and rattling windows, I can't hear him. He leaves the apartment and heads downstairs. Phượng and I look at each other. Mia stops cutting tomatoes. Phượng and I run to the window, and Mia joins us.

Uncle Handsome Harlemite steps quickly to the black Mercury Cougar idling in the driveway.

"Kiss Kenny goodbye," Phượng laughs.

"Shut up," Mia hisses.

Uncle Handsome Harlemite makes his way around the car and leans inside the driver's window. We can only see his backside as his head bobs as he speaks.

"This doesn't look good for you," Phượng turns to Mia and smiles.

Mia shoves her with her shoulder and says, "I said, *shut* up."

Uncle Handsome Harlemite stands up and jabs a finger at his own chest. He keeps jabbing and nodding before shaking his head slowly and points toward the street. Kenny reverses out of the driveway. Before he takes off, Kenny revs his engine a couple of times as Uncle Handsome Harlemite stares back with his fists on his hips. The Mercury Cougar's tires spin before Kenny speeds down the street, leaving a trail of smoke and black streaks.

Uncle Handsome Harlemite shakes his head, lets his fists fall from his hips and heads upstairs. The windows calm to minor vibrations until finally they are still. Uncle Handsome Harlemite slams the door behind him.

"If I ever see him here again, I will kill him. You hear me?"

"Yes," Mia mumbles.

"I said, did you *hear* me?"

"Yes," she says a little louder.

Uncle Handsome Harlemite goes into the bathroom and closes the door. I go back to reading the book, but I only look at the words. Mia continues slicing tomatoes.

"I wish he would just mind his own business," she says.

"Shut up," Aunt Pham Thi says. "Listen to what your father tell you. Don't be so, so, re-bell-ous."

"He didn't have to do *that*," Mia thrusts her face forward.

"Don't talk back to your mother," Mother interrupts. She puts down the knife and picks up the cleaver. "In Vietnam, children *never* talk back to their parents. You have become so spoiled here in America. You think we are crazy and strict," Mother waves the cleaver between herself and Aunt Pham Thi, "but it is for the best. We are not . . . *mean* because we want to be. Do you think we like to be mean? Stop *being* stupid."

Mother raises the cleaver and comes down hard on the catfish, severing the head. She raises it and comes down several times, cutting the body into three pieces. As she takes the second catfish and places it on the chopping board, she says, "In Vietnam, children *never* talk back or disobey their parents. In Vietnam, we kill the children."

She brings the cleaver down and cuts clean the head from the body.

"And no one ever asks any questions."

The Land of Dead Children

Tân Sơn Nhứt Airport, Hồ Chí Minh City, 1997

To some extent I can understand their suspicions. Long before we boarded the plane in Los Angeles, Uncle Ngô told me this would happen. It's not every day that they see a Vietnamese man with an African-American man in Hồ Chí Minh City. They can easily buy Uncle Ngô's story: he wants to return home, to see relatives he hasn't seen since leaving in 1972. In my case they'd think I'm a Vietnam vet making a personal journey to heal emotional wounds, but I am only twenty-eight.

And then when they asked me in English the nature of my visit, I told them I was here to see my mother. They became quiet before they turned to one another with opened mouths. They both studied my passport. The woman looked up and pursed her lips to speak, and I knew she wanted to say, "No. Really?" Instead she raised the passport up to her face and frowned into the black and white photo, at the name Long-Vanh Nguyen printed next to it. All the information was correct: place of birth (Nha Trang), date of birth (6/17/68), citizenship (U.S.); the name was distinctly Vietnamese, as was the long neck with the vulnerable Adam's apple, the large mouth. Everything checked out except the dark skin and the short, neatly cropped style African-Americans wear their hair nowadays. They didn't match with everything else.

So Uncle Ngô and I are now in a room with a picture

of a gaunt-looking Hồ Chí Minh hanging on the wall. His white goatee covers the buttoned collar of his shirt. Uncle Ngô and I stand side by side and watch as the customs officers slide and wriggle their hands inside tight-fitting latex gloves and snap them against their wrists. The officers in ill-fitting blue uniforms and caps pull neatly folded shirts and jeans from our suitcases one by one and shake them free of their perfect creases. Their hands plunge inside the pockets, front and back, and when they are through with each article of clothing, they pile them on the table. The woman opens my jar of Noxzema and sniffs it. She scrunches up her nose, holds it out to us and asks, "Cái gī đây?"

"Đê rửa mặt," Uncle Ngô says and he makes a circular motion with his hands in front of his face. He turns to me and asks, "Better than soap, huh?"

"Ah, yes. It cleans the pores." I clear my throat.

The woman stares at my face to see how well it has worked on my complexion. She peers inside the jar, frowning at the white substance. She replaces the cap and sets the jar to the side.

I want to look behind me and count the number of officers standing in front of the closed door. At times I hear them opening and closing the door, and only when they come and go can I hear other people walking about as they drag their luggage behind them, and a woman speaking over the intercom in a language I never learned. But I am afraid to turn my head. However many there are, I can feel them staring at the back of my head, and my neck burns from their constant gaze. Sweat forms on my forehead, and I wish they'd turn on the fan. There are no windows in the room.

I watch Uncle Ngô from out of the corners of my eyes. He's standing still, and I take it as a sign to do the same. So I leave my arms at my side and stare straight ahead, but my arms tremble. The way the officers go through our things with intense concentration on their brows convinces me they'll find something I overlooked. A part of me wishes they'd find something. Maybe something in my Noxzema doesn't smell right. Perhaps the ammonium level is too high by Vietnamese standards, or something as absurd as that. A part of me wishes they were crooked enough to plant an ounce of coke or dried-up buds in my suitcase. Anything to keep me from that moment I drive into Nha Trang and see my mother for the first time in seventeen years since she left Los Angeles.

When I got the phone call several weeks ago, I hadn't expected it to be Mother. How could I? It wasn't that I thought she had been dead these past seventeen years, but when I hadn't heard from her once, I simply accepted the fact that I had no mother, dead or alive. But there was her voice at the other end just as I had remembered it as a child, stern and absent of feelings. And I thought, *How can she speak that way? After so much time?*

But I was only able to say Mother, and I wasn't sure if I was stammering, or if my voice echoed in the receiver within the walls of white noise caused by long distances.

That was all I could say, over and over, before Uncle Ngô took the phone out of my hand. I stood beside him and listened as he spoke to her in Vietnamese, his voice low. All I understood were the rise and fall of syllables, just mere sounds. Then he hung up, and we stared at each other without saying a word.

The customs officers go through our things quietly, and when the man uncaps a tube of Crest toothpaste and squeezes enough of it to cover the tip of his finger, Uncle Ngô lets out a low grunt. The woman shakes the can of Gillette shaving cream and presses the tab until her hand cups foam. She holds it up to her nose and sniffs before wiping her hand on the table. The male officer tears open a box of Irish Spring soap. With a switchblade he pares layers off the way one would a fruit.

I reach inside my shirt pocket and take out my pack of Marlboros, and jerk one free with a quick flick of the wrist. Before I even have a chance to put it in my mouth, the woman says snapping each syllable, "Dừng lại. Cấm hút tục."

I raise both hands, and I hear the officers stirring behind me, but I don't look back. The man hurries from around the table and snatches the pack out of my hand and the cigarette from the other. Uncle Ngô reaches inside his denim jean pocket and produces his pack of cigarettes.

"Nó chì thuộc lá thôi. Coi. See." Uncle Ngô holds his pack out to the officer, but he doesn't look.

The inspector snaps the cigarette at the filter, sniffs it, and rubs one end between two fingers so that the tobacco spills onto the floor. Again, Uncle Ngô is showing the officer his pack of cigarettes and talking at the same time. The officer nods his head. He walks back to the table and sets my pack on the table.

"Đây," Uncle Ngô gives me a cigarette from his pack. "You take mine." He fishes inside his pocket for his Zippo lighter, and at the same time he flips the lid open, it lights, a trick I can't do.

I puff until the cigarette catches and I take a drag, holding it in for a moment before exhaling. The officers go back to inspecting our luggage. Uncle Ngô lights up a cigarette. After about the third drag I'm starting to feel dizzy, so I hold the cigarette between my fingers and stare at it, thinking how lucky Uncle Ngô is that he gets to keep his pack. But I can only stare at my cigarette for so long.

Our suitcases lie wide open and empty. The officers feel around the edges, smooth the palms of their hands against the lining. Hồ Chí Minh sits high on the wall, and he stares over our heads toward the back. I continue to smoke the cigarette despite how it makes me feel.

Then the male officer does something that makes me gasp. He stoops down to pick up a rectangular box and sets it on the table. I turn to Uncle Ngô then, but he only smokes his cigarette. The officer takes the switchblade and cuts the string that holds it all together. He tears away at the brown wrapping, and with the blade he slices the box right down the middle, parting the seams and corners where I've taped it.

He pockets the switchblade, opens the flaps, and together, he and the female officer bring out the *áo dàis*, long-sleeved satin gowns, and the black pantaloons that go with them. They turn them over in their gloved hands, smooth their palms over the length of the dresses, rub the material between their fingers, fondle the hem. The woman even holds one up against her body, checking the length. As though she remembers who she is and what her duties are, she quickly catches herself and looks at me, bringing the *áo dàis* away from her body.

"They're my mother's. She left them behind."

She merely blinks her eyes several times before folding the *áo dài* in half and setting it on top of everything
else. The man takes out two bundles of letters bound by
rubber bands. He inspects the cover of one of them and
notices the addresses in the center and in the left-hand
corner. He sets them aside and proceeds to the manila envelope. He digs his hand inside and extracts Polaroids of
me and Mother and Dad. The man says something, and
I take it to mean *look* because the woman leans in and
together they shift through each photo, frowning at them
for long moments, most likely dissecting Mother and Dad
to see their features in me. After they are through, he puts
them back in the envelope, but he catches sight of one he
missed, and he takes it out. It is an 8X10 photograph, the
only big one in the set. He raises it to his face, and slowly
his eyes widen.

"Lý Lôc," I say. "My grandfather."

The man looks up at me and he says something to the
woman. She nods her head and frowns, and it's as if the
darkness of my skin has turned pale for them, and my hair
became straight and gray. And I want them to say it, admit
how much I look like my grandfather despite my dark skin
and hair, admit that I am one of them. But the man simply
replaces the photo in the envelope and closes the flap.

The officers step away from the table, yanking the latex gloves off their hands. They speak to Uncle Ngô, and
he nods his head eagerly. He tosses his cigarette on the
floor and crushes it with the heel of his shoe. I let mine
burn between my fingers.

"Come on Long-Vanh," Uncle Ngô waves me forward

as he walks up to the table.

Uncle Ngô picks up a pair of jeans and begins to fold them. I set the cigarette at the edge of the table and sort through the pile. Both officers are speaking to Uncle Ngô. He nods his head at times, says *um-hm* as he folds the sleeves of his shirts behind their backs before doubling them at the torsos. Still, they continue to speak, and like Uncle Ngô, I don't look up at them. One of them, the male officer, extends his hand out and Uncle Ngô drops a pair of boxers onto the table to shake the man's hand. He pumps it several times while exchanging words. He even smiles. When Uncle Ngô lets go of his hand, the woman extends hers and he shakes it. The officers come from around the table with the box and leave the room.

"What's happening? Where are they going with Mother's things?" I whisper.

"Later," Uncle Ngô says. "Just fold clothes."

We continue to untangle long shirt sleeves from around pant legs.

········

"What next?" I ask.

Uncle Ngô lights his cigarette, snaps shut the Zippo, takes a long drag and exhales before he sits back into the bench.

"They keep our passports, your Mother's *áo dàis*, the letters, pho-to-graphs. For two days . . . maybe three. For now, we stay here."

"Here in the airport?" I point at the floor.

"No. Here. Hồ Chí Minh City. We stay. Besides, we cannot go an-ee-where without passport," he says slowly, enunciating each syllable so that he's not misunderstood.

I rub my hands together and look about the airport. Our luggage is beside us. In a room that looks like a warehouse, people stand behind a queue with slips of papers in their hands, the same slip they gave me to claim the items they are holding for further inspection. Officers stand on the other side, and shelved behind them are the people's luggage, and there must be hundreds. Other officers retrieve luggage from off the shelves and hand them to people.

Often, the officers are pointing at the luggage they hand the patrons, insisting that it is theirs. And it's funny. It's funny because they've spent so much time packing their belongings into suitcases, but once the suitcases are gone from them for the duration of the flight and placed with others, they forget which is theirs despite the differences in color, size, and weight. They can't recognize their own from the others, and they look confused, almost doubtful that they've been handed the right suitcase until they think to check the tags.

After they get their luggage, the people make their way past Uncle Ngô and me, and every one of them stares. I nod my head, even give a slight wave of my hand, but they don't return the greeting. They just continue parading past us, and some even bump into the person in front of them. One man is videotaping as he walks, and he turns his Camcorder in our direction, giving commentary. He, along with everyone else, makes his way to the far end of the lobby to where guards have holstered guns. Behind them, men, women, and children wait. Most of them hold up signs with names written on them, and I recognize some of the names: Phượng, Nguyễn, Thành, Huang. And although I know Mother is not here to meet us, I search each card expecting to find my name on one of them. But I don't see Long-Vanh, and even if she were here, I wonder if Mother will look the same, or if the only way I'll recognize her will be by a sign bearing my name in the hands of a woman I don't know.

Beneath

It is so dark it scares me to be out on the highway at this hour. I want to tell Uncle Ngô to turn back, to stay the night in Hồ Chí Minh City and sleep in a room where the lights can be controlled. Or at least pull over on the side of the highway and wait for daylight. But Uncle Ngô is sitting comfortably in the driver's seat of the '67 Benz we rented. He blows smoke from his nostrils, and for someone who is fifty, he still looks young in jeans and a T-shirt. There are only thin lines sprouting from the corners of his eyes. This is the only physical difference I notice since we were neighbors back in Nha Trang. He still rides a motorcycle, a Harley he resurrected from a junkyard, only no one would ever think so because of all the chrome parts he soaked in solvents for days until it shone like heaven. The Harley is an improvement from the Yamaha he used to ride around the marketplace, attracting young women whose prudish attitudes were façades he stripped away like the *áo dài* he unbuttoned, only to discover soft flesh so pale and virginal that sometimes he whimpered from the anticipation of touching something so pure, so sacred.

The headlights barely penetrate the dark, but Uncle Ngô keeps it steady at sixty miles per hour. I cannot see the trees on either side of us, and I can barely distinguish a gas station from a souvenir shop, a restaurant from a closed-up fruit stand.

"Don't worry," Uncle Ngô says. "I used to drive this

road when I go to Nha Trang and back to Saigon. Many, many times I drive this road."

"I'm not worried."

"Yes you worry. You're quiet. Also, you hold on to seat."

I let go of the seat and bridge my hands together in front of me and stare out my window. We wind through the valley. Moonlight shines on the valley below, and we can see small patches of a lantern lit town huddled at the base of surrounding mountains. We hit a fog so dense that Uncle Ngô has to slow down.

"God. Is it always this bad?" I ask gripping the car seat.

"Yes, but don't worry," he says as he hunches over the steering wheel, almost touching it with his chest as he squints at the fog.

"I'm not. I trust you won't get us killed," I chuckle.

"I mean your mother. She is fine."

I turn to him, and he looks at me briefly before returning his attention to the road. I want to tell him he is wrong, and that some point during this week she will finally go into hysterics as I remember her doing many times. I cannot see how Uncle Ngô can come to such a conclusion, especially when he witnessed the times she dropped everything and curled into a ball the way snakes coil themselves beneath brush and rocks. She would bring her legs up until her chin touched her knees and wrap her arms around her legs, fearful of losing herself. Whenever she was like this, she shed her responsibilities, and I watched and wondered how long before she shed her emotions. How long before her arms, legs, and body uncoiled so she could slither back into our lives in a new skin?

Mother has probably been sitting there for the duration we waited in Hồ Chí Minh City to get back our passports. Just sitting there, mute and still.

Every time Uncle Ngô slows down or lurches forward, I hear the things in the trunk and back seat move. Before leaving Hồ Chí Minh City, Uncle Ngô thought it was a good idea to buy Mother things she might need. So we bought packages of vermicelli noodles by the bulk, some twenty packages. We also purchased canned goods by the dozen: Grass Jell-O, palmed fruits and lychees in heavy syrup, pickled mangoes and limes, bottles of fish sauce. We even bought her catfish and slabs of beef and pork. Then it dawned on Uncle Ngô that she probably didn't have a place to store the meat and fish. So we bought a freeze box no bigger than the red ice chest every family in America used for picnics and barbecues, weekends on the beach, or attending little league baseball games. We bought so much stuff that the storeowner had his sons haul everything out to the car with a dolly.

When I asked Uncle Ngô how much everything cost and he told me four hundred dollars, I knew not to make a face or to utter even a sound. He'd think I was putting a price on my own mother, but as he took out our money to pay for the food and freeze box, I wondered if the cost of not having a mother for seventeen years could be calculated. And when Uncle Ngô set the wad of money on the counter, he glanced at me. Still, I didn't say a word but stood there and nodded in agreement like it all made perfect sense to give a woman who abandoned me four hundred dollars worth of food and a freeze box.

The fog is getting thicker the farther we drive. Uncle

Ngô braces one leg against the steering wheel to free his hands. He reaches over and takes up the soft pack from off the dashboard, extracts a cigarette and lights it with his Zippo. He replaces the soft pack and lighter on the dashboard and takes the wheel with one hand.

The fog is still thick. Uncle Ngô begins to accelerate from sixty miles per hour to seventy where the needle rests for a brief moment before rising in an arc to seventy-five. The needle does not stop at the next increment in speed, but continues to rise until it reaches eighty, then settles.

"Don't you want to slow down just a bit, Uncle Ngô?" I ask, sitting deep in the vinyl seat.

"I know this road. No problem."

He cruises at eighty, and he is very much relaxed with one hand on the wheel and the other propped on the door's sill. I peer into the white wall of fog and at the broken yellow lines painted on this newly paved road that curves left and right, and I imagine this is what Uncle Ngô is using to guide him.

"Your mother is like this." He holds out his hand before him. "There is fog very heavy, but I know what is beneath it."

I turn to him, and although he does not acknowledge me, he smiles all the same. He flicks ashes out the window before placing the cigarette back in his mouth. I return my attention to the road and stare into the white wall barely parting from our headlights, and I anticipate the moment we emerge from the fog, ready to breathe easier again.

········

We drive into Nha Trang, only now the heads of palm

trees stay afloat above the fog. We pass along a row of bungalows before we get into a section of the city filled with French styled villas with large verandas. It is 5:30 in the morning and people in black pajamas leave their homes carrying straw baskets filled with laundry. Some shoulder bamboo poles with empty baskets hanging at both ends; they walk in the opposite direction, and I assume they're heading for the marketplace we passed three miles back. They wear sun hats around their necks by the straps and some have tied handkerchiefs to cover their nose and mouth.

Uncle Ngô continues down the dirt road, which leads through a palm orchard. Before long we are out in the open again as we head toward the houses near the beach. The water is a dull green due to the fog drifting in from the sea. Uncle Ngô pulls up to a house, and standing on the porch filled with potted jade plants is a short woman whose hair is wrapped in a bun. I sit forward in my seat. Because there is so much fog, because she stands as still as the posts that hold up the veranda, she looks like a ghost come to remind those from the present of the past.

"Is that her?" I ask.

Uncle Ngô doesn't answer because we both know it is she. He turns off the engine, and we sit there. I don't know what we're waiting for, but we sit there and watch. And I guess I'm waiting for her to blink, let us know to get out of the car. I barely breathe through my mouth. The hot engine ticks. The sound of the door opening on Uncle Ngô's side startles me, and it is only now I realize I've been clutching the seat to stop trembling.

Uncle Ngô climbs out of the car, and I do the same. I

feel my legs cramping up, and I walk stiffly as I make my way around the car, but I refrain from shaking them loose. She may think there is something wrong with me.

"Hi Vu-An." Uncle Ngô climbs the steps with arms out. He kisses her on the cheek, then hugs her.

I take the steps one at a time, and finally I am standing in front of her. She comes up to my chest. The blouse and pants she wears are loose on her. She has thinned over the years. Her cheeks, which were once round, are shallow enough to expose her high cheekbones. The skin around her jaw is stretched taut. The lines beneath her eyes extend from the inner corners out toward her cheeks. Lines frame her mouth. The tendons in her neck are prevalent, her Adam's apple made prominent. The notch at the base of her throat is sunken and dark.

"Hi Long-Vanh," she says with a smile.

"Hi," I stammer, not from nervousness, but from indecision to call her Mother.

I do not know what else to say or do. Finally, I hold out my arms, force my legs to move, and when I am close enough I wrap my arms around her. I am surprised by how small and thin she is. I can feel the notches of her spine against my palm and the way her shoulder blades protrude. She pats me on the back, an American expression to let go, we've hugged long enough, but I hold onto her because of what's happening. My legs grow weaker, and my face begins to burn, and I find myself biting down on my bottom lip because I feel it coming. And no matter how much I try, I can't help it, but it comes out in one burst.

"It's OK," Mother says. "It's OK." She tries to pull me

away.

Uncle Ngô takes me by the arm, but I won't let go. I'm too embarrassed to let Mother see me cry like this, embarrassed that she can make me feel this way after so many years. It's like I'm ten years old again, and the moment I let go, she will be gone for another seventeen years. I hold her and think back to that morning she left, and I did not get to see her leave; she did not get to see me cry as I ran from room to room, thinking I had misplaced the suitcase, only to remember it was still outside, beneath the ivy. I hold her, believing she will curl up, wither away, and I am left holding only her clothes.

Bartered Hands

I wake up to the sound of Mother and Uncle Ngô laughing and talking in a way I haven't heard in years: when one finishes speaking, the other immediately chimes in without so much as a pause. Sunlight hits the shutters, but it doesn't make its way into my room. Sitting up, I look around the bare room and notice Uncle Ngô's thin mat rolled up tight and the folded blanket tucked in the far corner. After folding my blanket and rolling up my mat, I set them next to Uncle Ngô's. Dressed in jeans and a blue dress shirt, I leave the room with toothbrush and paste in hand.

I follow the sound of their voices. They stop speaking when the floorboards creak, and when I enter the kitchen, they are already staring in the direction of the doorway from which I enter. Mother smiles and points to a room behind me.

"In there. Brush your teeth in there."

I turn to look behind me, and before I go into the bathroom, I exchange glances with Uncle Ngô. He just looks at me as he holds the cup of coffee with both hands and massages it with his thumbs. Once I close the door behind me, their talking resumes.

It is a bigger bathroom than I expected, though like the room I slept in, it is bare. The enamel basin sits atop a table that serves as a counter. Water has been drawn for me, and a cup floats in place. As I brush my teeth and my mouth fills with foam, I look about the bathroom won-

111

dering where do I spit. I walk over to the far corner where there is a slight raise in the floor. From the hole, the smell of urine and waste comes up through the floorboards, and I realize it's a toilet. I peer into the dark shallow tub underneath the house to make sure I'm directly over it before letting the foam drip from my mouth in a long white stream. I push open the shutters to let in some air and sunlight, and I notice something I hadn't seen when I walked in: the shower in the opposite corner. It is the only area in bathroom that is tiled, and a bamboo screen courts it off. The chrome showerhead shines spotless of rust or watermarks; the brass rosary chain I assume turns on the water. And in a half coconut shell near the drain are several worn bars of soap.

I turn in a circle while holding my toothbrush, turn and take in the table, the hole in the floor, the bamboo-screened shower, the sunlight coming through the square hole in the wall, and the whole time I am imagining the way Mother has lived these past seventeen years. Though it is plain and the whole house is equipped with only the bare necessities, I know Mother is content with this.

········

"Hi son," Mother says as she stands up from her chair and comes around the table to hug me. Only one hand reaches up to hug her, afraid if the other one comes around I'll start crying again. "Would you like some coffee?"

"Yes, please." I take my seat at the table.

Uncle Ngô still massages the cup. Mother goes to the potbellied stove and pours a cup of coffee. I can feel the heat coming off the stove's bulging black belly.

"Thank you for all the food. My gosh, I can live like a queen with this much food." Mother says. Mother sets the cup before me and takes her seat. "And thank you for the package. I'm sure I can fit into my clothes."

"You're welcome," I say and wait for her to thank me for the other contents of the package: the letters, the jade pieces, the Polaroids. But when she doesn't say anything else, I take a sip of coffee and flinch from how hot it is.

"Ngô tells me you and Phượng are married," she says, her voice rising with her smile.

"Yes." I take another sip, careful not to burn myself. "Yes. We've been married for three years now."

"But no kids." Mother sits forward with her arms crossed and resting on the table.

"No. No kids," I shake my head. "We want them. It's just that we want to wait and be sure."

"Be sure?" Mother frowns.

I hold the cup to my mouth with both hands and blow. Uncle Ngô sits forward in his seat. And I realize as he sits waiting for me to answer that Phượng and I have never included him in our plans. Although he lives in the same house, in my old bedroom while Phượng and I have taken my parents' room, although he eats with us and we go out on the front patio to smoke cigarettes and watch the sun go down, we never tell him anything about us. I take a sip.

"We want to make sure we're ready to be parents," I finally answer. "We don't want to rush into it and not give them what they want."

"But you have a good job. And a house. You still live in the same house, right?"

"Yes. That's not a problem. It's just that we want to give them the attention they need. We want to give them *our* time. I don't want to disappoint them."

Mother doesn't move back as I expected. She remains seated forward with arms crossed and elbows on the table. Uncle Ngô sits back in his chair, and it is silent again. I slurp my coffee.

"Well, in time you'll have children, and then I can be a grandmother." Mother laughs and leans in Uncle Ngô's direction.

I look at my coffee, thinking, *You missed the first step as mother. You can't just skip.* I continue to sip coffee.

"I should stop bothering you about that. I'm sure Phượng gets enough of that from Handsome."

Uncle Ngô brings his cup away, coughing from swallowing wrong. He realizes that not all of this is a vacation, and in this moment he also realizes that Mother knows nothing.

"How is Handsome doing?"

There is a silence that lasts too long. Mother looks from Uncle Ngô and then to me waiting for an answer. And as she waits she takes no notice of our bowed heads, our eyes kept on our cups, and it surprises me that she cannot read our silence.

"He's fine," Uncle Ngô says, and I can hear his voice getting caught in his throat, like he wants to take back his answer.

I look at him. He blinks as he stares into his cup.

"Is he still working at the graveyard?" Mother asks.

"He practically lives there," I say.

"That's a shame. He is so smart. I thought he would do

better with all that school," Mother says. She rocks herself to and fro as she stares at her near-empty cup of coffee. "Well, if that's what he wants to do, then," she shrugs her shoulders.

Uncle Ngô picks up his cup of coffee and finishes the rest of it without looking up at anyone. Mother continues to rock to and fro in her seat, smiling from across the table.

········

Uncle Ngô and I walk down the boardwalk along Nha Trang Beach. There are small hotels and cafés and restaurants facing the South China Sea. We settle at a table outdoors beneath a palm-thatched veranda of a café. The breeze comes in steady waves. It is the afternoon and children run along the shore, tempting the waves as their mothers sit out on blankets and keep watch. Small boats oared by men and women in black pajamas and sun hats tied at their chins come from opposite directions and meet in a tight circle to trade what they have.

A waiter comes outside to take our order, and Uncle Ngô puts up two fingers and says a couple of words. The waiter bows before going back inside, and we sit in silence. Uncle Ngô takes out his pack of cigarettes and jerks two free, handing the second one to me. We light up and sit there and watch the boats stationed in a close circle, watch hands giving over bundles wrapped in cloth or paper.

The way they handle the bundles reminds me of strangers in uniform handling Uncle Handsome Harlemite's body the day he died. After Phượng spent the night at

my place, we walked back to her apartment in the afternoon. When we came down Montana Avenue and round-
ed the corner, we stopped upon seeing the ambulance
backed up in the driveway. Police cars parked along the
curb, their blue lights flashing.

"Oh no," Phượng muttered.

I stood beside her without saying a word. Police officers kept walking up and down the steps that led to her
apartment, and the paramedics unloaded a gurney. They
set the gurney down, collapsed the wheels and metal legs
so that it folded underneath, then carried it upstairs. Other tenants watched from behind the yellow tape.

Phượng started walking toward them. Her arms remained stiff at her sides, head straight. I followed right
behind her. She crossed the street without looking both
ways. She was able to duck underneath the yellow tape
and make it as far as the bottom of the steps when an officer seized her by the arm.

"You can't go up there."

"I live here," she muttered.

"Well, you can't go up there. Not right now." Before
she could say a word or shrug off his hand, we heard them
coming down. "What's your name, hon?"

"Phượng."

The officer led her to the side and bent down low
enough to look her in the eyes. As he talked, Phượng kept
her eyes on the steps, waiting for the paramedics to appear. She wasn't listening to what the officer said. She just
watched and waited.

The paramedics finally appeared with the gurney. The
body was covered with a white sheet and strapped down

in three places. Beneath the sheet we could make out the feet and the arms, but the sheet was soaked red where the head seemed formless. They didn't bother to set the legs and wheels on the ground. Instead, they carried the body to the back of the ambulance where a third person waited inside. He reached down with his clean white gloves, took a hold of the front rail and slid the body inside. They closed the back doors, went around each side, and climbed in. What surprised me was that Uncle Ngô came downstairs with an officer, and I figured someone had called him at work. He saw us, and without saying a word, he placed a hand on our shoulders and led us to his Monte Carlo.

I look at Uncle Ngô now, sitting across the round table as he smokes his cigarette, amazed over how well he took care of everything that day.

We remained silent during the ride over to the hospital, especially Phượng, but there was a stillness about her that made everything seem fine. Uncle Ngô pulled into the parking lot of Kaiser Hospital. As though he had worked here many years instead of the auto shop, as if he were able to read the English words aglow in neon or painted on glass doors like it was his first language, Uncle Ngô passed through many corridors, turned corners, went down stairwells, and parted any double doors he came upon until we were at the basement of the hospital, the morgue.

There were offices downstairs, no windows, and Uncle Ngô walked up to one of the doctors in a white lab coat and whispered to him. The doctor squinted behind his glasses as he looked over Uncle Ngô's shoulders at us.

"They will have to wait here. They can have a seat on the bench," he pointed to a metal one against the wall.

We sat down and Uncle Ngô followed the doctor through double metal doors. The doors swung shut and stayed closed for half an hour, during which time we were alone. I heard footsteps down different corridors, but no one ever came to our section, and I wanted someone to walk by, look at us even. They wouldn't have to say anything, just be present for a moment so I could place a face to the feet I kept hearing going back and forth.

Phượng remained still. She trained her eyes at the wall, and her breathing was even. Her hands were at her sides, and her feet, though barely touching the linoleum floor, kept from swaying. And I remember wanting to tell her to speak, just speak and her voice would fill our corridor. I don't know why I didn't take it upon myself to say something, to console her at least, or even hum, but I guess out of respect, out of some sense of wanting to give Phượng her moment of peace, I kept quiet. And being quiet was like we were invisible, as unseen as the man I read about that summer from the H.G. Wells novel. Just invisible sitting on the bench and we were waiting to be seen, to be discovered.

Uncle Ngô finally came from the room; the double metal doors flapped shut behind him. And although I was glad to see him emerge, the way he calmly walked—with head up after spending half an hour with the body and listening to the coroner—made me dizzy. It was the way he also kept quiet, like Phượng and Uncle Ngô had an understanding they did not have to communicate through words, and what he conveyed was that he was going to set things right. Being in the morgue didn't help my dizziness, for it was only hours before that Mother had left for the airport, and sitting here reminded me of her absence, her abandonment a form of death.

Uncle Ngô walked up to us, held out his hand, and Phượng took it. She stood up from the bench and together they headed down the long corridor, and I followed. It wasn't until we were halfway home I noticed the white gloves he wore, and I wondered why they made him wear them. Were they afraid he was going to contaminate the body, contaminate those who were already dead?—or were they considerate in keeping Uncle Ngô's hands clean? I imagined Uncle Ngô pressing a hand against a part of Uncle Handsome Harlemite's body to feel what the coroner was talking about. The white gloves were clean and I didn't mention them to him.

Uncle Ngô crushes his cigarette in the tin ashtray. The waiter comes out with two glasses of ice. Condensed cream sits at the bottom of the glasses. He sets two French presses filled with coffee grinds and hot water in front of us. Uncle Ngô pays and tips the waiter.

We press down on the knob, hold it for a couple of seconds before pouring the coffee into our glasses. We swirl the spoons around until the color turns brown.

"I'm sorry I lie," he says.

"Phượng would be pissed," I say. "Very angry."

"Yes." He nods. "Yes. But you know in Asia, one never dies."

I look at him and he meets me with a faint smile.

"Yes, but Uncle Handsome Harlemite is not Asian." I look away and drink coffee.

Uncle Ngô stabs the ice with his spoon.

That day when we drove up Montana Avenue and

Uncle Ngô parked the car, he reached down to undo his seatbelt when Phượng asked for his gloves. Uncle Ngô frowned at his hands and touched the fingertips, and his shoulders slouched. His mouth worked for words, but none came.

"Can I have them?" she asked. "I never got to see his body."

Again, Uncle Ngô touched the gloves that fit snugly over his hands. He pulled at the fingers gingerly until he could slide them off; he handed the gloves to her. She rubbed them together and muttered, "Thank you." She stayed inside the car for a while longer, alone with the gloves.

Phượng still has them. She keeps them in a dresser drawer buried beneath her bras and panties. Because she has so many of them, it takes almost a month before she has to do the wash. But when she's about to run out of undergarments she'll see the gloves. Once, I caught her standing there with the dresser drawer opened. She picked them up, brought them to her nose and sniffed, and she had probably hoped she could still smell her father or traces of the room in which they kept his body. I waited a while without saying a word, and I expected her to cry, to see her shoulders and back jerk in spasms as she covered her nose and mouth with the gloves to muffle her sobbing as she had that day she asked for them and sat in the car long after Uncle Ngô and I went into the house. I watched her and waited to see my wife cry, but after she had her fill of smelling, she hugged them to her neck and bowed her head. I stepped out of the room, careful not to make a sound.

"I'm sorry," Uncle Ngô says before taking a large swallow of his creamed coffee.

"It's OK," I say.

I continue to watch the people trade on the water. The circle of small boats grows larger. Men and women pass bundles and baskets from one boat to the next until they are safely in the hands of those who bartered well.

Letters to Vietnam

Mother stares at the bundle of letters in front of her. Her lips are pressed together, the corners stretched, and I can't tell if she's smiling or simply overwhelmed by them. She caresses the back of her hand. Uncle Ngô took the rental car and drove into the city.

"Do you know what is in these letters?" Mother asks.

"Yes."

"Uncle Ngô read them to you?"

"No. Phượng would listen to you and Aunt Pham Thi, and then she'd tell me."

"Pham," she whispers and smiles.

"But I didn't need Phượng entirely. I knew things were not right just by the tone of your voice . . . when you read them to yourself."

"So you know everything." Mother's smile fades as she turns to look at the potbellied stove in the corner.

"As much as I need to know."

Before her eyes narrow and well up with tears, she covers her face with her hands. I start to move toward her, but I pull back and watch her cry. She looks so old, not because of her wrinkled hands that have hardened over years spent in the fields working in the sun, or from the streaks of white hair, but because she can hide her whole face behind her hands. Her shoulders shake as she sobs. I sit there and watch her, watch her wither in front of me.

"What else would you like to know about him?" she manages.

"Where he's buried."

·······

Uncle Ngô is smoking a cigarette; his elbow rests on the doorsill of the Citroen, and I am seated behind Mother as she remains still. Ahead, there are rock formations off the coast, their bases hidden by low-lying fog, and we cruise the hilly road, and yet it appears we are getting no closer to the rock-mountains. And because the rock formations' tops are only shown, I expect Uncle Ngô to come through the fog and we find ourselves just inches from crashing into them.

But they are far off. Their round, yet jagged tops exposed above the fog look like knuckles, and this hilly road Uncle Ngô drives over is like the back of God's hand, and we are driving over His thick veins and the tender bones, and every time we dip and progress towards His knuckles it's like we are entering heaven the back way, like we're cheating, and Uncle Ngô and Mother are quiet like they've done this before and that it's no big deal on how one gets there, so long as one gets there. And I expect those knuckles to come alive, to rise up until we see God's fingers, the loose flesh, ridged and wrinkled at the joints, the nails polished like flawless pearls, manicured and cleared of any grime, dirt, or fungus.

Uncle Ngô takes a long drag and throws the cigarette out the window. Before he's about to enter heaven, we come out of the fog, and I see the rock formations off the coast, the salt mounds at the bases of the rocks. Workers wade the shore with baskets, and before we get to the rocks, the road veers to the left, through a small town. On either side of us are outdoor markets displaying mounds of mangoes, the purple pineapple-like dragon fruits, bunches of lychees, and bouquets of longans dusty from the traffic.

The vendors stare at us from behind mounds of fruits, tracking our progress through town, and then we are among the fields and trees again.

········

We get out of the car, and Mother wipes her hands on the front of her blouse as she begins walking toward a structure, and when I see it I stop. It is larger than what I imagined, but she walks to it and Uncle Ngô follows. They enter the quarter empty of cots, but on the wooden floor there are dark circles equally distant from each other, and I know they are where the legs of the cots were, and the darker they are, the more the people weighed down by dreams and the burdens of the day's labor. I search the circles for Mother's weight, for Lý Loc's weight. How much weight did she press upon these floors? How much did I weigh her down when she slept?

"Well, you wanted to see him. So here he is," Mother says, holding out her hand to the field before her.

Uncle Ngô reaches inside his shirt pocket for his cigarettes. Mother sits at the steps that lead to the fields and she places her hands on her knees and looks out at the fields long harvested of rice. The stalks are brown and wilted, and there are patches of land pale with dirt and clumped long ago by the rainy season.

When I don't say anything, she turns to me and says, "He wanted to be cremated and have his ashes spread in the very fields he worked, the fields where he said he died.

And then he can become alive again."

Uncle Ngô glances at me before he leans against one of the posts and stares out across the fields at the tree lines intermingled with bamboo shoots. I expect Uncle Ngô to walk over to them with switchblade in hand, snap the bamboo shoots close to their roots and start tearing off their leafy shoots to whittle their ends, connect them with holes bored into them, hook one into a faucet and turn on the water and watch the wooden sprinklers at work. The fields will flood, and the rivulets will gather Lý Loc's remains, and like God's Eden, Lý Loc will take shape from the ground and stand naked and dirty.

·······

Mother and I are in the kitchen making fresh spring rolls. She's washing the vegetables in a bucket she keeps in the corner while I sit at the table, stripping the shells off large shrimps and slicing them down their backs and bellies to extract their spleens and intestines. Black shit, Mother used to call them.

Mother is humming while she washes the green leaf lettuce and mint. She even takes a sponge to rub the cucumbers of their waxen texture though she's going to slice the skin off anyway. She stops humming abruptly, stops washing and looks up from her place in the corner and smiles.

"I still can't believe you and Phượng are married."

I nod and wish Uncle Ngô were back from the city so he can field any questions she may have regarding Uncle Handsome Harlemite. Continue the lies.

"It's nice. We know everything about each other so

there are no secrets. No lies to tell."

Mother goes back to cleaning the vegetables. She places them in a colander and brings it to the table. Standing over me, Mother reaches down and takes up a shrimp I just peeled, its tail missing.

"God," she says. "You are still bad at this." She laughs, shakes her head, and places the shrimp back in the bowl. "Here. Like this." She takes a shrimp, peels the shell from around the body, and then pinches the shell around the tail and plucks it off, leaving the tail intact.

"Phượng gets on my case, too."

"That is what a good wife is supposed to do."

Mother takes a pot from off the table where she keeps all the skillets, dishes, and utensils. She empties the water she used to wash the vegetables into the pot and sets it on the potbellied stove. She opens the hatch with a towel carefully wrapped around her hand to check the fire.

"Did you ever want to come back to Los Angeles?"

"Ummm," she pouts. "Maybe just to visit."

"Oh," I say, and look down at the shrimp in my hand. "I meant to live with us. Would you like to live with us? Not just a visit."

"Oh no," Mother's eyebrows rise in sharp arches. "No. I can't. This is my home. This is where I belong, not America. But you can come and visit when you and Phượng have your first child. Show your child where you were born," she says.

The tone of her voice upsets me because it doesn't fit with what I just asked. And the way she said it, making light of my offer as if everything is fine, makes me wonder why I even asked. But that's what I thought I was coming here for, to bring her home. I expected her—in that brief moment—to smile and say, "Yes. I've been waiting for you to ask."

I remember before I left for Vietnam I met Dad for lunch at Jerry's Deli in Marina Del Rey. Dressed in a three-piece, pin-striped suit, Dad peered at me from across the table as he chewed his Reuben sandwich with deliberate slowness when I told him about the phone call and my plan to go see her.

"Why would you want to do that?" he finally said after swallowing his food. "What do you expect to come out of this?"

I frowned at him and give him the obvious response.

"Because she's still my mother."

He took up his Reuben and just before taking another bite, he said, "Be careful of what you expect."

Now I wish I had run it by Uncle Ngô first. I peel the shrimp faster, and slice their bellies and backs almost deep enough to cut them in halves.

"How is Wil?"

"Who?" I say.

"Your father. Wil?"

"He's fine. He's doing well for himself. Lives in Marina Del Rey. With someone, a girlfriend."

"Aah, yes." She nods. "Uncle Ngô told me about working for an accounting firm. I also expected him to find someone."

I was up with Uncle Ngô that night he told Dad to leave. We were outside on the lower patio working on his Harley; I held the flashlight steady to where he pointed. It had been some three months after Mother left, some three months after Uncle Handsome Harlemite had shot himself in the head with the pistol he used during his graveyard shifts patrolling Forest Lawn Mortuary. Mia was off somewhere with one of her boyfriends, and Phượng was spending the night with Yên. I held the flashlight and thought of nothing but helping Uncle Ngô in any way I could as he restored what had been dead and broken and abandoned, held the light as sweat dripped from my underarms and down my back.

Though he had the Harley for almost a year, it still sat on blocks. It looked ready. Although the chrome shone even in the dark, the old, torn, crusty leather seat had been replaced, and the rust scraped clean and buffed, Uncle Ngô kept picking up pieces littered on the patio and screwing them onto the bike.

Just then Dad pulled up in his Firebird, and we could hear the loud shrill laughter of a woman. We peeked over the ledge at the street below and she was practically sitting in the driver's seat hugging Dad. Uncle Ngô worked a nut with the socket and continued watching them. As Dad turned off the headlights and engine, Uncle Ngô returned his attention to the Harley.

They got out of the car and walked up the steps with arms around each other. The woman's wavy blond hair fell around her face, and all I could see were her blue eyes—round and big—and her gleaming teeth.

"Hi Ngô. Hello son." Dad waved his free hand.

"Hi," Uncle Ngô said without looking up from where I shined the flashlight.

They went inside the house, and the woman sat at the dinner table while Dad went to the refrigerator for two

cans of Schlitz and joined her at the table. After tightening
the last bolt that held the shell in place to cover part of the
engine, Uncle Ngô set the socket wrench on the ground
and laid his hands flat against his thighs. He stared off
in the direction of the opened front door and sighed. He
picked up the rag and wiped the palms of his hands, then
each finger.

"She's sitting in mom's chair," I said.

"Wait here," he said.

I turned off the flashlight. Uncle Ngô headed inside
the house where he stood in the middle of the living room.

"Take her home," Uncle Ngô said.

I quietly went up and sidled my way to the window
and peeked through the thin curtains. Dad and the woman stared at him as he placed his hands on his hips, waiting. And when they didn't say a word he said, "She leave,
and you leave too. No more."

"What?" Dad frowned.

"No more. You leave this house. You shame this house,
this family with her." He pointed at the woman. "Long-
Vanh do not have to see this."

"Ngô, this is my house, and I'll invite any friend I want."

The woman sat back in her seat directing a smirk at
Uncle Ngô. That was when I came away from the window
and stood in the doorway.

"You bad example to him," Uncle Ngô pointed at me.
"Leave."

Everyone turned to me, and I blinked repeatedly and
moved my tongue inside my mouth to make sure the word
came from me.

"Leave," I said again, a little louder.

"What did your boy say?" the woman asked.

"You're sitting in my mother's chair, trash."

The woman glared at me with mouth opened.

"You're going to let your boy talk to me like that, Wil?"

"I'll talk to you the way I want to. You're in my mother's chair. *Get up.*"

Dad stood up and said, "Watch how you talk to adults. You show her some respect."

"I don't respect her," I said. "She called me 'boy'. If Mother sees her . . . If Mother sees her—"

Dad turned to the woman and told her to wait for him in the car. The woman exchanged glances with everyone before standing up and walking past mc. Dad and Uncle Ngô stared at each other for a long time without saying a word. When Dad looked away and shook his head, Uncle Ngô told him, "You stay at her house, not bring her home here. You not divorce."

"She left. That's as good as being divorced."

"She's coming back." I said.

They turned and stared at me. Frowns began forming on their foreheads, but at that moment, I believed what I had said. She had been gone three months, but I believed she was getting tired of Vietnam, and she was missing me, and now she wanted to come back to Los Angeles, come back to this house and start anew.

"She's not coming back Long-Vanh," Dad said and shook his head slowly.

"Yes she is. She left because of you, not me. It wasn't because of me."

"You not bring women home no more. *No more*," Uncle Ngô interrupted.

"What I do in my own home is my business," Dad jabbed at his own chest.

"No. It's mine and Long-Vanh's, too."

Dad came from around the table and left the house. I stayed by the door and heard him go down the steps, heard him get into his car and tell her he was taking her home. Dad started the car and I could hear the engine working as he sped off down Montana Avenue. Behind me, Uncle Ngô sighed. He joined me outside, fished inside his pocket for a cigarette and lit it. Just before he pocketed the cigarettes I asked, "Can I have one too?"

He looked at the pack and opened his mouth to speak. Instead, Uncle Ngô jerked his wrist and I took the one cigarette that stood up from the pack.

"It hurt the first time you take in your throat."

"I just want to puff on it," I said.

He held out the Zippo, and I puffed on the cigarette until it caught. He snapped shut the Zippo. I held the cigarette between two fingers, and every so often I puffed on it and watched the end light up like coals being stoked. I watched Uncle Ngô take in each drag and hold it in his lungs for the span of a breath before exhaling. When we were through, we went back to work on the Harley: I held the flashlight as he tightened parts in their rightful places.

········

There was a difference in Dad the following week. We didn't talk about that night and we rarely saw each other, but he did make himself a little more available. He requested to work swing shift five days a week instead of six. No more graveyards. Every morning he had a lunch bag packed for me to take to school and twenty-five cents just in case I needed something like a carton of milk or orange juice. Because he wouldn't see me by the time I returned home at 3:30 in the afternoon, there would be a note on the dinner table instructing me to heat up the rice and beans or pork chops or baked chicken. On the weekends, he'd study at the dinner table, filling graphing papers with equations he'd whittle down to single numbers.

Because Phượng spent the weekends helping Mia keep Yến company and Uncle Ngô worked where his hands marked the hours of fixing people's neglect of running their cars to near ruin, I did my homework at the table as well. Most weekends as it neared dinner time, Dad would start cooking. But one weekend I went to the refrigerator at noon. Dad looked up from his calculator with pencil poised in hand and watched as I took the bagged vegetables from the fridge.

"What are you doing?"

"I'm making spring rolls for dinner."

"Now?"

"It takes all day," I say. "Especially for me."

"You know how to make it?"

I looked at him, mindful not to frown. I nodded and said, "I've made them here and at Aunt Phạm Thị's."

"You need help?" he asked after noticing the armload of vegetables I carried to the sink.

"Can you peel the shrimps? I always tear off the tails."

Dad dragged the chair back and came into the kitchen where he took the bag of shrimps, a bowl from the cupboard, and set them on the dinner table and began peeling while I washed the vegetables and set a pot on the stove to boil the rice noodles. When he was through, he brought the bowl of peeled shrimps to the kitchen and just as I

opened my mouth to tell him what he needed to do next, I
saw that he had already removed the black shit.

········

Dad dipped the spring roll in the saucer of *nước mam*
and took his first big bite of something I made, and his
mouth stopped chewing for a moment. He nodded and
continued chewing.

"This is really good, Long-Vanh," he said. He dipped
the spring roll in the *nước mam* to take another bite.
"What else can you make?"

"A lot: stir-fried chicken and ginger, *bún chả*, bitter
melon soup."

He nodded at each dish I listed, and I had to make
myself stop because all he ever taught me was to behave
and to erase chalkboards and sweep floors, and then I remembered the things I couldn't do like speak Vietnamese,
read the letters Mother had received, or even use chopsticks properly.

"Do you think Mother is there? You think she made it?"

Dad shook his head as he chewed. When he finished
swallowing, he said, "I don't know." He shrugged. "I have
no idea."

"You think she'll write to us and let us know?"

Again, he shrugged and shook his head.

"Maybe I can write a letter to Vietnam. I still have all
the letters from Vietnam. I can write to the address on the
envelopes and ask if she got there."

"If you want to. Don't be surprised if they don't answer
you."

The morning Mother had left, Dad found a letter on

the table. It simply said that she was going home. Dad had gone into my room to wake me up and told me. He stood at the foot of my bed and stared at the letter in his hand. To keep from trembling, he pressed the crease where Mother had folded it in half, but I knew he was also trying not to cry. I kept silent as I waited to hear what else he had to say, but I also wanted to go to the closet to see if the Samsonite was gone.

Dad didn't say anything else. He just left the room.

I reached for another spring roll and said, "If she's there, you can go back and get her."

"No one can get in there," Dad said.

"If *she* got in, couldn't you?"

Dad stopped chewing and stared at me from across the table. He hooked his thumb in the direction of the living room and asked, "You been keeping up with what's going on in Iran?"

"Yes."

"Carter can't get his ass into Iran to get the Americans out. He can't even step foot in Vietnam."

It was then I put down my spring roll. I imagined Mother stepping foot in Vietnam and the soldiers asking her what she wanted. I imagined her smiling and telling them she wanted to see her father, that she came a long way. But then they took her to a field, whispered to her that they were taking her to see him, but they kept walking into the fields until she found herself in the jungle of tall banyan trees overgrown with vines thicker than ropes used for nooses.

"I'm sure she made it," I said. "And one day, when they allow people to visit, we can go back, even get Lý Lôc to come back with us."

Dad forced a harsh sigh. He began chewing his food, and then suddenly he stopped. All of him just stopped and he stared at me, his jaw slack, the spring roll clutched between his fingers, and his eyes began to get moist.

"You knew she wanted to go all this time?" he raised his voice.

When I just sat there with mouth opened, Dad leaned forward and the table sounded with a loud thud from his elbow planted at the center to point a finger at me.

"That's why you asked me all those questions at the diner that morning. You knew and you didn't say a word. What the hell is wrong with you boy?"

I sat away from the table, trembling from his voice, from his thick finger directed at me, and I just went limp at the sight of his eyes narrowed in anger.

"What the hell were you thinking?" he threw up his hands.

I looked down at my plate, unable to answer, and my ears began to burn and the burning spread to the back of my neck.

"Jesus Christ! I can't believe you told no one. Now look at you. You have no mother. I have no wife, and God only knows what the hell they did to her."

The sound of the chair dragging away from the table made me jump in my seat. He stood up and continued to glare at me.

"You're a poor excuse for a son." He went for his keys, the lighter and pack of cigarettes, and slammed the door hard enough that the windows rattled, the curtains stirred, and the dishes in the sink shifted.

Phượng

Ilie on my back and listen to the geckos crawling about the walls and ceiling for insects. Uncle Ngô stirs in his sleep. I haven't mentioned the question I posed to Mother, afraid he might get upset. I was glad she didn't bring it up in an offhanded manner during dinner. Mother is up marinating the pork Uncle Ngô and I bought in Hồ Chí Minh City. As she marinates, she sings. It startlcs me at first because I expect her to come into the room at any moment, get her things and leave. But she is where she wants to be. My heartbeat settles, and I listen to the song. My eyelids grow heavy, and I wait for sleep to come, but she stops singing and goes to bed.

"Ngô?" I whisper. I turn my head in his direction. "Ngô. You up?"

He stirs and the alertness and weight of his voice is something I didn't expect.

"What is it?"

"Nothing. Just—"

"What?"

"I want to call Phượng."

"She not want you to call her. She said, 'Don't call.'"

I blink at the darkness.

"But I want to hear her voice, even if she yells at me, I don't care."

"Then call her tomorrow."

We remain silent. Uncle Ngô fusses with the pillow

until he finds a comfortable position. I open my mouth to
say something else, but it remains open to the dark and I
am angry at myself, for I can't express my rationale, like
the evening Phượng and I talked in bed before I left for
the airport.

She had been just as surprised as I was over the phone
call from Mother. But what made her angry was my decision to go see her. That whole month I did what I was
supposed to do: get a passport only to send it to the embassy in D.C. I remembered through news reports, docu-
mentaries, and friends who had traveled abroad never to
relinquish your passport, so when I was told to submit it
so that it could be recorded and verified, my response to
the lady was, "Really? I have to give it up?"

"It's so we can grant you a visa. If we don't get it, you
don't get a visa. No visa, no entry."

That whole month it took to process my passport and
visa, Phượng only said "good night," "good morning,"
"yes" and "no," "thank you" and "please." She kept quiet
for long periods while watching television, washed dishes,
cooked, paid bills at the dinner table, sat hunched over her
knees as she painted her toenails or clipped them, ironed
the clothes she would wear the next day. Her silence had
a way of making me feel invisible in my own home, even
when I filled that silence with phone calls to the embassy
to check the progress of my passport and visa.

The night before Uncle Ngô and I left, she slept with
her back to me. I grew tired of watching her stomach rise
and fall beneath the sheet. Instead, I stared up at the ceiling. I opened my mouth to speak only to take in the darkness. I must have sighed, for she rolled onto her back and

said, "If that's what you want to do, then do it. I'm not stopping you."

"Yes, but you act like I'm not allowed. I want answers, so why not go and see her?"

Phượng turned onto her back and sighed. She said, gesturing to the ceiling, "She left you. I can't respect someone who left her family behind. She's my aunt. *My* aunt, but I can't. For seventeen years she didn't contact you and ask if you wanted to see her much less your grandfather? Now he's dead. And don't tell me you haven't been thinking about your mother all these years. You changed your last name."

At that point I had remembered Mother pointing to her maiden name the first time she received a letter from Lý Lộc. I was five then, and she said, pointing, that this was her name before she met my father. She said say it, and I stared hard at the name, and when I mispronounced it, she said, "No. It's pronounced Lee, not lie."

I drew back the covers and swung my feet onto the floor.

"Where are you going?"

"The sofa."

I was surprised to find Uncle Ngô at the kitchen table hunched over a pad of paper.

"Where you go?" he asked.

I motioned to the couch. He tore off the piece of paper from the pad and joined it to his makeshift map. He immediately started adding more lines and assigning street names: Vo Van Tan, 3 Thang 2, Hoang Viet, Ly Chin Thang. Each line ran into the other, but they all led back to the MAIN SQUARE.

"I try to remember city," he said, "but may-be they change names."

He got to one line and his felt tip pen rested on the paper. The ink began to spread, and I watched it waiting for him to write a name. But he frowned, and with the other hand he brushed at the very spot of his eyebrow where hair refused to grow back. He lifted the marker and brought it down again, hoping the name would somehow come to him, but he only managed to make what started off as a small speck grow into something bigger. The black spot spread until it blended into a nearby name and the name disappeared.

Beautiful

They say blacks have big ones, and Asians are small. Because I am half of one and half of the other, women have always jokingly said I must be somewhere in the middle. I must fit just right to where I don't hurt them, just right to where I don't disappoint them either. But the truth is I've never been able to fit anywhere. I had many relationships before my marriage to Phượng, but I was never considered their boyfriend. I never met most of the women's parents because many did not care to meet me. And if by chance I did, I was always introduced as the friend as if to keep away any ideas that their daughters could date someone like me, a *còn lại*, a half-breed. There were a few promising relationships, however. A couple of times I've been promised two things: that they loved me, and no matter what, they would stick by me if their parents disagreed with the relationship. But once their parents threatened them physically or vowed to disown them, the women broke it off. Always it was the same: their inability to make eye contact, the shaking of the head, the half shrugs, the "I love you, but—" And always it was me who'd watch them walk away, me who never fit just right, me who wound up getting hurt.

Truth is, I've never been on a dry spell. Women were always curious about my kind, and they wanted to know what it was like to sleep with someone like me. To them I was something of a curiosity, someone they could lay claim to, like a token, and say, "I've slept with one of them."

Generally, I dated whoever would take me, or try me
for that matter. But I had never dated an African-American woman or even an Asian. The black women feel I am
not one of them because I am half. They took every oppor-
tunity in high school to remind me of that fact by pointing and laughing because I had no ass. The Asians? They
cannot date outside their race for fear of being disowned.
Asian parents see it as a stain on the family, a disgrace,
and if their daughters date someone outside their race,
then the men are blond-haired and blue-eyed, and even
this isn't acceptable, but in their eyes, it's good enough.
At least, as far as they're concerned, the men their daughters date and marry are pure. Whole. I'm closer to Asian
than the whites, but again, it's the "half" they don't like,
for we are deemed worthless. In Asian countries, we are
overlooked, or looked down upon.

In America, however, it is a different matter. The ad-
jectives women use to describe me are always the same.
They say I am "exotic," "eccentric," "curious looking," but
most important, "beautiful." That's the one word that always comes up when they describe biracial people. We're
beautiful. Phượng, my cousin, heard that word a great
number of times while dating. We're beautiful.

That was the word Melanie used when we first spoke.
Melanie was my last serious relationship before Phượng
and I got married. She and I attended California Arts
Institute in Valencia. We were both advertising majors.
She was from New Orleans like my dad. She approached
me one day after class and asked me what I was. She said
she could see that I was something else other than black.
When I told her I was half Vietnamese, she said, "No won-

der you're beautiful." And she was beautiful too with her brown hair cut short to expose her slender neck, and her large blue eyes that bulged from their sockets and gave the impression she was always amazed at everything around her. We went out for a month before I brought her home to meet Uncle Ngô. Uncle Ngô immediately loved her because Melanie's father restored and owned four Harleys. And what impressed Uncle Ngô was that she'd take one of the Harleys out for a ride.

After taking her home that night, Uncle Ngô said, "She is very nice, very special. You love her, Long-Vanh, you do."

I remember chuckling and shaking my head and answering, "I don't know. We just started going out. It's too soon to tell." But I did know; I did love her, and I don't remember at what point I knew this, but I didn't want to tell Uncle Ngô, afraid I might jinx a good thing.

"Show her e-ver-ree-thing about our culture," Uncle Ngô said. "Tell her e-ver-ree-thing about Vietnam," he enunciated each word slowly so that he was not misunderstood. After living in the United States for twenty-five years, he still had the tendency to slow down when speaking. "That is how you know she love you."

So that was what I did. I invited her over for dinner at least once a week, sometimes twice. She'd sit at the table, and Uncle Ngô and I would tell her what we were having for dinner. I remember that first evening we cooked for her, she sat still the whole time and watched us as we peeled shrimps, slit their bellies and backs to "devein" them. Melanie studied us as we boiled the shrimp, broiled the chicken breasts, plucked the roots off bean sprouts, thin and white; washed bunches of spearmint, red leaf lettuce, and Chinese chives; pared cucumbers of their waxen skins to expose their white bodies; boiled water for the vermicelli rice noodles; sliced the chicken breasts and cucumbers, drained the noodles and shrimp, and set everything out on platters arranged from green to red, white to bland. Three hours later, Uncle Ngô and I sat at the dinner table, and we showed her how to dip the stiff circular sheets of rice paper into warm water, rest them on plates and wait until they soften. Then we plucked noodles, placed them on the individual sheet, a couple slices of cucumbers and chicken, formed a line of curled shrimp, added bean sprouts, tore spearmint from their stems, a sliver of Chinese chives, and a cover of red leaf, and we rolled the paper forward, tucking in the sides before finishing, making sure the chives extended from the rolls like tails. When we were through, we had a pyramid of fresh spring rolls, and we sat there staring at the thin pink wrapping of the rice paper, barely hiding the red, green, and white ingredients, but holding everything together.

········

Another night I made her bitter melon soup. Bitter melons are slightly longer than cucumbers, thicker in girth–warty pale gourds with white tasteless centers. I started by splitting them down the middle while Melanie slipped a white thread through a needle's eye. I emptied the melons of their hardened centers and began stuffing them with a mixture of puréed raw chicken, noodles, and seaweed. Melanie gave me the needle and thread, and I stitched the melons, closing the seams as tightly together as possible.

"My mother used to work in a sweatshop making dresses," I said.

"She did?"

The alarm in her voice wasn't what I expected.

"It's not that kind of sweatshop," I shook my head. "She only worked eight hours a day, five days a week, and she had an hour's lunch each day. It wasn't like the sweatshops we know them as nowadays."

"Oh," Melanie said as she kept watching me pull needle and thread through the hard, raw skin, and yank on the thread to cinch tight the seam I created, until there was little slack in the thread.

"I used to go with her every day during the summer. I had no choice. I had to go."

"You must have hated it."

"At the time yes. But now I wish I had paid more attention. That was the most time she and I spent together, those eight-hour days."

I told Melanie of Mother's efficiency in working at the shop: how she never left during lunch or for the day without setting a new spool of thread in the spoke, of making sure she had patterns ready to cut when she came back, making sure she had the thin papered patterns pinned to the fabric she wanted to cut so that she didn't have to waste time when she returned to work. The times I took a break from reading the novel I was forced to read, I'd watch her as she sewed sleeves to a blouse, stitched cuffs to the ends, attached collars to necklines, coupled buttons with holes, secured pockets, then hung the blouse on a hanger. She'd then bring it to the rack and place it with the other finished blouses, and I was always amazed by how she could take a yard or two of fabric, cut patterns, and piece them together until she had something whole. Because there were many women, each one was assigned a different colored safety pin so that the owner knew who sewed how many and how much to pay each woman. Mother was always blue.

·······

I showed Melanie all the boxes of news clippings of Vietnam I had collected over the years, on anything from their reeducation camps to the economy making progress, from tourism to agricultural life. I showed pictures of women walking the streets of Ho Chi Minh City, riding mopeds, working in the rice fields, or walking down an endless dirt road with bamboo poles balanced across their shoulders with baskets hanging evenly at both ends. I pointed to the women in the pictures and told her she looks kind of like her, only slender, or like her, but with a much thicker head of hair that comes down to her waist. Her face is round, I told Melanie, not so gaunt.

"Though, after fifteen years, she could have lost a lot of weight. They don't eat so well over there," I said as I shifted through more pictures. And I have intentionally aged Mother, added lines to her face and neck, grayed her hair a bit, subtracted weight due to malnutrition after each year, after each time I opened up a newspaper or magazine, especially *Time*'s and *Newsweek*'s annual special report on Vietnam. And I think perhaps this will be the year or month or day in which some photographer accidentally captured Mother on film, and she's standing somewhere in the background ready to cross the congested streets, or she's serving phở in one of the soup stalls, or bent double from carrying a large bundle of rolled rice stalks on her back. "They don't eat well," I repeated. "The average Vietnamese person's annual income is anywhere from two to eight hundred dollars."

"Wow," Melanie said. "Can't imagine living off that."

"No," I shook my head.

Melanie took up a *Time* magazine from 1990, and she turned the pages and a noise escaped her. She settled on a spread featuring Amerasian children, and the pictures were paired up, before and after, black and white, color; they showed the children posing in snapshots with their American fathers, then alone with their weathered looking mothers who had turned thin and gray. The grown children stared at cameras, trying to stand or sit and hold up their heads like their fathers.

Melanie marveled over the pictures of children who had their fathers' brown or green eyes, but they were shaped in tight ovals; she noticed the tallness they inherited from their fathers, but they kept their mothers' slender build, kept the sculpted jaw line, prominent cheekbones, kept the long necks, their names, their mothers' ability to make syllables rise and fall in tone. They even got to keep their mothers.

········

That night while in bed, she let her hand roam over me. She smoothed the palm of one hand along my goose-like neck, felt the protrusion of my Adam's Apple and said, "This is Vietnamese." I nodded, and she kept going, brushing her thumb across my full bottom lip while the other fingers braced my cheekbones. "And your lips and face are Vietnamese." I nodded and with her forefinger she traced my thick eyebrows, and then drew circles around my eyes, pressing her fingers toward the corners where they come to sharp ends and proclaimed, "Vietnamese."

"Yes," I said.

"Is there anything that's not Vietnamese?" she smiled.

I nodded. "The color of my skin."

········

At night, after making love, we'd cuddle. Always, she'd ask to hear a story, certain I could not remember things as a child growing up in Vietnam. I'd hold her close and tell her about the time Mother told me I was an embarrassment to her; about the time Mother abandoned me when I was ten, packed up her Samsonite and left one morning to go back to Vietnam; about the time Mother tried to teach me colors by holding up a Crayola Crayon, and each time I got it wrong, she'd hit me over the head with a coat hanger. It got so bad that I couldn't tell brown from green, blue from purple. But she beat it into me, beat me until I could identify blue and its different shades of powder, midnight, and Mediterranean; beat me until I could identify brown and its different shades of tan and burnt sienna; beat me until I could feel red dripping down the side of my head, and how when Mother suddenly realized what she was doing, she held me and said she was sorry, and from that day forward she decided not to teach me anything ever again. The colors never stuck. I had forgotten them the next day simply out of fear of being asked.

To each story I told her, Melanie would hold me close and whisper, "You don't embarrass me. You won't ever embarrass me. I promise." Or, "I won't ever abandon you. I promise." Or, "I'll teach you how to tell colors. I promise." I'd feel secure in Melanie's arms whenever she said these things, especially by those two words: I promise. And that's why I fell for her, believed Melanie was the one. I had never asked anyone to promise me anything because I understood how much was at stake when it was never kept, and also because much was asked of the person. Like when Mother packed her Samsonite one night with Polaroids from our years here in America, her *áo dàis*, long-sleeved gowns with tight clerical collars, the bundle of letters she received back home, and I stood there and watched, thinking it was impossible to go back. But I was ten then. And when she shut the Samsonite closed and told me not to tell Dad and Uncle Ngô, I kept it between us. I never got to see her leave. I woke up one morning, and I searched the house not for her but the Samsonite with the red, white, and blue tag tied to the handle, and when I didn't find it I knew she had boarded the plane back to Vietnam.

········

Things were great for eight months until one night we lay in bed for what would be the last time. After making love, we laid in a spoon position. The moonlight came in through the window, casting her pale white body in soft blue. I placed my hand between her breasts to feel her heart beat in my palm. She didn't say anything, didn't ask for a story, and I knew something was wrong. But I continued to let my hand wander.

"Long-Vanh," she said, "do you ever think of getting married?"

I smiled but immediately stopped, for I sensed something in her tone.

"I've thought about it, yes. Why?"

She took my hand and held it close to her chest.

"Well, do you ever think about having kids?"

"I'd like to have kids. You've talked about wanting kids."

"What do we call them? I mean, they'll be mixed, so what do we call them?"

"This may sound funny Melanie, but we call them by their names." I chuckled.

Melanie bumped her back into my chest and torso, and said, "No. I'm being serious."

"I'm serious too. We have a boy, we give him a boy's name. Likewise for a girl. Why? What's wrong? What brought this up all of a sudden?"

"Beth asked me. She wanted to know if we've discussed, you know . . . the race issue. I told her no."

Beth was her older sister. I met her a couple months ago when she flew out to California not only to visit but also to attend her husband's convention. Thomas was a doctor nearly twice Beth's age. She had heard all about me and she wanted to meet the man that made her little sister happy, so the three of us met for coffee. Beth asked me questions while Melanie kept her hands beneath the table and stared at her cup of coffee. And I remembered the whole time it felt like an interrogation, answering question after question: What did I want to do with the degree?

Do I plan on living in Los Angeles forever? Would I like to live anywhere else? Do I like children? It felt like I was being screened, and at the end, Beth jokingly said that I was good for Melanie as if it were her decision to make.

"Beth," I mumbled.

"Yeah. She was just wondering if we spoke about it that's all. She said that whenever she and Thomas go to functions, people go up to him and say, 'Gee Thomas, I never knew you had a daughter.' Or, 'Your daughter is about the same age as my son.' She said no matter how many times it happens, it hurts to hear them say things like that. And she was wondering if we're handling all the attention we get."

"Well, are we?" I asked.

Melanie nodded her head against the pillow.

"It's just that sometimes, I notice people staring."

"Of course they stare. Does that bother you?"

"Sometimes. Don't get me wrong," she looked up at me. "Please don't get me wrong. I'm happy when I'm around you. I really am. The thing I love about you is that you don't care what people say or think. You don't care because you're happy and you're comfortable with who you are, and I love that. It's just that some days, some days when we're out, I could feel their eyes on us and it makes me feel uncomfortable."

"Have you heard anything? Has anyone said anything to you?"

"No," she shook her head. "But—"

"But what?"

"It'll happen and when it does I don't know if I can take it. I mean, if they say something, I don't know how

I'm going to handle it. And if and when we get married and have kids, we have to worry about them as well. And I don't know Long-Vanh. I don't think I can do this."

I didn't know I had done it, but Melanie looked over her shoulder at me.

"Why did you move away from me?" She asked.

"What?" I said.

"You moved away from me. Why did you do that? You're mad at me, aren't you?"

"I was just thinking. Just thinking is all."

I wrapped an arm above her waist and held her.

"Look," I began, "let me shoulder the looks and comments."

"What?"

"I said let me take the brunt for everything."

"You can't do that."

"Yes I can. This isn't new to me. I've dealt with this all the time. Besides, this isn't the South."

Melanie shook her head, "No, you can't. What about the times you're not around and I have to hear my co-workers talking behind my back? Or when I go somewhere with the kids and they see how much . . . darker they are compared to me? They'll think I'm their babysitter or something. What about then? You can't do it. You can't."

We were silent. At times Melanie wanted to say something but she took in air each time. I laid there thinking about the times Mother had held my hand while crossing the street, and I felt all the motorists' eyes on us, but Mother kept her head up as she walked straight; or the times we went to the store, and wives turned to husbands and whispered behind their hands to *look, look*. I laid there imagining the same happening to Melanie when she took our kids to the mall to buy clothes, and I wondered if there would come a day when Melanie would have to pick up our son or daughter from school because of fighting, as my mother had done several times because I beat up some kid who called me "yellow nigger" or just nigger. And I wondered if Melanie would turn to our son and tell him, "You embarrass me," as Mother had done when I was eight, and she was fed up with having to listen to the principal as she nodded her head as though it were she who had done the fighting, as though it were she being scolded.

"I'm sorry. I really am sorry." Melanie said.

"I didn't know this," I said. "I thought you were different."

"You're mad at me aren't you?"

"I thought you were different in that none of this mattered. It shouldn't matter. If you love me, if you love me—"

"But I do love you," she insisted. "I really do. It's just . . ." She faced the wall and sighed.

I let my hand roam her body even though I knew she wasn't in the mood to be touched.

"You want to hear a story?"

"*Now*?" she said. "I don't feel like hearing a story now."

"This one is good. Remember I told you about how my dad worked for a construction company back in New Orleans when we first came to the United States?" Melanie blew air from her nose. "Well, I was about eight then; it was the summer before we moved to Los Angeles. Mother and I would bring Dad lunch almost every day. The architects, the ones who owned the business, thought it'd be a good idea if Mother mowed the lawn and planted flowerbeds. They'd pay her of course and Mother accepted. It gave her something to do.

"The old Victorian house where Dad worked at the time was near some apartment complex in the projects close to the French Quarter. For a whole week Mother and I came every day, and there were always things left out on the lawn ready for her to plant. She planted Azalea bushes underneath the windows, roses on either side of the walkway, and Crepe Myrtle saplings all around the house. I sat on the porch reading a book. Dad always made me read during the summers. Dad and the others were inside the house taking down the shutters before painting the walls white. Well, on the last day, Mother mowed the lawn. It wasn't the motorized kind of mower, but the manual one where you had to push and the blades rotated. It was always best to push those kinds of mowers as fast as possible. Any slower and the blades got caught on the grass and you had to backtrack to untangle them.

"Mother was mowing and there were these two black boys hanging onto the chain linked fence watching her. They were a little older than I, probably ten or eleven. Anyway, one of them said, 'Hey. Hey. Hey you.' But Mother kept mowing, and this upset them. When Mother didn't answer them or turn to look their way, they started calling her names like Chink and Jap and yellow bitch. They told her to go back to China. They called her so many other names, names I can't remember because I was too stunned and angry by what they were saying."

Melanie turned around to look at me. Her eyes were big and moist.

"But Mother didn't say a word to them. She just kept

mowing the lawn. She didn't look their way. She just kept mowing, and they kept calling her names and I wanted her to say something to them. Tell them to shut up or call them names back. I closed the book, stood up and said, 'Hey!' And that was when Mother spoke. She said for me to shut my mouth and keep reading, and I didn't understand her. I was upset at Mother for directing her anger at me when she should have directed it at those two boys. I wanted to come down from off the porch, run to the fence and hurt those boys. I wanted to grab their fingers that clutched the fence and just bend and twist them until joints popped out of their sockets. I wanted to hurt them. Mother stared at me until I sat back down. Now the boys knew I was there. They saw the color of my skin, the way I looked, and they figured it out. They knew I was her son. This made things worse.

"One of them said, 'I see you like dark meat. Oh shit!' they laughed. 'Well, come over here and get some dick. There's plenty. Maybe too much for you to handle. I know you want some.' But Mother continued mowing, and I grew hotter each time she passed by them until finally it came time to mow the grass by the fence. That was when they started spitting at her and I prayed the mower wouldn't get caught on the tall grass, stalling her progress until she could untangle the blades. The more they worked their mouths to collect enough, the more I thought I'd run up and just hurt them, but I knew Mother would get angry. I knew Mother would stop me before I could even get to the fence. So I watched them spit at my mother as she passed back and forth in front of them. I wanted to run inside and get Dad and the others, and hopefully their presence would run them off."

Melanie curled up into a ball and cried. Her whole body shook as she tried to cover her face in her hands, and she was probably imagining the same thing happening to her–kids spitting at her and our child while shopping or walking down the street.

"I remember hating Mother at that moment for doing nothing, for pushing that fucking mower back and forth, for not shouting at them. When she was through, she came to the porch, picked up the towel and began wiping spit off her arms, face, legs, and out of her hair. What upset me even more was the slow way she did it: the patience of running that towel over herself. That was when the men finally came outside for a cigarette break, and they didn't know what had happened. It was summer, very humid, so it looked like she was wiping sweat."

I grabbed Melanie by her shoulder and tried to turn her over so that she could look at me, but she wouldn't budge.

"For a long time," I continued, "for a long time I never understood why Mother didn't do anything. But later I learned why. Do you know why? Do you fucking know why? Because nothing those boys said, nothing those boys did could ever compare to the shit my mother went through. I mean, she went through a war, her brother died in the war, she was disowned by her own father for a year for marrying my father; she left everything behind: her country, but most important her father. She understood what loss meant and that was something those boys didn't understand. She kept mowing the fucking lawn because she went through more shit than those boys will ever go through."

I finally forced Melanie on her back and I brought her hands away from her face. But she wouldn't look at me. She shut her eyes and cried.

"I love you," I told her. "I still think you're different; I believe you're different. And if you love me, then this shouldn't matter. Mother went through it because she loved my dad, and that was all that mattered. Nothing. Nothing stopped her. But if you're sure you can't . . . then you might as well get dressed and leave."

Melanie shook her head as she tried to speak. Her lips moved, but she kept crying. The arm I used to cradle the back of her head was wet. Finally, she fell against me and buried her face in my chest. I held her and told her I understood if she were to get up at this moment and leave. I held her, kept telling her this until she fell asleep.

We woke up the next morning. We didn't say a word to each other, and when Melanie began sobbing again, we both knew what that meant. I watched her get dressed; her hands fumbled with the zipper to her trousers, the clasp to her bra, the buttons to her blouse, the laces to her shoes. The whole time I watched her cry as she got dressed, I couldn't help but think she was like all the rest.

I took her purse and handed it to her, and with my hands in my pockets, I walked her to the car. She fished inside her purse for her keys, unlocked the door, and climbed in. Melanie drove off. I watched her leave.

· · · · · · · ·

After that it was hard to concentrate in class. We had a semester left and every day we'd keep conversation to a minimum: hello, goodbye, how are you? At times when I was working on story boards for a commercial, I'd sneak glances her way when I knew she was bent over her work, busy cutting up colored construction paper. I couldn't help but think of the nights in bed, all the stories I told her, how she felt in my hands, the moonlight on her body, the evenings cooking dinner as she watched, and the promises. And I wanted it all back.

One day after class I asked her out for coffee. We sat at the only available table in the café amid the other patrons who stared from above the rims of cups, from behind fashion magazines or looking up from notes they jot in the margins of their textbooks. It was more awkward than I imagined. I thought conversation would be easy since we always had something to talk about. Instead, we spent most of the time staring into our cups, trying to think of something to say.

"I miss you," she said, and it took me by surprise, for I had thought it would be I who would break down and admit this.

"I miss you, too," I said.

She reached over and caressed the hairs on my forearm.

"I haven't touched you in so long."

I reached over and touched her hand, then turned it over and traced the lines of her palms with my finger.

That was the extent of that afternoon. I wish I could say we went back to my place to hear us pant from our regrets for breaking up in the first place, to take her breath into me and feel the sweat dry on our bodies. We sat and caressed each other's face and arms, thoughtful not to do any more than that or say anything we would later regret.

Melanie's absence hit me at different moments. Like one day I had to go and buy markers, and as always, I had to buy the ones that were labeled. My fingers paused over a rainbow of markers and I realized that was something she never followed through with–teaching me how to tell colors. I distinctly remember thinking to myself at that moment, *Here I am at twenty-five, and I still can't tell my damn colors.* Oddly enough, while I was standing there with fingers poised over the rows of markers, I realized I was back where I had always been. I didn't fit anywhere because I was half, and because of this, I was never completely accepted, like half was all I was ever good for, never the whole.

Usually at the end of class, Melanie would leave with another student, a white guy, and I'd think to myself, *It's best she stays with her own kind. That way she doesn't have to worry about stares from everyone, or worry over what people will say about her dating someone outside her race; nor does she have to spend a week, a month, a year, or even a whole lifetime worrying over what she should call her children; she won't ever have to answer her parents and friends with a look that says, "A half-breed was the best I could do for myself"; and most important, she won't ever have to make any more promises she can't in the end keep. It was best,* I told myself, *that she drove off that morning.*

But what about me? Who do I marry or date for that matter? How do I date my own kind? Biracial people tend to date and marry whites, or someone other than their biracial make-up, whatever that may be, because they don't want to be reminded of being denied by their own respective races. They assume if they marry white, for instance, they have elevated themselves past their previous status of half-breed. In that person, a half-breed seeks to become a whole person, which places a great burden the other person may not want to undertake. To marry someone pure is also a way of denying who they are and their pasts. I had invested so much in Melanie and the burden was too great.

But there was one person who could field that burden, for she had gone through the same problems as well. Several months after graduating, I proposed to Phượng. Although we had known each other all our lives, we had never "gone out" for the simple fact that we were first cousins. She immediately said yes like she had been waiting all her life. Phượng and I never discussed it, but I guess our marriage was a way of accepting each other's doom since no one else wanted us. It was a way of giving up on people and the many disappointments they brought us.

One evening just before going to bed, the phone rang. It was Melanie. She was packing her belongings and moving out of state for a job. Like me, she had accepted the first job offer that came her way. We talked about how we were doing, wished each other success in life, and before we hung up, she gave me her number. And as I jotted it down, I knew I would never call her.

After hanging up, I climbed into bed. Phượng asked me who it was. "No one important," I said and rolled over and went to sleep. To this day, I haven't heard from Melanie, and like I said, I haven't called her. But some days I get this feeling that she will call, perhaps apologize for things not working out, or that we should have gone straight to my place after our afternoon at the café. I still have her number tucked away in one of the compartments of my wallet. It's just like me to hold onto the past, but I still have it though I know it is a senseless thing to think about, wish for, or even keep, because what good will come out of calling her? Melanie lives in Montana or Wyoming, I forget which. All I know is that it snows there most of the year, some place where it is always cold and white.

How Is Not Important

It just happened is what I tell friends and family after Phượng and I went out to a movie. The jokes of kissing cousins and only a short stroll down the hallway ensued, and always, Phượng and I would laugh, but as soon as our eyes met, we looked away, cleared our throats, and lowered our heads. It was that way for some time until we didn't laugh anymore, much less crack a smile.

But how it happened. It was seven months after Melanie's teary departure, and Phượng had been dumped by her last boyfriend, Chuck, the one we had all thought was the one. During that long spell, Phượng and I spent our Friday and Saturday evenings at home, having dinner, watching television, and if one of us happened to rent a movie from Blockbuster, we'd watch it together. Sometimes I worked late at the studio, drafting storyboards for commercials, and when I'd come home, I'd find her on the sofa, the colors coming off the screen and lighting her face as she watched comedies or violent films, anything that had little to do with romance. But even these films had subplots of interoffice or on-the-road romance, and with them came betrayal and make-up scenes.

The violent films are the same, and at that time, there was a string of films in which cops protected female witnesses: *China Moon, Someone to Watch over Me, Witness, The Bodyguard, Year of the Dragon,* and *Stakeout.* Sure, they stand each other, after all she is scared and he's just doing his job, but he's angry with her because she's rich, because the Klimt, Kandinsky, and Van Gogh paintings, the vases and bowls from the Ming Dynasty, the large kidney-shaped pool with the mini waterfall, the intercoms in every room, even the white carpets that are always clean, are constant reminders of a life the cop once desired but learned to despise. He understands they are of a different class. It is her husband who got killed and now the killer wants her because she's the actual target, or because she saw the killer and she can identify him.

Likewise, she is disgusted by the cop for the tough, vulgar way he talks, and most important, he's a blue collar worker, a class of people she always looked down on all her life or from the moment she married rich. However, when they are kept in close quarters, when they get over the initial arguments and parameters they have established for themselves, and their quick quips at each other's society and even the clothes they wear, they begin to know each other. Their conversations become light, and there is that scene in which she takes a morning swim, and he must watch, and you can see it in his eyes, even behind mirrored sunglasses, that he wants her. Or there's that scene where he walks down the hall and happens to catch a glimpse of her just getting out of the shower and toweling off, or better yet, he sees her through the fogged-up shower door, steam rising and billowing from the top, and the water beats against her breasts, between her thighs, and the cleft of her buttocks. Or they have dinner, and she happens to cook him her favorite dish, undoubtedly something she has cooked for her dead husband many times, or regrettably, not enough, or perhaps she had never received any compliments about the dish. Until now.

Or he cooks, and the woman is impressed because, after all, he's a cop, a blue collar worker, and cops aren't known for cooking, but he gives some sob story about learning from his mother, because what cop doesn't love his mother, or better yet, from his dead wife, undoubtedly killed because he couldn't get to his gun in time, or he was at a stake out or playing softball against a rival police department or fire department and someone broke into his house and killed her. He won the game that night by the way, coming home with the trophy to show his wife, only he had to follow a trail of blood, broken vases, upturned tables that once held trinkets and framed photographs, followed the trail into the bedroom where he found her lying in her own pool of blood.

And so they have something in common, and they want each other to fill the hole in their hearts, that emptiness that had made them bitter to the world.

They have to fuck, of course, and it goes either way: it can be fierce and biting, all their aggressions and pent up frustrations exhibited on the living room floor or on the dinner table, but never the bedroom. No. The bedroom is where it goes the other way, gentle and with close-ups of his hands sliding down her backside, or the veins on the back of his hand show as he massages a round, unblemished breast, and there are the close-ups of her legs wrapped around his waist, her hands gripping his back and shoulders, her red lips parted by moans. The audience prefers the gentle version because it shows they understand and love each other. Something fierce and biting only foreshadows the inevitable—they will break up at the end, he goes back to his life and she remains secluded in her huge house, or she dies.

That is how it happened, the need for protection, the need to fill what someone else left empty.

I had come home early, and Phượng worked only half a day at the bank on Fridays. Neither one of us had taken anything out to thaw, so we decided on a Thai restaurant in Los Feliz. Halfway into our meal we both stared past the glare coming in through the window and realized the sun was still out, and though neither of us admitted it, we knew that after dinner, even if we decided on dessert—coconut ice-cream, fried banana, or fried green tea ice-cream—there was still the rest of the evening, and most likely it would be spent at home.

"What do you want to do after this?" I asked.

"I don't know, rent a movie?"

"We always do that. Why not stay out all night? I mean, when was the last time you went *out* to a movie?"

Phượng chewed her food, scrunched her forehead and tilted her head to the side.

"Oh, I'm sorry. I forgot." I said, playing with my prawns with the fork.

"I wouldn't laugh. It's been a while for you too. How long has it been since she left?"

I was ready to say fourteen years, that it had been fourteen years since Mother left, but I realized she meant Melanie.

"Just about as long as you." I returned to playing with the prawns. Before she could say anything, I asked, "So? A movie then?"

Phượng finished chewing her food and nodded.

There was a revival house that specialized in festivals every week, and that week they had a Hiroshi Teshigahara Film Festival, a different film every day of the week, except on Fridays and Saturdays: there were double features. That night they were showing *I Have a Stranger's Face* and *Woman in the Dunes.*

"You want to stay for both of them or just one?" I asked.

Phượng brought both hands to her temples and rubbed as she shut her eyes. "Let's see…I've been sitting on my ass all day at the bank. All day. Sitting in a chair at the bank."

"OK, OK. Jesus, just asking. Half a day by the way."

After paying for both tickets, we went in and sat in the dim theater, surprised there were more whites than Asians. Surprising still were the Asians with white men and women, and Phượng and I slumped in our seats and observed the couples, and we figured the Asians were teaching them something about their culture.

"It's like they're taking them to the museum," Phượng whispered.

I laughed but immediately stopped, for I had done the same with Melanie. Hadn't I taken her to see films like *The Lover, Platoon, Apocalypse Now, Heart of Darkness, Good Morning Vietnam, Full Metal Jacket,* and *Indochine*? Hadn't I cooked her dishes like fresh spring rolls, phở, and bitter melon soup?—showed her Chinatown, went through the markets and pointed out the different types of fish, octopus, mung beans, dried seaweed, bok choy, pickled mustard greens?—showed her how they were sliced and chopped, gutted and stuffed, boiled and skewered, and eaten?

For that moment I thought of Melanie, I wondered how the couples around us fared, if they were introduced to family members as boyfriends or girlfriends, and most important, have they had the talk. Not to be reminded of Melanie, I looked down at my hands bridged in front of me and kept quiet. As I looked over the couples, the back of my neck began to warm. I hoped that one day they get that talk where their white boyfriends or girlfriends say, "I can't do this. You're nice, but—"

It was always the "but" they could never explain, the "but" they toiled over for days, maybe even weeks before the first date, the "but" they held reserved in their mouths for that day, the "but" they dredged up enough courage for, yet managed to fumble through it like people who stuttered. And like those who stuttered they thought they sounded stupid and wished they hadn't opened their mouths. I looked at each couple, and the back of my neck was now hot, and the fever rose and consumed my ears. They kept burning, burning until my head was hot, and I could feel sweat form beneath my hair.

The theater dimmed and *Woman in the Dunes* began, and Phượng and I sat up in our seats. It was clear where the movie was going. A man, an entomologist, and an existentialist at that, came across a sandpit, descended the rope ladder and met a woman who shoveled sand from her house all day into buckets; he fell asleep, woke up only to find the ladder had been taken away, and he was stuck there with the woman.

There was nothing for him to do but shovel sand, stop and hold his breath every time sand dripped into the hole, fearful of his own existence swallowed whole. They were in closed quarters, and the sand was too loose, too fine and dry to even attempt to climb, and if he raised his voice in anger or cried out of frustration, there came the threatening hiss of sand wanting to avalanche the two.

I could hear Phượng catch her breath each time she heard the sand slide down the walls, hear everyone breathe again. After a while, it became claustrophobic watching them go about the house, shoveling sand to maintain their existence beneath the ever present glare of the white sun.

Before long, in the middle of the day, the woman of the dunes recognized the look on the entomologist's face, and at first she resisted his advances, but it was not long before they were on the floor. He kissed her neck and shoulders, her face and lips, and she held his head in her hands, eyes closed, lips parted by moans. My body suddenly began to itch from seeing them roll on the hardwood floor. Her exposed wet arms and shoulders collected sand, and I could hear it moving beneath their weight, their rolling and slow writhing.

Phượng pushed air from her nose, and I could hear everyone's breathing, interrupted by sighs. Like myself, I imagined they were thinking of the first time they explored each others' bodies and delighted in the foreign soft skin, pale or brown, triangles of hair, the hardness of nipples, swirling tongues tasting the difference they had heard or were always curious about. And I imagined them resting side by side—sated—and falling in love from hearing the person next to them breathe.

The man continued to deliver clumsy, hungry, thirsty kisses upon her body, and she accepted them as her skin did the sand. Suddenly Phượng threw her hand over her mouth to stifle her giggling. Several people turned their heads, and some even laughed.

"What's so funny?" I whispered.

She leaned over and brought her hand away long enough to say, "*Don't suck, don't suck,*" and quickly closed her hand over her mouth. I immediately bit down on my bottom lip to keep from laughing.

"I wasn't sucking," I said. "You just couldn't kiss."

Phượng bent forward and used both hands to cover her mouth. She got up from her seat and ran up the aisle. A white rectangle of light fixed itself upon the screen where it stayed for a while, then was swallowed by the darkness.

After all these years she remembered our first kissing lesson when we were twelve. It was the clumsiness of the actors kissing that reminded her of us. One summer we went to the school playground to throw a Frisbee around when we came upon her sister Mia making out with some guy in the back of the equipment shed among the barrels containing soccer-, basket-, and footballs. It looked strange to us because for a while after Handsome Harlemite's death, Mia hardly left the apartment. It was like watching her kiss for the first time, though we had seen her do it so many times before.

They didn't see us, and I knew they weren't aware that the door had made its way open. Like the many times I had seen Mia making out with all her boyfriends, I watched. She was sitting on his lap, and he was gentle compared to Pedro, compared to the tattooed José who groped her breasts and thighs so hard that veins stood out on the backs of their hands. This boy only ran his hand along the length of Mia's bare thigh like he was afraid to explore or afraid Mia would slap his hand away if he reached for her breast or went for her zipper and button.

Though we did not stand there long, it was enough to feel that itch starting in my crotch and underarms, the tingling in my penis, the feel of it slowly beating as it grew inside my shorts. The tingle traveled throughout my body, raising bumps along my arms and legs, the hair rising like blades of grass following the sun.

"Come on," Phượng whispered.

We went to the open field, away from all the older boys playing baseball to a patch of grass and we began tossing the Frisbee. I couldn't take my mind off Mia and the boy inside the equipment shed: the slow gentleness in their kissing, the patience and care with which the boy's hand moved over her thigh. It was after a couple of throws that I started thinking about Phượng that way, and I began to notice how she had grown in two years. Every time she took the Frisbee and crossed her arm over her chest to fling the disk, I watched her stance, the way her leg muscles tightened, the stretch of her T-shirt against her ribs and waist, and how her long, thick, black hair swayed from her throw or when she bounced on the balls of her feet in one place with raised hands, face lifted to the sky as she tried to judge where the Frisbee would come down. During those moments she waited to catch, I noticed her chest: they were small, swollen.

After a while, our aim was off. We threw it everywhere, and we ran in hopes of catching it before it touched the ground, but we were running so much that we started to pant, even glared at each other for having to chase it down. It was at least half an hour before we just stood there—a good distance apart with shoulders slouched—sweating and trying to catch our breath before we decided to quit.

During the walk home I listened to Phượng breathe. She had pulled her hair into a bun the moment we left the park, and from out of the corners of my eyes I could see her profile, and I studied the fullness of her lips, her long thin neck, but especially the way her shirt pulled at her chest when she swayed her arms, and I wondered if she was studying me from out of the corner of her eyes.

When we arrived home, we poured ourselves a glass of Kool-Aid. We stood in the kitchen taking large gulps, and when we were through, we licked our lips, breathing heavily from having finished too quickly. Phượng stared at me while tucking in her lips and running her tongue along them for its sweetness. I set my glass on the counter and went to her, and before she could put her glass down I had my arms around her and my lips against hers. She finally set the glass down and placed her hands on my shoulders. I mashed my lips against hers, breathing through my nose, and she pulled me away and said, "You're doing it wrong. Open your mouth."

I closed my eyes and opened my mouth. "Not too wide," she said, and leaned in and slipped her tongue inside my mouth. It felt cold from the Kool-Aid, and while she moved her tongue about, I clenched her upper lip between mine and began sucking. I liked the sweetness I tasted from her lips and thought this was what kissing was supposed to be like—sugary. Phượng laughed, and pulled me away again, and said, "Don't suck. You're not supposed to suck. Just do as I do."

....

When the film ended, everyone filed out. I didn't think there were this many people. They pressed against us in their hurry to leave or stand out front for a cigarette break before the start of *I Have a Stranger's Face*. Even when we finally got outside, we had to work our way past smokers. I took a hold of Phượng's arm to keep her close to me.

Uncle Ngô's Harley was parked just off to the side of the steps. Knowing he wasn't going anywhere, I unlocked the door to the garage-bedroom he hadn't lived in since Dad left. Phượng and I entered, and I drew the door closed behind us. Before I could turn around, Phượng had reached for the rosary chain in the center of the garage and tugged on it. She stood underneath the light. All around us were chairs we had stored over the years, their legs too weak to even support themselves, boxes filled with magazine and newspaper clippings, clothes we had outgrown, lamps whose cords strangled their bases and stems, and stacks of lantern-thin lampshades.

"Do you…uh," I stopped.

As Phượng pulled on the sleeves of her cardigan sweater, she kept her eyes fixed on me and shook her head.

"Do you…remember—"

Phượng draped the cardigan over one of the boxes.

"Stop talking Long. You're making me nervous." She giggled and looked away. The place hadn't been opened in months, and I could smell the dust that veiled the stored items and lay in the shadows. "You're the boy I want." She gave a crooked tight-lipped smile.

I approached her, brought my hands to her waist, and she placed her hands on my shoulders. We stood there underneath the light like a couple getting ready to slow dance for the first time, keeping in mind the distance between us, where our hands settled, if our feet touched, where our noses met, where her chest met mine, and whether or not it felt soft if I held her against me. I drew her nearer, our stomachs touching and her breasts pressed against me.

I tried to look into her eyes, but she was staring at my lips. Standing this close made her become a stranger to me, though I had known this face all my life. Though we were about to kiss, it was going to be with someone who knew everything about me and that was what made her unfamiliar to me. This was not a kissing lesson. Cocking my head to one side, I tasted her lips at first and I expected something sweet and cold like that afternoon we drank Kool-Aid. Instead I tasted dry warmth, and I wet my lips. Phượng turned her face up and tilted her head in the opposite direction. Before long, our tongues circled within each other's mouth. Her hands left my shoulders and she wrapped one around my neck while using the other hand to cup the base of my head. I cinched my arms around her waist, and I felt her breasts give. Feeling them against me made me pull away, and I wanted to ask her if she wanted to stop, if she was certain we should go on, but she leaned into me, still kissing.

We continued with wet, noisy kisses. Soon our hands went to different places. We finally stopped and held each other, and I could feel her heart pulsing in her neck. As we stood there catching our breath, I lifted her shirt just enough to slip my hand underneath. Through her plain cotton bra, I kneaded her with my thumb. From the top of her blouse I saw her brown skin, and I never realized how dark she was in contrast to the white of her bra. Her breasts were small, and I took my hand and cupped her smallness before settling my hand between them and felt her bone, felt her breathing pushing against my hand, her heart beating in my palm.

Honeymoon

We inherited my parents' room where it was sunny and where Mother had screamed accusations at Dad all those years. After our honeymoon in San Francisco, we gave some furniture to Mia and her boyfriend and moved the rest into the garage-bedroom. We bought a new bedroom set and as a gift, Uncle Ngô got us an antique mahogany armoire that almost reached the ceiling. We loved the room despite the fact that I had known it all my life. The new bed with iron head- and footboards, the armoire, the thin-legged night stands, blue flower-embroidered cotton sheets, and white comforter made the house new again. They made our marriage seem legitimate, less circumspect.

For the first few months, Phượng and I were like adolescents, staring across the dinner table, lounging on the sofa and stroking each other's arms while watching television, leaning down or rising up to kiss the other on the forehead or neck. On weekends we'd drive to Venice Beach, hold hands while walking along the boardwalk and buy T-shirts, wind chimes, blankets, hemp bracelets and anklets, framed black and white photos of fog-covered mountains and waterfalls—things we didn't need.

Most nights, we'd dress up and go out for dinner. We always took our time in following the hostess to the table, and often she'd stand at the table waiting for us to arrive and seat ourselves so she could hand us menus and tend to the next party. We took our time ordering. Often, we told the waiter or waitress we needed another minute. After dinner, we'd pass on dessert but order coffee, let the check sit there. The waiter or waitress who passed by would look at the leather pocketbook to see if it had moved, or if a credit card or bills were visible.

Some weekends when Uncle Ngô was gone, we cleaned house. In walking toward the bathroom to dump the mop water, I'd catch a glimpse of Phượng in jeans and a T-shirt, her hair done up in a bun as she bent over to sweep underneath a table or chair. And I'd watch her and wonder how our marriage had grown from our childhood and blossomed into a comfortable union. I'd stare until she noticed me, and she'd stop sweeping or polishing. Sometimes she wouldn't notice me. Either way I'd set the bucket down, walk up behind her and place one hand on her hip or the smaller part of her back and taste the thin film of sweat on her neck.

With Uncle Ngô gone, we took advantage of space and time, and when we finished, we'd lie in bed, on the sofa, or on the recently mopped hardwood floor, feeling the other's heart beat against the chest, feel the sound thicken in our ears.

But my heart thickened and concealed what I had forgotten about those first few months of marriage. It seemed when we had to cancel evenings out or weekends to the Venice boardwalk or Third Street Promenade because of conflicting schedules and project deadlines, that was when Mother returned to me. She was the other woman with whom Phượng had to compete.

Instead, I spent my weekends going through magazines, newspapers, and supplements whose headlines or featured articles were about Vietnam, the unrest along the northern and western borders of Vietnam and their war against China and Cambodia; of Amerasian children trying to find their American fathers; of newly-arrived Vietnamese who went to zoos or parks and captured ducks and geese for dinner and thought how generous America was, that they would have wildlife available for them to eat; veterans whose strongest muscles were their memories; and the steadily rising interest in tourism.

I'd spend hours reading each article, and what I discovered was that they interviewed so many people. Rarely did the same name come up twice. I'd read slower to write down every name, city and village, and provinces. In color or black and white, women shouldered baskets on poles as they walked in the background or foreground. I'd study the women, some in profiles, some facing the camera from across streets, fields, or streams and they were too short or thick in the mid-section, their necks too long, or cheeks too sunken to be Mother. But I studied each picture adding age and subtracting weight from malnourishment over years to form my mother.

At first, Phượng only glanced at me when passing. She had always known I did this—sat at the dinner table and read articles, jotted down names, cut the articles and pictures from magazines and newspapers and filed them inside manila folders and labeled them by publication and year. She never said anything then, but after several weeks when we didn't go anywhere, Phượng stopped on her way to the kitchen and sighed.

"If you ever find her, then what?"

I looked up from the picture I studied and frowned

at her.

"Why does this bother you so much?"

"Because you'll never find her. You think I don't know about all those letters you've written to people whose names you write down. To government officials?—to the Department of Immigration and Naturalization? You think I don't know that? That you send them photos of her?" She snatched up the pad of paper filled with names. "And what have you received from them?" She waved the pad at me. "Nothing. You know why? Because you write to them in English."

"The letters are not in English." I grabbed the pad out of her hand. "They're written in Vietnamese." I slapped the pad back down on the table.

Phượng's shoulders went slack, her head tilted to one side, and her mouth opened wide. As she stood there, I picked up the pen and waited for her to speak.

"Don't tell me Uncle Ngô wrote those letters for you?"

"No, I did. It's called a Vietnamese/English dictionary. They're quite handy for a *còn lại* like myself."

Her jaw went rigid before she began grinding her teeth. "I told you not to say that word. You're such a fucker sometimes."

She left the room, leaving me to my pile of magazines and newspapers.

That night, she had turned in early. I knew she was still awake though she stayed in one position, facing the window. She took short breaths, then spaced them out as if trying to figure out the breathing pattern of a sleeping person. I too kept still and stared at the ceiling with my hands over my chest. Finally, she breathed in deeply, stretched and rolled over on her back. She blinked as though awaking from sleep only to go back, but in doing so, she caught me watching her. Unable to pass it off any longer, she looked at me.

"I'm sorry." She muttered.

"There's something I need you to do for me."

········

"Just read. One a day, but just read," I said.

Phượng stared at the bundles of letters Mother left behind. She sat with one hand covering her mouth, and from behind her hand she said, "You already know what's in them."

"Remember when we were kids?—we'd listen to our mothers talk about the letters? You'd translate. But not all of them. There are several I'm sure we haven't heard about. And in them, maybe Lý Lộc or this woman, one of his wives who wrote to Mother, mentioned something about moving. Something like that. Maybe he decided to move to his birthplace wherever that is, or after his release he worked on a farm in another province. Or, or…or he went to live with one of the other wives."

Phượng wiped her hand on her shirt and stared at me with lips tucked in.

"We could even start with that letter, the one where he's released. I'm sure of it. If we start with that one, then we probably know where he went. Then you won't have to read any more after that. And then I'd be all over."

But that was not the end, for that letter was brief. It simply said he was released, and one of his wives picked him up and he went home, thinned and stooped, scarred and purpled, knotted and disfigured. Home, I assumed, was Vinh-Long, a place I had written to several times, but no one ever replied. I wondered if I conjugated the words correctly. I had sent the officials pictures and Xeroxed copies of letters as well, yet no response. I imagined the officials coming around to every hut, home, and hovel to collect Mother's pictures, confiscating all my letters. I imagined these officials placed them in one big box, and some veteran from the war, some general wallpapered a private room with her pictures along with Nancy Sinatra in knee-length white boots, Marilyn Monroe, Annette Funicello, Sophia Loren, and "Barbarella" lying on a bed of furs. After reading the last letter first, Phượng sighed, for she realized she would have to keep her word.

········

She lacked the inflection, or rather the urgency, the anxiety of finding out what was coming next. The syllables did not stay cupped in her tongue, nor did the consonants bloom fully in her throat. She'd read one line, then translate in English. She read the letters sentence by sentence, and though Phượng spoke with a flat tone, in her head she knew the meanings. The dips and rises were necessities to understanding. Her voice did not crack or tremble, went dry and useless. I told her this, told her to read it right.

"I *am* reading it right," she said. "What you're looking for, what you want is your mother's voice. I'm not your mother."

"Lý Lộc is your grandfather too. My mother is your aunt."

"I never met Lý Lộc. And I don't think highly of a deserted aunt, a half one at that. Now, do you want me to keep reading, or do you want to do this yourself? Save me your shit."

We sat there staring at each other until we looked elsewhere. Phượng placed the pages in order, skimmed through sections to find where she had left off, and just as she opened her mouth to continue, I said, "Forget it. I don't want you to read anymore."

Phượng shook her head, folded the letter in three sections and placed it in the envelope. She dragged the chair back, stood up, grabbed her keys and purse, and left. Just as I collected the letters to bind them with a rubber band, the front door opened again, but I stayed seated with my back to her.

"Do you want to go with me?"

I turned my head enough to show only my profile. "Where are we going?"

"I don't know."

Rising

Her name means Phoenix, a bird that rises from
its own ashes. I think of Phượng rising above all
that has happened to her and her family, my inability to let
go of the past, rising and staying put in one place without
the desire to leave for a short time or abandon completely.
Phượng is my Phoenix.

I am in the back room of a store. The store owners
have a phone where they keep their livestock. Chickens
are cooped up in bamboo cages, stacked atop one another.
Feathers float around the back room, and with the sunlight seeping through the wooden slats of the roof, they
look like large dust particles. Flies swarm slabs of rib bones
barely held together by flesh. I have to breathe through my
mouth because of the stench, but it's caught in the back of
my throat, thick and gathering.

It is an old phone, a rotary Uncle Ngô paid the store
owners twenty dollars for me to use. From a piece of paper
the store owner used to jot down numbers, I dial them
before my own. The silence lasts so long that I thought
I missed a number somewhere or the rotary is just too
old to make such a connection halfway across the world.
I hold the receiver away from me and stare at the coiled
chord. I'm about to hang up and try again when the phone
rings. But the ringing is low and far apart, a sign that no
one is home. I look at the chickens sleeping in their cages
as I listen to each ring. There is another click, white noise,
and the machine comes on. It is her voice on the machine,

185

and rather than hang up I listen to the whole message. And when the beep sounds, I open my mouth to speak, maybe say "Hello. It's really beautiful here. I love you." Or, "I miss you. Please pick up."

But I hang up the phone. I leave the back room immediately and enter the store where the owners and Uncle Ngô are talking, most likely about America and how he has fared well over there.

He sees me and asks, "Did you talk to her?"

"She isn't home."

Uncle Ngô turns to the store owners and explains. The husband reaches inside his breast pocket and withdraws the money, and as he extends it to Uncle Ngô, he waves it off, but the store owner is quick in grabbing Uncle Ngô by the wrist and slapping the money in his palm.

Uncle Ngô exchanges a few words and laughs with them before leaving. We step out onto the sidewalk. He begins to walk away, but I stand where I am. When he notices that he's walking alone, he turns around.

"What's wrong?"

"I just want to breathe a little. I'm thankful, but I nearly choked from the smell."

"You see that soup place right there?" Uncle Ngô points down the sidewalk to where a group of people sit around a soup stall, hunched over their bowls. "Meet me there."

Uncle Ngô makes his way to the soup stall. I look back at the entrance to the store and consider asking them if I can use the phone again. And if I get her on the line I know what to say that I couldn't that night: That she didn't have to treat me like her leaving was my fault.

I turn to walk inside but the wife is busy stocking cans on the shelves, and the husband hangs a Coca-Cola poster on the window. He squints behind his glasses, smiles and nods as he tapes the corners to the window. After he is through, he steps outside and studies the poster. He leans back like he's staring up at something tall, and he tilts his head from side to side and squints. He turns to me and smiles.

"It's straight. It looks good," I tell him.

"Aah, good," he erects a thumb in the air.

"By the way, can I use your phone again?"

The husband frowns at me.

"That's okay. Never mind." I begin to step away, and as I do, the store owner says something to make me turn around, and he's miming holding a phone up to his ear. "No, no, that's okay," I wave to him as I walk away, certain that when Phượng plays back the message, she'll know that stretch of silence on the machine is me.

The Summer that Failed to
Retain Spring's Bloom
Los Angeles, 1979

Asia Minor and a Year of Door Slams

Asia Minor was coined not by the Chinese who settled in Los Angeles after the railroads were built or by the Japanese after their internment, nor by the newly-arrived Vietnamese refugees, but by the whites who drove through Silver Lake to beat the rush hour traffic on their way home. They'd slow down just to marvel and point at the Japanese, Chinese, and Korean homeowners walking about their gardens putting the trowels, hoes, and bamboo rakes to use. They'd pluck dead leaves, set up wooden trellises for vines to crawl up, or tie white nets around pepper bushes under the close watch of whites. But they never looked up to return the friendly waves hailed at them from passing cars.

The Asian homeowners thought it was futile to keep a lawn. They saw no point in mowing grass. The moment they moved into the houses they now occupied, they dug up the lawns. They spent weeks shaking loose dirt from the roots of grass and threw away the clumps. They waddled about on their haunches and scooped up handfuls of dirt into colanders and flour sifters to catch the pebbles, dirt clods, and roots. After which, they tiered the ground with 2X4's so that the lawns resembled steps.

Now their front lawns were gardens. Snow peas and potato vines crawled and covered chain-link and white picket fences. Rows of baby corn stood alongside sugarcane stalks. Lemon and Purple Ruffle Basil and spearmint hovered one tier higher than the small bushes of Serrano

peppers bursting with an abundance of dark green peppers. Some had grown mango trees, but after discovering
that the neighborhood children had been stealing mangoes, the homeowners uprooted the trees and planted
them by the front stoop out of the reach of thieving hands,
hungry for the green, thick-skinned fruit. Some, like the
Japanese, constructed lily ponds with Koi fish. They swam
about and slurped at the surface.

Asia Minor pleased Mother, not for the obvious reason that there was a small community of Asians, but that
the gardens reminded her of home. Mother wanted a
home with a lawn to uproot, but the only thing available
was a two-bedroom house on Montana Avenue with two-
tiered concrete patios on both sides of the steps which led
to the street down below. Uncle Ngô and Dad fixed up the
garage into a bedroom where Uncle Ngô now lives. Because he didn't have a bathroom in the garage, Uncle Ngô
used ours to shower at 5:30 in the morning before going
to work at the auto shop at 6:30. And every morning, he
could be seen walking down to his garage-bedroom wearing only a towel around his waist. Sometimes he'd stand
at the edge of the curb carrying on a conversation with
neighbors across the street as they were getting ready to
leave for work—he standing with one hand clutching the
towel to make sure it stayed in place, the neighbors talking
to him as though he were fully clothed.

The house on Montana Avenue disappointed Mother due to a lack of a lawn to uproot, so Mother ham-
mered holes in the bottom of the coffee cans, built wood-
en troughs, cut the tops off two-liter Pepsi bottles and
one-gallon milk containers and planted basil, spearmint,

Chinese chives, tomatoes, Serrano peppers, and the perky yellow blossom flowered bok choys. She even filled water buckets and Styrofoam egg containers with soil and grew cilantro and radishes. Ginger roots grew above soil after filling out the forms of chipped deep-dished soup bowls. Potato vines and lemon grass stalks floated and took root in metal washtubs. Six *mai* trees in separate pots lined the ledge. Only during the day the tiny flowers bloomed in clumps of fiery yellow, and at night the buds closed as tight as fists.

Mother didn't stop there. The only patch of land that could be considered a lawn was a narrow strip by the side-walk, but it was crowded with wild wide-leafed cacti. They grew out onto the sidewalk so that people had to walk into the street to get around. One day Mother uprooted every one of them and dumped them in the aluminum trash cans. The lids didn't fit properly. Halfway through the day, the severed cacti pieces bled white. They looked like hacked off limbs of Cambodians at uncovered gravesites I had seen pictures of in *Newsweek* and *Time*.

In uprooting the cacti garden, Mother evicted all the geckos, garden snakes, and mealworms, and sent them scurrying for the shadows. The geckos inhabited the stuc-co walls; the garden snakes somehow found their way up the concrete steps and into Mother's makeshift garden and curled themselves around the coffee tins. The mealworms stayed in the dirt patch where Mother replaced the missing cacti with baby bamboo shoots.

For weeks the geckos overran the place. They clung to the stucco walls, the screen doors and windows, and at night they came out in great numbers. When I lay in bed

waiting to fall asleep, or to listen to Mother and Dad argue, I stared at my window. Their silhouettes covered the
edges of the window screen. They appeared plump, bigger
than their actual size, and they'd cling to the screen, waiting for mosquitoes and gnats. I was scared at first, scared
that they might find a hole in the screen and inhabit my
bed. The way so many of them clung to the screen reminded me of a Saigon train station overflowing with people.

Uncle Ngô said I shouldn't be scared.

"They our ancestor. They protect us from evil," he had
said.

Mother tended to her makeshift garden every day
during those first months. She replanted any stalks or
bushes into bigger pots whenever they outgrew their space.
She tied every young plant whether it was mint, tomato,
or pepper to a chopstick spiked in the soil to make sure
they grew straight. She hand-watered everything, clipped
any branches that grew too big, plucked dead leaves and
killed any bugs that landed on the leaves, and each time
she did, I wondered if she had killed a relative of ours or
Aunt Pham Thi's.

After several months, the garden bloomed. Small, tight
buds blossomed during our first summer in Los Angeles.
The garden only took up one patio. Mother set up wicker
chairs on the patio next to it. As for the lower-tiered patios, there was nothing on them. One of them, the larger of
the two, was over Uncle Ngô's living quarter. Mother said
nothing could go on the patio over Uncle Ngô's place. She
told Phượng and me never to step on it for any reason.

"You shouldn't walk over Uncle Ngô's head. It is bad
luck to do so. You will ruin his karma if you do. His head

should be clear of trouble. Step over it and I will kill you myself."

So none of us ever stepped on the patio. When autumn came, felling the leaves and small branches, and the wind blew them into the corners of the patio, Mother wouldn't allow herself or anyone to sweep them. The wind and rain will take care of them, she told us.

The move to Asia Minor from New Orleans was hard for me to watch. Mother didn't have the job at Hernandez's Sew Yourself, so she stayed home and built the garden. But that wasn't enough to keep her mind off Lý Lôc.

Although she kept herself busy by cooking three meals a day, washing and air-drying the dishes, learning to separate the whites from the colored and the importance of bleach, folding the clothes and putting them away in closets and drawers, sewing missing buttons on shirts, darning the heels and toes of socks, ironing creases into jeans and slacks and shirt sleeves, mopping the hardwood and tiled floors on hands and knees, scrubbing watermarks from around the toilet and wiping piss off the seats, Ajaxing mold, mildew, and grime from the shower walls, Lysoling the wastebaskets, taking down the screens and scrubbing them with a hand brush, washing the windows—inside and out—with distilled vinegar and newspaper, replanting vegetable or herb into bigger pots, plucking bug-eaten, faded yellow leaves, sweeping the patio—except for the one over the garage-bedroom—walking to the store because in the middle of making phở or *bun* she realized she needed bean sprouts, it still wasn't enough to take Mother's mind off the letters and Lý Lôc.

And when the letter didn't come, she'd slam the front

door.

Uncle Ngô and I got so used to the door slams that we didn't bother to look up to see who it was. The door slam followed by the rattling of every window in the house meant Mother just returned from checking the mail. The soft shut of the door meant we had visitors. We also got used to seeing Mother going out to the mailbox in the evenings long after the mail had arrived. Then her need for letters branched into Saturdays and Sundays, though in 1979, mail wasn't delivered on Saturdays. But we grew used to her walking to the end of the walkway to check the box, come back in, and slam the door.

One day Uncle Ngô suggested she should get a job, maybe at Hernandez's Sew Yourself working with Aunt Pham Thi. Why he waited a whole year to suggest it was beyond me. Mother declined at first, and a week after Uncle Ngô's encouragement, she decided to work, not because Uncle Ngô claimed he heard the door slamming and windows rattling in his sleep, or that he almost suffocated himself one morning when trying to drown out the sounds from his dreams with a pillow, but because the marbled statue of Buddha fell off the shelf over his bed and hit him on the corner of his brow. The cut required six stitches, and hair never grew over the scar again.

Strays

Uncle Ngô parks the car in the liquor store's lot, and as we get out of the car, we see Tú Đức leaning up against a Mustang along with China Dog, Fat Chan, and some other boy with pimples, most full and dark except for the tips, which are pale and ready to burst. Uncle Ngô stares at the cigarette in Tú Đức's hand. His hand suddenly shakes so much that he has to switch it to the other. He even takes a drag, but it's a short one because of what little smoke comes out.

"I see you like smoking," Uncle Ngô says.

"Yes," Tú Đức blinks his eyes. "I like smoke. Very much."

He takes another halfhearted puff and flicks the butt of his cigarette. The ashes fall on the hood of the Mustang, and China Dog leans down to blow it off. The acne-riddled boy keeps his eyes to the ground, one hand stuffed deep in his pants pocket while the other continually flicks ashes from the cigarette. Fat Chan stares me down.

"Have a nice e-ven-ning," Uncle Ngô says, and we enter the liquor store.

"Hey *carnal*," Miguel looks up from his copy of *La Opinion.*

Uncle Ngô nods his head and stands in front of the counter as I go to the back of the store to get bean sprouts, limes, and pickle-sized cucumbers. Uncle Ngô keeps looking out the front door as Miguel speaks to him. After I bag everything, I bring them to the counter. Miguel rings up the items on the register.

"That'll be ninety-eight cents, *carnal*."

Uncle Ngô hands Miguel a dollar, and he punches a couple more buttons and the cash register lets out a series of rings before the drawer opens. He dips his finger into the penny slot for two cents.

"Thank you for your business, *carnal*," Miguel says, "and pray for the Americans."

"I will," Uncle Ngô says.

Miguel folds *La Opinion* and picks up where he left off. On the front page there is a big picture of an American embassy hostage waving to photographers from a second story window. His eyes are small behind the round spectacles he wears and his tight-lipped smile is nearly hidden beneath the beard that covers his neck and collar. In the window beside him, an Iranian holds a machine gun to his head, but only his hands and arms and the short barrel of the gun are in view.

Uncle Ngô and I walk outside just as the Mustang drives by. Tú Đức is in the passenger seat holding the cigarette up. China Dog looks at us and a corner of his lips is turned up. They pull out into traffic and head down Silver Lake Avenue.

········

Uncle Ngô parks the car in the dirt lot next to the apartment building. When he turns off the engine, he grabs my arm before I can get out of the car and says, "Don't tell what you see. OK?"

I nod, and he says, "Your Uncle Ngô will take care of e-ver-ee-thing."

"I won't say a word."

Uncle Ngô nods his head and lets go of my arm. We walk upstairs, and when we enter the apartment filled with women, we notice Yên sitting at the dinner table. Her head immediately turns to Uncle Ngô who stops just inside the living room. Her eyes widen as she opens her mouth to speak, but she closes it and looks down at her hands.

Uncle Ngô bunches the rim of the brown bag and walks into the kitchen. He hands it to Aunt Pham Thi who announces that dinner will be done soon. Mother is busy stirring the *nước mam* while Mia and Phượng sit in front of the television watching *Fantasy Island.*

Uncle Ngô gets Yên's attention, and I catch him mouthing *later* to her.

Uncle Ngô drove us all back home. Mother turned in for the night, and I'm outside on the lower patio crouched behind the ledge, careful not to shift too much and hit the motorcycle parts Uncle Ngô has lying about. Uncle Ngô sits on a stool while Yên paces the sidewalk, moving in and out of the light coming from Uncle Ngô's room.

"They come every day," she says. "They come with beer, cigarettes, laugh, and curse. They stay 'til past one. I try to sleep, but they make so much noise. I wake up to go to work, and Tú is not there. They are not there. Only empty cans, cigarettes, ashes, big mess. Someone put crack in picture of my husband."

"Do you tell them an-ee-thing? Tell them leave?"

"I am afraid. China Dog hits women. I am afraid. So I stay in my room, lock my door and listen. I do not know what to do. I tell Tú not to bring them home. He says OK, but when they come, he forgets and lets them in."

"I do something. Do not worry. I take care of e-ver-ee-thing."

Yên stops just outside the light and shakes her head.

"I wish. But—"

Yên continues to pace.

"The other night, I hear China Dog talk about his father to Tú. How his father is disgraceful, and how he wants to do something."

"To his father?"

"No," she shakes her head. "No. He wants to prove himself. He wants to make people understand he is not like his father, a failure, and he wants Tú to feel the same way, to restore his father's name. If he proves himself, he can tell people he is better than his father."

Just as Yên passes by Uncle Ngô, he reaches out and takes her by the arm. He pulls her toward him until she is standing close enough to place her hands on his shoulders.

"I do something. It is my fault for making them apologize to Tú Đức. Now they become friends. I do something," Uncle Ngô says.

"I don't know," she shakes her head.

"I do something," he nods his head.

Yên keeps shaking her head, and I believe he will make things right. But none of us would have ever guessed that in several months, all regular television programming would be interrupted by a special news bulletin. There will be crowds as helicopters circle the city and the world will watch Fat Chan and China Dog's attempt at redemption.

"Don't worry," Uncle Ngô insists. "I do something."

Uncle Ngô draws her nearer. She leans with one ear against his chest, listening to his heart.

Tú Đức

When I first met Tú Đức, I saw him climbing out of a dumpster and I remember thinking, *How can anyone stand being that smelly and dirty?* This was before he had his bicycle; he carried large Hefty bags home. He had Uncle Ngô take them to the recycling centers. Some days when he was off, Uncle Ngô drove Tú Đức around the neighborhood, parked the car, and sat smoking cigarette after cigarette while Tú Đức made his way down the block, crossed the street, and made his way back. They passed the whole day that way until his back seat and trunk were filled.

Coming home from the shop, I see only the top of Tú Đức's head bobbing up and down inside the dumpster behind a pool hall. He sees me from over the rim and says, "Hiii. Wait. You wait a minute." I stand among the litter of bottles and cans as he pushes himself up and over, and he lands hard on his feet.

He smiles, eyes blinking rapidly. Tú Đức balloons open the Hefty bag a couple of times and begins collecting what he threw onto the lawn and sidewalk.

"I collect cans," he says, talking directly to the ground. "And bottles."

"I know that Tú Đức."

"They bring me many money."

I sigh and look around to make sure no one is staring at us. When he's through filling the bag, he ties it up several times into tight knots. But there are still some left over and he looks at each bottle and can, and his eyes stop blinking long enough to squint at them. He moves with a start before picking up as many as he can and placing them into the steel basket of his bicycle.

"Help. I need help," he says. "You take bicycle; I carry."

He heaves the Hefty bag over his shoulder with both hands. "Very heavy," he grunts, and begins walking bent over.

I swipe up the kickstand with my foot, take a hold of the handlebars, and walk the bike alongside of him. Although the bag is full and bulging, although he walks hunched over, Tú Đức keeps a steady pace as he follows his shadow. As we climb up the hill, he leans closer to the ground, and I am convinced he can put out one hand and touch his shadow. It gets worse when we come to Montana Avenue. We have to stop at times so that he can catch his breath, and the last hundred feet or so, Tú Đức drags the bag all the way to the Casa de Maria Apartments. We enter the courtyard where the fountain has no water, and the statue of a naked boy holding a dish in front of him is scarred by white water marks. Large fern and ivy grow from within the fountain and spill over the edges and cover part of the cobblestone walkway.

I put the kickstand down and set the bike to lean. I tell him I have to go, and he wheels around and hollers, "No. Don't go. Come. Come," he beckons. "Have Kool-Aid. I give you Kool-Aid for thank you."

I say OK, but that I must go soon. He grins and sets the Hefty bag down. I follow him upstairs, and Tú Đức reaches inside his shirt and pulls out the key he ties to a leather string and lets himself in. The apartment is clean because there isn't much in the living room and kitchen. For a one bedroom, they have a balcony where Uncle Ngô set out the wooden troughs he built for Yên to grow vegetables and herbs. The plants are tall, almost reaching up to the top of the railing, and the plants look ridiculous growing out of something so narrow, long, and short in depth.

In one corner of the living room is a coffee table with many propped-up framed photographs of relatives. The table is dusty from the spent incense sticks Yên burns every day. A low table is in the center of the room, and I take it that's where they eat. And their sleeping bags are tightly rolled and stashed in another corner along with blankets. There isn't a television or sofa, not even a chair for me to sit, so I stand at the counter, which separates the kitchen from the living room.

Tú Đức goes to the refrigerator and brings out a pitcher of Kool-Aid. He fills two glasses to the rim and carefully hands one to me. I immediately take a sip so that I don't spill.

"Thank you," I say.

"You welcome." He takes a big gulp and holds it in his mouth so that his cheeks bulge. He swishes it around before swallowing and sighs. He laughs while his eyes blink and I turn away from him, not only to keep from staring at his eyes but to keep from smelling him. Inside this small apartment, his smell is stronger, contained, and it's making me so sick that I have to breathe through my mouth. I hold the Kool-Aid up to my nose. In one attempt, I drink the rest.

"Thanks Tú Đức," I hand him the glass, but he doesn't

take it. He just stares at me with his mouth open. Rather than wait for him to take the glass, I place it on the kitchen counter.

"Wait. You see photos," he points with the hand that holds the glass and he spills some Kool-Aid on the floor. "Look at photos."

The more I protest, the more he insists, and he runs to the table, takes one and brings it over to me. It is a picture of Yên sitting in a cane chair, and standing beside her is an American dressed in a pressed uniform. Both of them stare straight ahead, neither one of them smiling. The man's mustache grows over his upper lip, and his hair is cut close to the scalp. He has one hand on the chair's backrest. Yên clasps her hands in her lap. Because of him, because he brought them to America, set them up in this apartment and with enough money to last them a couple of months, then abandoned them, the Vietnamese people of Asia Minor keep their distance from Yên and Tú Đức. One who can't keep a husband, Mother once said, is a sign of failure on the woman's part. So they do whatever they have to in order to keep the family whole, and I guess Yên didn't do enough.

Just then someone knocks on the door, and eager to leave, I open it only to step back. China Dog, Fat Chan, and the pimply boy are just as stunned to see me.

"Hiii," Tú Đức sings from behind me. "Come in, come in." He moves around me, waving his hands in an inviting gesture.

The three of them step inside and look me up and down as they walk past. Fat Chan smiles.

"Well, Tú Đức. I'll see you later. Uncle Ngô is waiting

for me."

But he doesn't hear me because he is too busy smiling and talking to the others. Without saying anything I close the door behind me, and I hear one of them snicker, "Fucking half-breed."

Taking a hold of the railing, I run down the steps, past the fountain, and leave Casa de Maria Apartments for my empty house.

· · · · · · · ·

"Here," Uncle Ngô hands me the four blackened bolts.

I take them from him and place them in a silver washtub filled with a solvent that burns my nose when I breathe it in. Uncle Ngô is busy taking apart the old Harley he saved up for and bought from a junkyard on the outskirts of downtown. It has no wheels. The chrome parts are dull and scratched, and the handlebars are rusty in places. The gas cap is missing, and the headless eagle's wings are smudged at the tips, and what's left of the symbol is almost scraped off. The leather seat is faded and cracked, and the seams are coming undone. *Maybe Mother can sew it together?* I think to myself.

We are on the patio atop Uncle Ngô's garage-bedroom. Remembering Mother's warning about stepping onto it, I keep my distance and stay on the steps and wait until he hands me the parts and even then I'm tiptoeing. I want to tell him he shouldn't be on here, but when I got home he was already taking the motorcycle apart. I figure since it's his space above his room, Uncle Ngô already understands the consequences. Or maybe he doesn't, and if so, then my telling him will only make him aware of what he's done, and bad luck will come.

"Here." He holds out a large portion of the engine covered with a thick coat of oil and dirt. I have to use both hands to hold it. I drop it into the tub and splash the lower part of my jeans. Uncle Ngô's mouth twists as he lets out a sound. "Be careful.""I'm all right," I say.

"No. With my engine. Be careful."

He takes the monkey wrench to the rest of the engine, and with each bolt he loosens he places a metal piece of the bike on the patio. Uncle Ngô's hands are black with old oil. He wipes his hands on a dirty rag but he only manages to smear them.

"Come here Long-Vanh, and light my ci-gar-rette for me."

I take up the pack of Marlboro from off the patio, and put one in my mouth. I hold the Zippo in both hands, flick the wheel until it lights, and puff on the cigarette. After it catches, I place the cigarette between his lips as he works the rag around each finger and between them.

"Thank you," he says with the cigarette in his mouth.

I remain at his side. By this point I figure if Mother is right about bad luck, then something should have happened, and so far nothing has. The bone-white cut through his eyebrow seems to be wider than usual, and it's probably the angle at which he tilts his head, but I'm hoping he'll use some of the oil to color it in, make his eyebrow whole again.

"What's it called again? The motorcycle?"

"Harley," he says. "Da-vid-son. The best."

Uncle Ngô throws the rag on the ground, takes the cigarette from between his lips, and exhales. He stands up and stretches, and his neck and back crack and pop. He lets out a sigh as he shakes his arms and flexes his hands.

"They came by. China Dog and them came to see Tú Đức."

Uncle Ngô's eyes go straight to the apartments next door, and he gazes so hard I'm convinced he can see through all of them and into Yên's small apartment.

"They're gone already," I say.

He doesn't turn away but continues to smoke his cigarette.

After leaving Tú Đức's apartment, I watched from my living room window. Not five minutes after they arrived, Tú Đức left with them in the Firebird. What caught my eye were the sunglasses Tú Đức wore. They probably couldn't stand to look at his eyes, the way they never stopped blinking. But I remember feeling jealous while watching them walk to the car. Of all the boys in the neighborhood, even someone like Tú Đức could be accepted over me.

August 15, 1979
Friday

It's a rare treat to leave our neighborhood of Asia Minor and drive half an hour into the valley, an area of Los Angeles County where whites live. Going to the valley to watch a movie is like visiting another country because the mountains are closer, and everyone stares at us like we've wandered too far from home, lost.

Dad wants to get a good view of the screen, so we arrive at the Van Nuys Drive-in Theater early enough to get a parking space in the center of the lot. After paying admission, we file into a single line and slowly drive past the tall white movie screen made silent by the sun. Although there are many people who have already arrived, I still feel foolish for being here so early. I stare at the screen in front of us. The sun is too high, and I don't think it will fall in time to begin the movie, but Dad doesn't want to take any chances. He learned his lesson from the previous times we came late and watched the movies from the far left or right side of the lot. The actors were too tall and thin from those angles and my eyes hurt just from watching them stretch their mouths to let out small words.

As soon as Dad turns off the ignition, Mother uncovers the brown shopping bag beneath the pillows and blankets, pulls lids off Tupperware bowls, and fixes each of us a plate of egg rolls, shrimp fried rice, and mushroom, broccoli and Chinese snow peas stir-fried in oyster sauce. The scents of oil, rice, vegetables, and oyster sauce fill the car. Mother and Dad roll the windows down to let in fresh air. She sets the Tupperware atop the dashboard.

We eat slowly knowing it will be some time before the movie begins. Dad has talked about *Apocalypse Now* for weeks. "It's about the war," he said when I asked what we were going to see. "And it also has Marlon Brando," he added. When I didn't respond he said, "You know, Superman's father."

Dad and Mother eat with their eyes on their food. When they wipe their mouths to take a sip of Coke, they stare out the window on their own side or look ahead at the screen. People arrive in droves. The sun's rays glare off the hoods and windshields of cars as they make their way from aisle to aisle searching for the space they want, or for a speaker that works.

People let down the tailgates of their trucks or station wagons and sit on them as they fix cold cut sandwiches, precooked hot dogs and hamburgers. Some make their way to the playground area below the screen to cook their food in brick barbecue pits while children climb up ladders and slide down chutes, or they try to outdo each other on the swings. Their feet come out from under them as they kick out for height. And still the cars come and I feel less foolish.

People who brought nothing walk to the concession stands. They dig into the pockets of their tight bell-bottom blue jeans and corduroy pants for crumpled bills and loose change. Young couples wander about the lot looking for others they may know, or they just walk to wear down the sun. Mother wipes her mouth and puts away her plate.

"Do you want some more, Long-Vanh?" Mother asks.

"No."

"Here," she reaches behind her and I hand her my plate. Mother sits forward and from off the dashboard, she scoops rice onto my plate. As she takes up the spoon for the vegetables she says, "You don't eat enough. That's why you're so skinny."

She hands back my plate.

"Is there another Coke?" Dad asks.

"It's in the bag." She picks up the brown bag and sets it between them on the seat.

They continue staring out the windows. A car pulls up to our left—a teenage boy and girl—and before he turns off the ignition, the boy wearing a baseball cap leans forward in his seat to look past his girlfriend, who slightly turns her head to our side so she can look out of the corner of her eyes. He keeps his hand on the gear as he glances out of the rearview mirror before scanning the lot in front of him and to the sides. But the cars keep coming, and the spaces are filling up. He turns off the engine, and they sit there talking, their eyes barely meeting each other. The teenage girl moves her hands freely while she talks, and at times the boy gives a faint smile. He sits leaning against the door away from her with his elbow resting on the sill.

The sun is behind the apartments and townhouses across the street. The eucalyptus trees that border the drive-in are tall enough to keep tenants and homeowners from standing out on their balconies and rooftops. The wide white screen looks bigger as the day grows darker. People are still walking around; fathers make their way back from the concession stands with carry-out trays filled with popcorn, hot dogs wrapped in tin foil, and drinks.

Groups of men wander around with Coors and Schlitz in hands. From across the lot they wave at those they know and yell with the promise of meeting up with them later.

Still, the children swing higher and higher, and my parents sit facing the screen, waiting for night.

········

I don't know when I fell asleep. A whirring sound fills the car. It fades in and out, in and out, and then Indian music. I open my eyes and it is dark and there is a dull glare coming into the car. Still the whirring continues—in and out, in and out—and it sounds like someone swinging a bamboo shoot. I sit up and stare at the palm groves on the screen.

"Did I miss anything?" I ask.

"No," Dad says. "It just started." He clears his throat.

A man parts the blinds in the hotel room and looks out over the city's business district: women wearing *áo dàis* walk by and it's like I'm seeing Mother by the masses walking about. Pedicabs and mopeds and bicycles swarm the main square.

"Saigon," the man says under his breath. "Shit!"

"That is not Saigon," Mother shakes her head.

"I know Vu-An, but what do you expect? You think they can just walk in and shoot a film in Vietnam?"

As the movie progresses, Mother picks out things that are out of place: the Viet-Cong's uniforms, the shape of the sun hats the villagers wear, even the waters of the Mekong Delta are too calm. Its green is too dull, too light. Dad only slumps in his seat and sighs every time Mother opens her mouth to point out inconsistencies, and at one point he raises his voice: "Will you just watch the damn movie? I want to watch the movie." It is the first time Dad has turned to Mother all evening.

I keep quiet and watch the screen. For someone who has to find a deserter and kill him, the film is taking too long. The company comes across one incident after another. An orchestra bombards our car, and helicopters fly against the backdrop of early morning. One of the helicopters carries a boat attached by cable, and like dragonflies, they swarm the coastal village. Bombs drop and fire blooms from the ground and rises above tree lines. A spray of bullets shoots sand and water and they rise like geysers. Mother covers her face with one hand. The more shootings and bombings and screams there are, the more Mother slumps in her seat. She covers her eyes and shakes her head from side to side.

"Let's go," Mother says.

"What?" Dad snaps his head at Mother.

"I said let's go," she repeats.

"We can't go now, we're not even halfway through the film," he says, pointing at the screen.

The airborne commander in sunglasses and a neckerchief struts along the coast of the small village and urges several of his men to strip down to their shorts and surf. While villagers scramble from burning huts and bombs flower into tall columns of fire, the commander praises the waves and how they break.

The teenage boy and girl in the car next to us are kissing. The windows are nearly fogged up, but I can see them holding each other, lips mashed together. One of his hands is on her breast. And I stare at his hand squeezing and changing the shape of her breast, imagine the softness giving in to his hunger.

"Long-Vanh, stop staring," Mother says.

Dad turns to look over at the couple, then gazes at me in the rearview mirror. I stare straight ahead. At times I turn away, pretend I'm rubbing my nose, or yawning off to the side so I can watch the couple. I think of Mia in the laundry room or in the back bedroom with a boy, any boy, and how their hands always held the weight of her breasts. The couple keeps at it. The boy pushes her back onto the seat and they are out of view.

Mother looks off to the side with her head down. The helicopters continue to swarm above the village as they shoot anyone running.

"I need to use the bathroom," Mother says and gets out.

Dad keeps his eyes on the screen. She slams the door and I watch her heading for the bathrooms near the concession stands.

"Is she all right?" I ask.

"Yeah, she'll be fine," he says without looking back.

After some time I ask, "Was this how it was?"

Dad breathes in and lets it out slowly. The air hisses from his nostrils.

"I was just a cook," he finally says. "I just cooked. That's all."

They had been fighting again at four in the morning: she demanded to know her name and he denied everything until he told her to shut up so he could fall asleep. Mother threatened to find out so she could kill whoever kept him out late at night.

"Start with your imagination," Dad told her. "That's where you need to start: in your head."

The crew continues the journey up the Mekong. Faint drumbeats come from the dim light in the night and it grows louder as they approach. The men get off the P2 boat and join other soldiers in the middle of nowhere for entertainment, and I am glad Mother is not here because three women, one dressed as an Indian, the others as cowgirls in short shorts and tied tops, get off the helicopter and dance to Dale Hawkins's "Susie Q."

"Close your eyes," Dad says.

I look at him in the rearview mirror and say, "They're just dancing Dad."

He exchanges glances between me and the three women strutting in front of the soldiers. The men suddenly jump over the barriers and storm the platform; the helicopters take off with the women inside, and men hang onto the rudders of the chopper before falling into the water.

Mother gets back inside the car, and we still haven't seen Marlon Brando. Just pictures that Willard, the main character, goes through. I want to ask Mother if she is OK, but that might make Dad huff and stare at me in the rearview. She sits quietly. Her hands go to her temples and she moves her head in a rhythm so that her hand doesn't have to move.

The crew in the P2 boat comes across a junk and stops it. Chef, a New Orleans cook with a handlebar mustache, is ordered to go on the junk, check identification papers while shoving the two men and woman around. Chef walks along the length of the boat, opening sacks, lifting lids off pots and barrels, and spilling over baskets of fruits and vegetables, and suddenly the young woman shrieks and runs at Chef, and the American soldiers shoot up the boat and everyone on it. Smoke comes off the machine guns. Chef uncovers the lid to a straw basket and pulls out a black-spotted white puppy. He holds it by its neck and shows everyone what she was running for. The woman is face down and moaning, and Chef checks on her. The commander of the P2 boat calls for medic, but Willard takes his pistol and shoots the woman dead. Chef leans against the sacks of rice, crying and pulling his helmet over his head.

"I told you not to stop the boat," Willard says to the commander. "Now let's go."

"Let's go."

Mother has her head in her lap, her hands over her head. Dad and I look at each other and wonder at what point she went down. Suddenly I can't hear the movie. Mother is gasping for air as she covers her face and cries. Dad unhooks the speaker from the window, replaces it on the pole's cradle, and starts the car. He backs out of the slot and makes his way down the aisle. Gravel pops under our tires, and clouds of dirt rise. Although there is no sound, I continue to watch the movie.

The P2 boat makes its way up the river. The water is calmer as it becomes narrower and narrower; the wall of trees and bushes and tall grass grows thicker along the banks. The trees along the banks are smoking; bodies drape over tree limbs or float in the water. One tree's branches and vines hold a helicopter above the water.

We leave the packed drive-in theater surrounded by

eucalyptus trees and head down Roscoe Boulevard for the 405 Freeway. I turn around in my seat and watch the screen between the trees. There is a clearing along the river's bank. The P2 boat passes this clearing where a small house stands among fallen banyan trees. An old man steps out of his home and watches the boat pass, watches us head home as Mother cries into her hands.

Parade

Lý Loĉ sits out on his porch smoking a cigarette and drinking cream-sweetened coffee. The P2 boat drifts by, and Lý Loĉ jerks in his seat to the sound of gunshots. Soldiers jog down the road carrying M16s. They tie men's hands behind their backs to one long piece of rope fashioned with slip knots. They march down the dirt road and wait while the soldiers surround houses. The awaiting prisoners flinch from the noises of upturned beds and floor boards, tremble at the sharp commands to surrender, and hang their heads from men pleading. Their eyes flood with tears the moment they hear the pin-pull and hiss of smoke bombs. From the open shutters and doors, gray smoke blooms into round, fat clouds. Billowing clouds burst from the windows, and the blind and choking men run outside and into the hands of soldiers who bind their wrists. The men plead, and when they open their mouths they speak smoke.

They progress to Lý Loĉ who watches the line of men double in number as they emerge from the lingering smoke. Their single file shuffle stops before his house and the men begin to cough smoke from their eyes and ears. Blood cakes the lips and ears where the butt of M16s made their marks and their eyes swell to ripe bruises.

The soldiers in black pajamas gather at the porch steps. Lý Loĉ sits up in his chair with legs crossed at the knees, a cup of coffee in one hand, and a hand-rolled cigarette in the other. He looks out over the Mekong at the opposite bank; Willard and Chef are carrying pails as they search for man-

goes in the jungles.

"Catch them, and let me go," he motions to the other bank with a jut of his chin. "Americans are worth more."

The soldiers turn to look at two white men carrying pails and climbing over the large gnarled roots of banyan trees. The pockmarked soldier of the group turns to Lý Loc, shakes his head and says, "Americans were worthless the moment they stepped foot in our country."

"I am almost finished," Lý Loc says and places the cigarette between his lips.

The Communist soldiers remain standing. They look at one another, at their loosely fitted clothes. Some have clipped the hems with bobby pins and kept the shirt from flapping about with extra notches bore into their holster belts. They've rolled up the sleeves to show off the Timex and Bolo watches hanging off their slender wrists, and they've cinched tight the collars with neckerchiefs and dog tags.

Lowering their weapons and holstering their revolvers, the soldiers squat. The pockmarked soldier produces a pack of cigarettes from his shirt pocket. He extracts one for himself, and passes the pack around. He offers a light from his Zippo with the word Cowboy engraved on one side. From the other shirt pocket, he produces a deck of playing cards. Marilyn, wearing a white strapless dress, is on the back of each card. She blows a kiss with her hand. He deals a round of Twenty-One.

Lý Loc continues to smoke his cigarette and refills his cup. The soldiers ogle Marilyn. Some pick up their winning hands and kiss each card. Lý Loc keeps smoking and drinking coffee as the soldiers use whatever they have on them to play each round. They reach in their pockets, knapsacks, beneath the pith helmets and caps, within the rolled-up sleeves, the compartments of their holster belts, and even stretch the elastic waistband of the pajamas and take out white and yellow packs of Wrigley's Spearmint Gum, buttons with cannabis leaves, Salems and Lucky Strikes, bottles of ginger ale, fingernail clippers, nail filers, Swiss Army knives and switchblades, straight razors, magazines and clips, Bic lighters, handkerchiefs, compacts, handheld fans, betel nuts, an orange here, a mango there, and tree limbs with tamarinds whose green skins had hardened and cracked.

Lý Loĉ crushes his cigarette and uncrosses his legs and says, "I am ready."

He stands up ands steps down from off his porch. They get to their feet, raise their rifles and fumble for the triggers. Lý Loĉ stands head and chest above them. The soldier with bad skin motions Lý Loĉ to the line, but when they all turn to the road, the captives are gone. They look down opposite ends of the road, peer across the river where Chef and Willard pee against a banyan tree; their rifles are slung over one shoulder and their pails hang from the crook of their arms. There are no signs of half-naked, bloodied and bruised men, just a slithering track in the dirt disappearing into the fields.

The bad skinned soldier barks at his men. They separate and enter smoky houses. Others follow the slithering trail into the field of tall cane grass and mai trees afire with fully bloomed yellow flowers. The slap of the soldiers' sandals on hardwood floors fills the village. Overcome by smoke, soldiers run from the houses, coughing and rubbing their eyes. The bad skinned soldier flails his arms and screams at them to continue their search, but they remain outside, bent double, vomiting smoke. The bad skinned soldier swings around *and strikes Lý Loĉ who spins around and around, and the soldier shuffles from side to side with arms out, ready to catch Lý Loĉ when he stops. Lý Loĉ's legs buckle from under him, and he is down on his hands and knees when they rope him around the neck and arms and waist and parade their only prisoner through town, past Francis Ford Coppola wearing sunglasses, barking at them not to look into the camera, but to keep going to where he points at the horizon.*

Monday, August 18th

"I didn't like the movie," Mother says with pins clenched between her teeth. She takes one from her mouth and sticks it in the hem of my brown corduroy pants. She stands up among the steady hum of sewing machines—needles stamping thread into fabric. She removes the pins from between her teeth and says, "We left halfway through the movie."

"You didn't see the rest?" Aunt Pham Thi asks.

Mother places her hands on her hips as she tilts her head from side to side to check the straightness of the hem she just finished.

"No. We didn't see the rest of the film," Mother continues. "I couldn't stand it. All that shooting and killing." She brings a hand up and lays it flat against her cheek. She squints before bringing her hand away from her face. "OK, Long-Vanh, take off the pants."

I unzip the brown corduroy pants that don't even have a clasp or button, or the belt loops sewn on, and there is only one front pocket. I step out of them, careful not to prick myself. I hand her the pants and quickly get into my old jeans. The Mexican ladies whistle and hoot and make kissing sounds as I'm putting on my jeans. They've seen me in my underwear all morning, and each time I take off my pants to try on the ones Mother is making for me, their cheering gets louder.

"OK, go sit down," she says and folds the pants. "You're growing too fast."

I take my seat by the door where sunlight comes in and turn to where I left off in Mark Twain's *Huckleberry Finn*. It is still morning and already the sun shines brightly and it is getting hot. Guessing from the telephone pole's shadow parallel to the sidewalk, it's probably ten, ten-fifteen. The shirtless children swarm in front of the liquor store with their fingers in their mouths. Some are wearing the same shorts and pants day after day and their brown skin turns darker.

"You wouldn't have liked the movie," Mother says as she hangs up my pants on a hanger, then places it on a rack along with other dresses.

"And my God, Pham, so many mistakes w-w-with costumes, and the city itself. The city doesn't look like Saigon. Who is that fat ass Coppola trying to fool? 'I am Vietnam.'" Mother holds out her arms, mimicking Coppola at a press conference she caught on the evening news. "If he keeps eating, he'll be as big as Vietnam. Stupid jackass."

Aunt Pham Thi laughs as she leans over her work, presses her foot down on the pedal and feeds the fabric through. She is sewing her third green dress for the morning. Because it will be autumn soon, the dresses are as simple as the summer ones, only thicker in material.

Mother takes her seat behind the machine. Reaching over to take a precut pattern, Mother places the two pieces underneath the needle, turns the wheel until the needle lowers onto the fabric, then presses the pedal. Her hands feed it through, guiding it past the curve and continuing to the bottom.

"How did Wil like it?" Aunt Pham Thi asks.

Mother lifts up the needle, cuts the thread, and goes to

work on one of the sleeves.

"He likes it. He likes it a lot because when we got home he was angry." Mother glances at me before returning to her work.

I slept during the long ride home after we left the drive-in, and I don't remember climbing the stairs and getting into my own bed. I do remember going in and out of sleep, the darkness of my room, the absence of geckos on the window screen, and Mother crying in the bedroom down the hall. She took in short bursts of air and let it all out with one slow push. Dad paced the kitchen, boots stomping the linoleum floor as he jerked open the refrigerator door, and all the bottles and jars on the side shelves rattled, only to clatter again when he slammed the door shut. The tab to the beer can spat and hissed, and Dad swallowed deep and hard: each gulp grew louder and farther apart. He crushed the can in his hand, slapped it on the counter, and went back to pacing. The whole time I kept my eyes closed I knew I wasn't dreaming, knew Mother was crying in her hands while Dad paced the kitchen, angry for having missed the film, for not getting to see Marlon Brando killed.

The front door slammed and I could still hear pacing even going away from the front door. Sobbing. And I slept.

Mother completes the sleeve. She takes the small pair of scissors and cuts the thread. It bothers me to see her working and talking about the evening like it was nothing. I'm pretty sure Aunt Pham Thi doesn't know that Dad hasn't been home since Friday evening. Mother went about the house cleaning and cooking, and the only things she said to me the entire weekend were, "Eat a bowl of cereal for breakfast," "Come here. Lunch is ready," and "Dinner is done. Eat."

Mother looks up from her work and notices that I've been staring at her. Her hands automatically reach to the side of the extended board for pins. Without looking, she attaches the cuff to the sleeve. I return to Huckleberry Finn drifting down the Mississippi River with Nigger Jim.

Closed Buds

Tuesday and Dad hasn't come home. Mother stays home instead of going to work. She just sits on the sofa and stares at the front door or looks out the living room window. After a lunch of bologna sandwiches, I tell her I am going over to Aunt Pham Thi's to play with Phượng. She only looks in my direction, blinks her eyes, and then goes back to watching the front door.

So I leave for several hours, come home, and find her sitting in the same spot. She hasn't changed out of her clothes or even turned on the television. Her face has hardened: lines form underneath her eyes, and her frown caused from worrying becomes permanent.

She didn't cook anything, so I make myself another bologna sandwich, and, like before, I eat at the dinner table and watch her. Mother's knuckles and fingers are purple from trying to crack them. She has stopped fiddling with her hands. After dinner, I go into my bedroom and just lie in bed, and slowly the room, the whole house, grows dark, and I think how sad it is for Mother to sit in a silent house and watch things grow dark around her. I don't want to be around for this. The idea of her not getting off the sofa until Dad comes home frightens me because it feels like I am home alone. She is a fixture like the Buddha statues on the shelves, or the photographs of Lý Lộc she keeps on the low table in the corner, the same corner where she burns incense. I figure it would be kind of weird watching television in the living room while she sits on the sofa. It's like having a stranger claim he is a friend of your parents, and so he waits for them to come home. But the whole time you can't get yourself to relax although he tells you stories about a time when you weren't even born, and your own parents become strangers to you because you couldn't picture them existing in another house, another city, alone. Before your parents even met or ever said each other's name. Or even worse, the stranger doesn't say a word the whole time while waiting.

The thought of this spooks me, so before it grows any darker, I get out of bed and turn on the light. From the dresser drawers I take out a pair of jeans and a T-shirt; I fold up pajamas, gather my toothbrush and a towel from the bathroom, and take them all into the kitchen to pack into a brown shopping bag. I keep the lights off. Though it is dark, I can see Mother on the sofa, and I can't stand the way she continues to sit there the way people in movies sit behind their desks or at the dinner table and then suddenly die on the spot, because that's exactly how she looks, dead.

"I'm going to stay with Aunt Pham Thi," I say.

Knowing I am not going to get an answer from her, I leave the house. I walk downstairs and Uncle Ngô is sitting on a chair just outside his garage-bedroom drinking a beer. The other door is propped open by a toolbox.

"I'm going to Aunt Pham Thi's place to spend the night," I tell him.

"OK. You stay at Pham Thi. Your mother will be OK."

I walk down the hill holding the brown bag to my chest. Everyone is home, even Uncle Handsome Harlemite. When Phượng opens the door, she doesn't say anything; no one says a word for a long time. Uncle Handsome Harlemite and Mia are staring at me while chewing their food, and I feel ridiculous holding the bag.

Aunt Pham Thi wipes her hands on the napkin and gets up from the dinner table. She takes the bag from my hands, leads me to the dinner table, and goes into the kitchen to fix a plate for me.

....

We sit in front of the television after dinner. Though it is *The Jefferson*s, hardly anyone laughs except for Uncle Handsome Harlemite. No one says anything, and in between commercials I want to ask him if he knows where Dad is. The way he keeps his eyes glued to the television, the way he keeps his laugh lasting as long as possible, tells me he doesn't want to talk about it.

The 10 o'clock news comes on, and in the center of the screen the words appear in big letters: DAY 287 The Iran Hostage Crisis. Men and women in the streets of Tehran burn the American flag and the black fumes barely hide the men and women's dancing and chanting as they strike the air with fists. Ayatollah Khomeini sits in a cushioned velvet chair, hands laced in front of him as he nods his head, and his beard comes down past his chest. The man sitting forward in the chair next to him is dressed in a two-piece suit—the negotiator. I'm listening to what the anchorman is saying, but the negotiator is probably telling the Ayatollah about the long lines at the gas pumps and if he can do anything about it; help bring down the price of oil, then deal with the hostages. When this segment of the news ends, we all get dressed for bed and brush our teeth.

Only Mia, Phượng, and I are sleeping on the living room floor. Not long after Uncle Handsome Harlemite and Aunt Pham Thi go into the back bedroom and close the door, the moans begin followed by *shushing*. Phượng and I are staring up at the ceiling, listening to the bed squeak. I can hear Phượng turning her head in my direction, but I stay quiet and still. There's nothing to say. Dad is gone, and Mother is staying up until he comes home.

There is a heaviness that settles on my chest, a heaviness that keeps me from moving because I tell myself, *It's wasted movement. Everything is wasted.* I've lost one parent and maybe by tomorrow the other as well. For a moment, the thought of finding her gone the next morning lifts some of the weight off of me. The more I think about it, the more I think it's best she gets it over with so she can stop making me feel this way. She'd have to find the suitcase, and I think of calling home and telling her to climb out my bedroom window, dig through the vines to get it, and leave. It makes sense. I'm here, Dad is at work; all she'd have to do is call a taxi and leave and I won't have to worry anymore. And if I call, she'll pick up thinking it's Dad. Mother is most likely on the living room sofa, watching the darkness and allowing it to swallow her whole.

Wednesday afternoon and Uncle Handsome Harlemite is sleeping and Mia has gone off to be with Pedro. In the lot next to the apartment building, Aunt Pham Thi cleared away a section of the weed-grown field last summer. She borrowed the Japanese family's hoe and rake for a day and dug up an area big enough for a vegetable and herb garden.

Phượng and I are squatting in the garden, picking Serrano peppers off the bush: "Pick them green," Aunt Pham Thi told us. The weeds bordering the garden are taller than us; they grow into the garden providing unwanted shade for spearmints that need the sun. Aunt Pham Thi is on her knees chopping at the thick stalks of weeds with the kitchen cleaver and tossing them into the fields so that they can dry in the sun and die.

"Don't worry Long-Vanh. Your Mother fine. Just need time to herself," Aunt Pham Thi says, though I haven't said a word about her all morning and afternoon.

Phượng keeps picking the peppers; her fingers pause over the light green ones before separating them from the darker ones.

"Really," Aunt Pham Thi continues, "I see her like this before."

I look at her. Even though she's panting from struggling with the weeds all afternoon, she manages a smile.

"I remember this in Vietnam. She tell Lý Lôc she marry your father. He say no. Because he is Catholic. Because he is black. Because he is American. He say marry him, and you no longer my daughter. So she marry him, and he not talk to her for a long time. A year. Very long time."

Aunt Pham Thi wipes the sweat from her forehead with the back of her hand. I've heard this story before, of how he came to see me after a year. Amazed by how much I looked like him, Lý Lôc allowed Mother back in the family again.

"And then he contact her and say I want to see baby. Your mother say OK. So she wait. It take Lý Lôc a week to come. For one week, she wait for Lý Lôc. She not do anything: cook, clean, work in garden, take care of you. Just *whoop*," Aunt Pham Thi throws out her hands, a gesture of quitting, and in doing so, she almost catches Phượng's head with the cleaver, but neither one of them realizes how close it came. "Your father take care of you because your mother wait for Lý Loĉ. One week she wait. And then he come, and he surprised of you. Very surprised."

Aunt Pham Thi digs about a foot or more around the stalk to get at the roots.

"So don't worry. She OK. OK?"

I nod and Aunt Pham Thi takes a hold of the stalk and pulls it with both hands. The tendons in her neck stand out as she grunts and strains to pry the weed from the ground. Finally it comes loose and she holds it up. The root is about two feet in length.

"Weeds," she sighs. "They like disease." With the cleaver, she points to the pale hairs dangling off the main one. "You leave a little behind, and it has chance to grow back. Just like disease. Can never get rid of it."

Blossom

When Mother doesn't come by the apartment, Aunt Pham Thi leaves for work. I stay at the apartment until ten before going home, and I find her sleeping on the sofa. I shake her by the shoulder, and she immediately wakes up. Her eyes move left to right. The pouches beneath her eyes are black, and her lips are dried and cracked. Mother raises herself and blinks at me.

"Get up and take a shower. Get dressed," I say.

She takes a long time in the bathroom. I'm still waiting for her to get dressed, and as I eat two bowls of Cheerios the mailman arrives at the top of the steps. I go outside to get the mail and in the bundle is a letter from Vietnam, the first in two months.

"Mother," I call out. "Mother, there's a letter for you."

She immediately comes out of the bathroom with a towel wrapped around her head. I hand her the letter and she tears it open, unfolds the pages, and her eyes and lips move over the words. Mother folds the letter and pulls the towel off her head. She looks about the living room and grabs her purse and keys.

"Let's go," she says.

....

We take the bus into Downtown L.A., and we have to get off and transfer onto another bus into Chinatown. Mother walks fast down the busy sidewalk. Gold and red

233

streamers stretch from storefront awnings to lampposts, and they continue across the streets to the other posts. Paper lanterns hang from the streamers high above. Jewelry and grocery stores and Chinese and Vietnamese restaurants butt up against one another. A long line of markets advertise posters of foreign films taped to the storefront windows. Beautiful women in *áo dàis* smile, and I assume they are big stars in Vietnam, China, or Japan.

Mother enters a store with its double doors wide open. Men in white coats and black rubber boots stand over rows of fish tanks filled with mussels, clams, live mackerels and catfish, crabs, lobsters, octopuses, and squids. They dip nets into the tanks and pull out the ones people point to. As soon as the men in white coats scoop out the fish and octopuses and squids, they weigh them on scales that hang above the tanks.

The floor is wet, and flies swarm the area. Mother and I wedge ourselves between the crowds of men and women waiting to be served, and head into the store. Mother takes up a handbasket and walks down an aisle of canned goods, plucking cans of lychees in heavy syrup, glazed palm fruits, and Grass Jell-O off the shelves. She makes her way down the next aisle for vermicelli rice noodles.

I follow her with people watching us. They peek over the tops of cans and bottles from the next aisle, or turn to look behind them as they dump their produce on the conveyor belt at the register. But I keep to Mother's side. At one point I take the basket from her, and this makes people stare even more.

We make our way to the checkout counter, and Mother suddenly stops before a stack of boxes filled with dress shirts wrapped in cellophane. She picks up a navy blue shirt and turns it over in her hands; the sleeves are folded behind the back and pinned in place.

"Go ahead Long-Vanh. Pick out a couple of them."

"Who are they for?" I ask.

"Your grandfather."

She sorts through the untidy stacks of shirts. I pick out a white shirt and a yellow one and hold them up to Mother. She frowns at them and even brings them close to her face as if to make out the fabric.

"Yes," she nods. "He will like them."

········

The bags of canned goods and shirts sit on the empty chair between Mother and me. We eat phở at the neighboring Vietnamese restaurant. Tired of noticing everyone watching us, I stare into my bowl when I eat. Or I watch the bag on the chair. The top part of the carton of Salem cigarettes is showing. Mother caught sight of the different brands of cigarettes stacked on shelves behind the cashier as she was checking out.

"When are you going to send these things to him?" I look up from my bowl to ask and look back down before she can answer.

"Maybe today."

"The letter. Is it good news?"

Mother nods as she shoves a mouthful of noodles into her mouth. When she finishes swallowing, she says, "Your grandfather was released from the camp nearly a month ago." Before I can ask another question, she says, "He's free. After four years, your grandfather is free."

The dark areas beneath her eyes have disappeared. Only the heavy lines remain. I stir my noodles and beef around with my chopsticks.

"Does this mean he's coming to America?"

Mother sighs. The smile disappears when she presses her lips together in thought.

"I don't know. We don't have an American Embassy anymore. Not since 1973. I don't think he can leave. But we will see." She smiles again.

"Why can't he leave? Why not buy a plane ticket and leave?"

Mother shakes her head sharply and she gives me a look that makes me lean away from the table, and I am ready for Mother to scream at me for asking too many questions, or the wrong ones.

"It's not that easy," she says. "No one can leave. If they do, it is by boats. They have to pay a large amount of money just to get onto a boat. Sometimes, the boat makes it here. Most of the time, it does not. They are captured. And if they are captured, they are sent back to Vietnam and put in prison. Or the boat is no good and they wander for months and don't know which direction to go."

I picture a rusty boat crowded with Vietnamese people. It is so crowded that the people have to bring their knees to their chests when they sit. I imagine them growing sick and thin from lack of food, and vomiting on each other because the open sea is too hard on their stomachs. With nothing in sight but water, they'd probably cry and go crazy from the idea of never seeing land again. The thought of Lý Lôc being on one of these boats worries me, but not to let on, I stir with the noodles as if getting ready to eat. Mother tips her head back and drinks her iced coffee drenched in condensed milk. The muscles in her throat move each time she swallows to take in plenty.

The Care Package

When we get home, Mother goes through the cupboards, the closets in her bedroom, and the living room for a box big enough to pack everything. Not to give her a chance to go looking through my closet and discover the Samsonite is missing, I find a box with all my old school papers and dump everything and give it to her.

She sits in the middle of the living room floor with all the items spread out in front of her. She takes the canned lychees, palm fruits, and Grass Jell-O and places them inside the box. As she sits there deciding what to put inside the box next, the phone rings. We look at the phone at the same time. Just as Mother takes up the packages of noodles and set them inside the box, she tells me to answer the phone.

It is José, the owner of Hernandez's Sew Yourself. He wants to know if Mother will return to work any time soon. Out of the corner of my eyes, I watch Mother as she takes up the shirts wrapped in cellophane and stacks them inside the box. My heart beats faster. Cancer crosses my mind. A car accident. Her leaving.

"She's, she's sick."

Mother doesn't look up. She tries to put the whole carton of Salems in the box, but it won't fit, so she tears open the carton and takes out each pack.

"No. It's just the flu. She has a high fever. She's sleeping right now. No, I don't know if she'll be in tomorrow. It depends on how she feels. OK. Bye."

As soon as I hang up the phone, Mother looks up.

"Good, Long-Vanh, now get me some tape."

I hand it to her, and she picks at the seam with her nail, unwinds a long piece, and seals up the middle and corners.

········

After Mother went to the post office to mail the care package, she came home, arranged incense sticks like the tail of a peacock behind a propped up picture of Lý Lôc, and lit them in the far corner of the living room. As they burn, Mother and I watch television and drink iced coffee. It is good to hear her laugh, to see her whole body shake. We watch show after show and when I think she's going to get up and turn off the television only to sit back down on the sofa and stare at the front door, another show comes on, and we watch and laugh until it is midnight and *The Twilight Zone* begins. Mother sips the last of her coffee and swirls the glass so that the ice clatters against it. She sets the glass on the coaster atop the coffee table and stands up to turn off the television.

"Come on Long-Vanh. Let's go."

She takes up the house keys from off the kitchen table and heads for the front door.

"Where are we going?" I ask.

She undoes the top and bottom locks and opens the front door, then faces me.

"Let's go," she says.

I follow her outside. After she locks the door behind us, we walk downstairs. Although it is warm, Mother crosses her arms and slouches forward a bit. She stops in front of Uncle Ngô's garage-bedroom door and sorts through the keys on the ring. She holds one up to the light and says, "Wait right here."

Mother unlocks the door. Afraid to let any streetlight in, she wedges herself inside and closes the door behind her. I stare at the door, wondering what she's doing in the dark among the geckos. I look around and all the lights in everyone's homes are off except for the porch lights. The lights in downtown burn, and the head- and taillights from the few cars at this hour travel up and down the freeways.

The door opens, and Mother squeezes herself outside, and immediately locks the door.

"Let's go."

We walk across the street to Uncle Ngô's Monte Carlo.

She gets behind the wheel, reaches over and unlocks the door and even opens it. "Come on. Get in."

I climb in and immediately put my seatbelt on, re-membering the last time Dad gave her a driving lesson. Mother bends down to find the ignition. She keeps jam-ming the key against the sides before she finally gets it in. She starts the engine but holds the key in position too long to where the car trembles, and she lets go. She places both hands on the steering wheel and looks straight ahead to where the lights flood the street and curb side.

"You know where Dad works. Do you know how to get there?" she asks, and it seems she's asking the head-lights and the darkness in front of her.

"I know how to get there."

She points ahead and asks, "Can I get out this way?"

"I only know this way," I hook my thumb over my shoulder to where Montana Avenue descends in a steep slope. "You'll have to reverse," I say, my voice shaking at the thought of her doing so, for Dad had told Mother that reverse scared people because they could not see what was behind them.

"OK," Mother nods. "OK," she keeps repeating it like prayer.

She takes one hand off the wheel, grabs the gearshift, pulls it toward her, then down three times. She grips the wheel with both hands and presses on the gas pedal. The car lunges forward, and she steers it straight ahead, hitting the curb a couple of times before she drives down the center of the street. She gets to a part where the divider has a break and makes a left into a driveway. The headlights cast against the huge living room windows with long curtains and I can see furniture, lamps, and the far wall, and I wonder if Mother has her high beams on.

"Look back for me Long-Vanh, and tell me if I'm going to hit anything."

Mother pulls up on the handle and takes her foot off the brakes and lets the car roll down the driveway. Before I can tell her to stop, Mother steps on the brakes. She sets the car into "D," turns the wheel until it can't turn any more and steps on the gas. We speed down Montana Avenue, and I sit back and grip the seat as she drives close to the parked cars. We pass up our house, the Casa de Maria Apartments, and I want to tell her to slow down, but Mother is leaning over the wheel, following the headlights.

Mother steers the car into the parking lot next to the pool hall and pizza place. Down one aisle I can see Dad's lime-green Firebird. She parks away from the other cars two aisles down, turns off the headlights, and sits there staring at the yellow lines on the black pavement. Although she grips the steering wheel with both hands, her arms are trembling. Mother lets go of the wheel and rubs the palms of her hands together until her heavy breathing is under control and the shaking stops.

"I want you to take me to the building. You know where," she says.

I look at the entrance to the community college, the gates wide open, the poorly lit hallways. I turn to her and say, "He works in the Liberal Arts building."

"No," she shakes her head. "Not Dad."

I frown for a moment and then my heart thumps so hard against my chest that I think it's going to break. Mother opens the door and climbs out of the car. I get out, and Mother is jingling the set of keys in her hand as she waits for me to walk ahead of her. I lead her between parked cars, past Dad's Firebird, across North Vermont Avenue, through the iron gates, and down the hallway. It is nearly one in the morning and no one is around. The farther we walk the shorter my strides become. All day I felt happy because Mother asked for my help. All day I felt useful up until this point, and I wish she had gone back to sitting on the couch, waiting for Dad.

When we come out onto the quad and I see the double doors of the infirmary, my legs wobble. We cross the quad, trampling over the thick grass, and I am having a hard time breathing. My whole body shakes and my legs get tired from taking short strides. I fear we will walk in on Dad holding Sharon's legs over his shoulders as he pushes his hips into her and mops the sweat off her body with his

large hands. And Dad will turn and bear his teeth at me
for having broken my silence.

"What's wrong?"

I shake my head and clutch my chest to keep the heart
from beating so hard. "Nothing. That's the infirmary," I
point. "She'll be behind the counter. Her name is Sharon."

I think of anything else I can tell her. Maybe the way
she wears her blond hair in a bun, the gold cross on her
necklace, her breasts I never got to see, anything to stay
outside. But Mother says, "Come on," and I follow right
behind her. The moment she places her foot on the black
mat the doors open, and Mother walks right up to the
counter. Sharon looks up in time to see me. She smiles
and says, "Long-Vanh. What are you doing here?"

I am held in place by her even white teeth, her large
blue eyes. Mother looks at me with disbelief, hurt that Sharon knows my name, that we have met before, that Dad
brought me here. Sharon finally notices Mother standing
beside me, and her lips close slowly like secret caves in
movies.

"I am Vu-An," Mother says.

Sharon's tongue moves inside her mouth. She straightens up in her chair and fumbles with the magazine before
closing it.

"He…He's just staying with me until—"

"Bull-*shiiit!*"

Although Sharon flinches from Mother's burst, the
word sounds mispronounced coming from her, and I do
what I can to keep from laughing. Mother takes in the first
syllable like a person who drinks more than what a mouth
can hold, then spits it all out, "Bull-*fucking-shiiit!*" Mother

leans over the counter with her finger in Sharon's face, and I expect Sharon to fall back in her chair. "You take me for stupid? You send my husband home. You send him home. You hear me?"

Sharon's mouth is still working for words. Mother looks into the room where I slept the last time I was here, and I'm thinking she's staring at the bed. I'm thinking she's going to turn on me for sleeping here, for having Sharon watch over me. But I realize it is not the bed by the window she is staring at, but Dad sweeping the floor in the Liberal Arts building. His back is to us as he moves the desks around to sweep. Mother continues to stare at him. Her shoulders slacken and her head drops for a moment before turning to Sharon.

"In Vietnam, we kill cheating husbands, and their women," Mother says, and she turns and leaves the infirmary, and I follow her.

········

Friday. I wake up with a start after realizing there is too much sunlight in my room. It is 9:30 and Mother is probably at work, but I hear noises coming from the living room. Forks and knives hit and scrape plates.

When I go into the living room, I find Dad and Mother sitting at the table eating breakfast. Dad realizes I am standing in the hallway and stops chewing long enough to say good morning. Mother looks over her shoulder. Her eyes stay on me for a moment, and remembering the piece of toast in her mouth, she continues chewing.

September

The start of the school year falls on Tuesday because of Labor Day, and already I'm sitting outside the principal's office with a busted lip. I can taste the exposed meat, soft and pussier. One of my front teeth is loose. At times I hit my tongue against it, and I feel it move, hear the sucking that comes from the tooth parting from the gums. The skin beneath my right eye feels like it's been stretched tight and it gets more numb each moment. Fat Chan glares at me from across the room as he holds a tissue to his nose. His right eye is nearly swollen shut from the red bruise turning purple. From behind the bloodied tissue he mouths Vietnamese curses I can't understand, and this makes Fat Chan smile. The only word I know is *còn lại*.

When he notices that I have sat up, he says in English, "Yellow Nigger."

His whole body shakes; the stomach rolls up and down beneath his tight fitting shirt as his eyes shut to near slits, yet no sound comes from him. His eyes open wide all of a sudden as he stops shaking long enough to repeat the words.

It is this that made me go after him during lunchtime. Now he sits across from me—with one eye swollen shut, a tissue to his nose—cursing. I turn to the secretary to see if she notices what is going on, but she is at her desk, typing. I want to get up, walk across the room and slap Fat Chan upside his head. But they already called Mother, and any minute now I expect her to walk in.

Fat Chan continues to mutter under his breath as he seeks an unused part of the tissue. I grab the armrests with both hands, ready to lift myself up out of the chair, and Fat Chan sits back with his mouth open and his eyes round as dimes. I stare at his nose, wondering if I can make the other nostril bleed. But Mother is coming. So I lean forward in my seat and whisper beneath the typewriter's uninterrupted chime and ring.

"Fat *Chin*. You cry like a girl." I wipe the corners of my eyes.

He lowers the tissue, smearing blood over his upper lip. He sits up in his chair and pushes out his chest.

"Fat *Chinnie-Chin-Chin*. You cry *worse* than a girl."

He looks at the secretary and studies her profile. The blinds are open, and sunlight collects in the clear plastic frame and large round lenses of her glasses, causing her to sit forward and squint. Fat Chan keeps going from me to the secretary, weighing his chances, but just then Mother walks in.

She jingles the house keys in her hand. She sees me slouched in my chair and the jingling grows louder. The secretary glances over her shoulder, stands up, and knocks on the principal's door. Without waiting for a reply she returns to her desk, reads the last line, and continues typing. The door opens, and Mr. Patterson steps out. He makes his way around the counter with his head down, hands stuffed in his trouser pockets.

"Mrs. Stiles." He looks her in the eyes. "Your son lost his temper with Chan here," he motions with a jut of his chin, "when he called your son names."

Mother turns around to face Fat Chan. The jingling increases at the sight of his black eye and the bloodied tissue.

"I'm going to suspend your son for three days beginning next Monday. Even though his behavior is unacceptable and warrants immediate reprimand, I do feel it is important that he at least finishes out the first week of school to get assignments and get situated. But Mrs. Stiles, if this happens again…."

Mr. Patterson takes his hands out of his pockets and holds them in front of him with the fingers laced. He twiddles his thumbs. Mother stares at me. Her eyes narrow, and not once does she blink. She grinds the backs of her teeth. I imagine her grinding them until they become chalky and when it's time for her to speak, gritty foam will pour from her mouth. Aside from her jaw, the only thing moving, the only sound coming from her is the keys in her hand.

I look away. Impatience shows in Mr. Patterson's pursed lips, the brows clamped together, and the thumbs twiddling faster. There is the continuous sound of the keys, and even the secretary's typing slows so that the bell that signals the end of the line never comes.

"If it happens again, then I'll suspend him for a week. A third time, I will have to expel him. This is only the first day of school, and already a fight," he finishes.

"And what do you want *me* to do?" Mother asks.

Everyone looks at her, and Mr. Patterson's eyes widen as he straightens up.

"A promise that he won't fight again," he stammers and finally collects his speech in the end.

Mother reels her head and her frown scrunches up even more.

"*I* can't make that promise. Only *he* can," she points to me. "If *you* want to suspend him, go ahead. If *you* want to expel him, do so. But don't ask *me* to make promises. *I'm* not the one in trouble. *I'm* not going to have you talk to me like it's *my* fault he beat that boy. It's that jack *ass* right there who's in trouble, not *me*. I was sewing dresses for pay when you called. *You,*" she points at Mr. Patterson, "interrupted *my* job. Why?"

Mr. Patterson just looks at Mother, mouth slack and open.

"Could you not keep him here until I got off from work? Was he going to escape? Cause more trouble?—in *here*?" she looks about the waiting area.

Mother turns to me, and for that brief moment she stares at me, she's grinding the backs of her teeth again.

"Go ahead," she turns back to Mr. Patterson. She holds her hand out to me and says, "Did you ask him? Ask him *why* he hit that fat ass?" She points at Chan with the other hand. "Do you even care why he hit him?—what he called my son?"

I sit up straight and realize I've had my mouth open all this time to breathe. Mr. Patterson leans away from Mother, head tilted up like he's staring at the fluorescent lights. Fat Chan's mouth has dropped open, and he holds the tissue to his nose more from dismay than to stop the flow of blood. And the typing has ceased altogether.

"*He* will promise you, not me."

She turns away from Mr. Patterson and heads for the door. Before she leaves, she stops in front of Fat Chan, leans down, and points a finger so close to his face that he sits back in his chair.

"If you ever touch my boy again or call him names, I am going to kill you myself. You're lucky we're in America. In Vietnam we kill children like you, and if your mother and father had any sense, they'd have killed you and your brother a long time ago."

"Mrs. Stiles, please," Mr. Patterson says.

"A *long* time ago," Mother repeats.

She straightens up and walks out. I look at Mr. Patterson who meets me with the same stunned expression. I get up from my chair and hurry out of the office and follow the sound of keys jingling down the hallway. I am right behind Mother as she cuts through the black-topped playground. She swings her arms high and one foot barely touches the ground before the other lifts forward. I jog until I am at her side.

We leave school from the corner gate and wait for the light. The cars pass in front of us and I start counting seconds until it is our turn to cross. I fidget with my hands. I don't want to put them in my pockets, but at the same time I feel clumsy letting them hang at my sides. And I know it is because I want to hold Mother's hand, or at least place my hand on her shoulder and promise her I'll be good from now on. So good she won't ever get another phone call from the school.

I glance at her, pretend I am looking down the street, but she stares straight ahead at the other side. She turns and looks in my direction and I flinch before realizing she is not looking at me, but past me. Before I know it, Mother steps off the curb and walks across. I look up to see that our light is still red. Mother keeps walking. Cars slow down and drivers watch her pass in front of them.

I step off the curb and a car honks at me, and I hop back onto the curb. The driver leans over the passenger side and hisses, "*I* have the green light, jackass."

Mother steps onto the sidewalk and keeps walking. I want to yell at her to wait for me. She didn't even turn around upon the screeching of tires, the honk and yell to see if I had been hit. She keeps walking, and I stand and wait for the light turn green. I run across the street until I catch up with her. Mother's arms swing back and forth in wide sweeping arches, her pace steady.

I stare at her out of the corner of my eyes while catching my breath. Aside from that, I keep my head down trying to figure out what is going on when suddenly Mother throws all of her weight behind her shoulder and shoves me into the street.

"Get away from me!" she yells. "You're walking too damn close to me."

Mother continues walking, but then she stops, turns around and says, "You embarrass me."

Just as she turns away, I say, "What does that matter?"

She stops and faces me. "What?" she asks.

"I said, what does it matter? You're going to leave anyway, so who cares if I embarrass you."

Mother and I stare at each other. Her jaw grinds and her eyes narrow. I fidget with my hands at my sides and I want to look away, but I keep my eyes on her. Mother nods her head. She walks away and I stand there and watch her. She picks up her pace. The first day of school and I've done the one thing I've always done and never knew it:

I embarrass her. I continue to stand there wondering if I'll find her gone by the time I get home or standing out on the patio with the Samsonite waiting for a cab. I get onto the sidewalk and stare at her back. She grows smaller and smaller, a woman in black jeans and T-shirt, and black hair coiled in a bun. I watch her until she becomes a small black thing, so small, so black that she begins to waver, and it hurts to squint.

········

   Although my door is closed, I can hear Dad snoring. Mother is beside him sound asleep despite the noise, and I'm hoping she can't sleep. She doesn't deserve to sleep. I lie awake and stare at the geckos, but it isn't long before I climb out of bed, and in lifting the window, the geckos scurry off. I remove the screen and set it inside. Knowing the ivy-covered ground is unstable, I jump from the window sill, placing both hands on the ground for balance.
   It takes me a while to locate the Samsonite because the ivy I had torn from the fence that night shriveled up and dried. But it is where I left it. I wrap my arms around the big suitcase after clearing away all the dead vines. Making sure my feet don't get tangled up or caught in a hole, I carry the Samsonite to the window, hoist it onto the sill and let it drop. It falls flat on its side with a loud thud. I stand there, hands on the sill, waiting to see the light come on in their room and flood the bottom of my bedroom door. But I don't care if they come into my room and find me outside or see the suitcase.
   There is only the faint sound of Dad's snoring, so I lift myself back inside the room, replace the screen, and

shut the window. I drag the Samsonite across the room and tuck it just inside the closet where Mother can find it. I even leave the door open just a little.

Brutal Bloom

"Long-Vanh. Wake up and get dressed."

Mother is in the doorway, hand on the knob. As soon as I raise my head off the pillow to see her glaring at me, she closes the door.

After brushing my teeth, taking a shower, and getting dressed, Mother and I leave the house. The sun has just come up, and already the yellow flowers on the *mai* trees begin to blossom. Mother still walks with the same urgency in her step as she did last Tuesday after school. There is a tight swinging motion of her arms as she allows the hill to carry her down.

When we get Aunt Pham Thi's apartment, I wait downstairs while Mother goes up to get her.

"Good morning," Aunt Pham Thi says once she gets to the bottom of the stairs. I follow right behind them with my head up. People are locking their front doors and walking to different corners to catch the bus for work. Mother maintains the fast pace and Aunt Pham Thi has to jog to keep up. Ahead, the two Korean women are walking side by side, one speaking, the other listening. I slow down when I notice Mother doesn't make a move to the side. Aunt Pham Thi even slows down: she looks from Mother to the women ahead. She wants to speak, but she closes her mouth. The Korean women keep walking, and the one listening frowns at Mother's approach. She says something and the other woman looks up just as Mother bumps them hard enough to make them stumble. They gawk at Mother as they watch her walk by with Aunt Pham Thi jogging to catch up. Mother keeps walking. The Korean women turn to me, their mouths and eyes wide.

"Excuse me," I say, and walk between them.

A Theater of War

Past

Mother waters the jade plants lined along the edges of the porch while Uncle Ngô and I sit in cane chairs, smoking cigarettes. She hums while she walks about the porch, and the whole time I'm wondering if that is the same song she hummed the morning I watched her wait for the taxi.

Mother's humming rises when she comes to the last jade plant. She scoops a handful of water into the soil and just as she sets the bucket in the corner, she finishes the last notes before turning to me. I take a big puff and exhale. Because it is humid, because there is no breeze even for a coastal city, the smoke lingers and it's a while before it clears. Mother sits herself down on the porch steps.

"So how do you like Vietnam? I know I asked you before, but it is different with each day."

"It's beautiful," I say. "Nice."

The sun submits to the weight of oncoming night. The stars pale. They barely glint against the light blue sky.

"So, have you lived here all this time? In this house?" I ask.

"Yes. When I came here, they detained me for some time in the camps before they let me go. I didn't spend much time there. Only six months."

"Six months?"

Mother snaps her head in my direction and I wonder if I'm being too blunt.

"Yes. Your grandfather spent four years."

259

She turns back to face the fields and the road that leads to the palm trees in the distance, and the glow from the hidden sun.

"I had to renounce my marriage before they would let me go. Admit that everything I did was a mistake. That my time in America was a shameful period in my life, spent poisoned by the ideas of capitalism, of wanting to rise above everyone, and always to have more. And the freer way of life was harmful to the body and mind because there was no guidance, no structure: you were not completely devoted to Vietnam. Whatever they said, I repeated, believed in it just to get out."

"So then, I was a shameful period in your life?" I ask.

Mother straightens up and twists herself around at the waist to face me.

"No, but they knew about you. They knew everything about everyone. I swear it surprised me. I told them I left you in America, but that was not good enough for them. I had to…" Mother faces the road again. "I had to consider you dead. To sever my past, you and your father were dead to me."

I make the mistake of looking at Uncle Ngô; he gives me the are-you-happy-now look.

"That's it? Just six months of hard labor, and everything is fine? Six months of admitting wrong and you're forgiven?"

"Long-Vanh!" Uncle Ngô says sharply and sits up straight.

Mother closes her mouth and stares at me, and I know she's considering what she wants to say next.

"Six months. I thought I was going to die, harvesting

rice for fourteen, fifteen hours a day. We didn't get much to eat, or sleep. Every day I worked I reminded myself why I came back, but also every day I regretted it. But it was too late. They were not going to let me go. Unless."

Mother looks away and sighs heavily.

"I thought that was it. Until I tried to mail you a letter to let you know I was safe. But they opened it. They open everything. And when they rearrested me, I knew then that every letter I wrote, every care package I sent, never made it to your grandfather. So I had to do more time. Four years like your grandfather to set my mind right." Mother leans forward to cover her face in her hands.

Uncle Ngô slouches in his seat. I stand up and step off the porch and begin walking away, and before I can get to the road, I hear Mother say she made a mistake. I turn around to face her.

"I made a big mistake by coming back. But I was here. They would never let me go. Once you returned, you were done. There was no letting go of anyone. So *I* had to let go," Mother nods.

I turn away and start walking down the road and I get to the main strip after successfully crossing the boulevard filled with scooters, mopeds, bicyclists, and cars. I keep walking as I wave off vendors who approach me to buy their goods, even the children who are still out this late hustling fruits, cigarettes, postcards, chewing gum, and though they are small and thin-limbed, they do not look like children. If anything, they look like small adults. They are dirty and emaciated, their faces old from walking the streets all day looking for buyers. Their faces wear the smog of the city, the noise of the traffic and the harsh,

constant bickering of the adults trying to negotiate pric-
es. And the children's voices mimic the same rough tone
when they argue back. It's like they died as kids once they
were born and were forced into one choice.

I stop in front of the entrance to a large café filled with
tourists and locals, and it is noisy. I think of going inside to
listen to them speak and laugh, have their noise drown my
thoughts, lose myself with a drink beneath the thatched
roof and Tiki torches, but I spot an old woman at a soup
stall across the street, ladling broth into bowls for the few
customers sitting at the tables. Everyone looks up from
their bowls when I approach, and I sit down at the only
round table small enough for one.

The old woman whose white hair is braided wipes her
hands on a towel and nods her head at me.

"Phở bà," I say.

The old woman nods and grabs a handful of white
noodles and places them into a steel basket and dunks it
in the cauldron for a minute before dumping the noodles
into a bowl. She places thin slices of beef on top of the
noodles, then spoons in the broth and sets the bowl before
me along with a saucer of basil, bean sprouts, sliced peppers, and lemon wedges.

The two fingers she holds up indicates the cost, so
I reach inside my pocket and extract two, ten thousand
đồngs and hand them to her: $1.25. The woman nods sev-
eral times before she goes to tend to her other customers.
I prepare my bowl and take my first bite, and immediately
the sour taste and the spiciness of the peppers lock my jaw.
A sharp pain travels from my tongue, through the very
bones of my jaw and hardens the area beneath my chin. I

have a hard time working the food, and the more I chew, the more the pain subsides until I can finally swallow. My shoulders slacken.

"Good," the old woman smiles.

I nod my head and continue eating, remembering the hours Mother spent in the kitchen slicing onions, crushing ginger, grinding peppercorns, and tossing anise in a large pot of boiling beef bones and ox tails. I keep eating, thinking about Mother coming away from the kitchen every so often after stirring the pot, setting the flame at a certain level to allow the ingredients to saturate the bones and beef, boiling them for hours until they all lost their individual taste to become something altogether.

Even though everyone at the soup stall is watching, I let the sweat wash over me. My pants stick to my legs and the hair on my arms is matted. I have to sniff so I can breathe. I devour the whole soup, barely taking time to chew. Lifting the bowl to my mouth, I sip the broth until empty, and I set the bowl aside and just remain on my stool.

"Enough?"

"Yes. It was very good."

"Drink?" she points to a row of sodas, but I shake my head, for I don't want anything to wash away the taste in my mouth, that taste of Mother seventeen years gone. I just sit there, sniffling, and let the sweat continue to pour down my face and collect at my chin and above my lips. I sit there and the crooks of my arms become pools, and the wet spots on the lap of my jeans spread, and underneath my arms the hairs are soaked and dripping. I get wetter just sitting there, wetter as I let my clothes cling to me, allow the humidity, the people's constant staring, the fragments of their conversations and whispers, their lit cigarettes, the horns of the cars and mopeds, the bells from the bikes, the unending drone of engines, the smoke from the exhaust pipes, the petrol fumes, and the scent of food to change me altogether.

········

By the time I get back, it is dark, and although it is slightly cooler, my shirt still sticks to me. I have to use what little light is in people's homes to find my way to Mother's. I finally make it home where there is only a light on in the kitchen, and I find Mother sitting at the table with a cup of tea. I assume Uncle Ngô is sleeping, or trying to before waking up tomorrow morning to drive us back to Hồ Chí Minh City where we will stay for a day before flying back to Los Angeles.

Mother rubs her temple, and already the circles underneath her eyes are darkened, and it is like I am ten years old again when I used to watch her eyes moisten, only her other hand is empty of a letter. When she notices me standing underneath the doorway, she stops rubbing her temple and sits up in her chair. She takes up the cup of tea in both hands and begins sipping, and I take a seat across from her.

We sit for a while—she staring at the tea and I looking at my hands clasped upon the table.

"Would you like some?"

"No. I need to go to sleep eventually."

She makes a sound and returns to sipping her tea and looking off at another part of the kitchen.

"I'm no different from you," I say.

Mother frowns at me.

"I'm no different from you," I sit forward. "After you left, people, especially teachers, asked if you were coming to pick me up after school; if you were coming to PTA or parent-teacher meetings. I was too embarrassed to tell them you had left. So I told them you were dead."

"You told people that?" she sits up.

"I was ten when you told me to tell people who called anything I wanted to. Even that you are dead, so," I shrug, "I told them you died in a car accident. Later, I changed it to cancer."

I sit back. Mother resumes staring into her cup of tea.

"I killed you off to save myself the embarrassment. If I told people the truth, then they'd think there was something wrong with me. They'd think, *What did he do to make a mother leave her own child?*"

Mother's fingers begin to move along the sides of the cup, and although her head is down, she is staring at something else. Suddenly her shoulders begin to shake, and even though her head lowers I can see that her eyes are shut tight to stop from crying. And this surprises me because whenever I remember all the times Mother cried it was because her mind was always on Lý Lôc and how he fared in the reeducation camps. I didn't understand her constant need to check the mailbox until the first time Phượng translated a letter. Mother would go to the mailbox at all hours of the day, pull down the door, and look inside. And when the mail did come, she went through each piece carefully, looked on the back of each envelope as if it were possible for letters to stick together like new dollar bills. When she didn't find a letter with blue stripes bordering the edges, she'd look inside the mailbox. She'd even go so far as to stick her hand all the way inside and it made me think she was a magician. Some days I thought she would pull Lý Lôc out by the hand, and he would stand doubled over from old age and the years of beatings he endured while imprisoned. He would straighten up like a flower beneath the sun, gaze out over Los Angeles buried underneath the smog. Mother was always reaching for not just a letter, but to pull Lý Lôc through, and anything short of that disappointed her. But a letter was what she settled for until it wasn't enough. During the rare times I caught her, I imagined what the neighbors who lived across the street below us thought when they looked up to see a woman with her arm in the mailbox up to her elbow and her head tilted to the sky: she was stuck, and there was nothing anyone could do to set her free.

Departure

We're standing in a long line at the airport, waiting to be questioned by customs before boarding. There is only one officer checking tickets and destinations, asking questions, and briefly eyeing any form of picture ID the patrons present over the counter. He brings the rubber stamp down on their passports and visas with finality, waves them through and waves the next person forward. Several officers stand aside waiting to check bags if necessary. The people in front of us keep looking back to make sure they have enough distance, and those behind look me up and down. They even look at my suitcase. Uncle Ngô smokes a cigarette.

"Can I have a cigarette?"

He reaches inside his pocket and fishes one from the soft pack. Just as he hands it to me, they open up another line. Instead of lighting it, I tuck it behind my ear. We get up to the counter, and the man takes our passports and does a double-take. He asks questions and Uncle Ngô answers him. He stoops down and picks up his suitcase and I do the same, only I lay mind flat on the counter and begin to undo the lock. Uncle Ngô grabs my hand and shakes his head, but I already have it opened before I realize the officer just wanted to see the suitcases.

The officers standing by are only able to take two steps toward me when the customs officer waves them off. The officers look at each other and step back, clasping their hands in front of them. The customs officer says something while opening our passports to a blank page and stamps them. Uncle Ngô nods his head and smiles at whatever the man is saying. He hands us our passports and gives a polite and patient wave of his hand. We pocket our passports, take our suitcases, and leave the line.

We make our way to the line of people setting bags on the conveyor belt for X-rays. People pass through the metal detectors, take up their bags at the other end, and leave the building through the double glass doors and join yet another line of patrons waiting to get on a plane. But no one gets on. They sit on their luggage in the humid weather, and some have even gone beneath the plane's wings for relief. The bag checkers and metal detector attendants stop what they are doing and press walkie-talkies to their ears.

"What's going on?" I ask.

"I not know. I hear the word *delay*." Uncle Ngô shakes his head.

He leaves me in line and walks up to one of the officers. They speak for quite some time, and the officer nods his head several times before waving people forward.

"What happened?" I ask.

"There was ee-lec-shion in Thailand. Some people were very upset. They take o-fi-shals hostage. But they are fine now. We can fly to Bangkok."

Uncle Ngô takes our suitcases and sets them on the conveyor belt. They pass through and Uncle Ngô takes out his Zippo, cigarettes, pens, and keys and places them in a basket before passing through the detectors. Outside, the people stand up, form a single line, and begin climbing the roll-away steps. They present their tickets to the stewardesses greeting them at the top. They make their way inside the plane, traveling down narrow aisles for their assigned seats. The baggage handlers stuff the people's luggage in the side of the plane. And still the people continue to ascend the steps and disappear inside the plane.

Uncle Ngô pockets his things and takes the bags off the conveyor belt. He looks around for me and discovers that I am still on the other side.

"Come on Long-Vanh."

The people who have been waiting behind me go around me and walk through the detectors. I cannot move. The officers watch me. One stands beside me not saying a word. I begin to feel queasy. Still, the people climb the steps, and one by one, they disappear inside the plane where they will be confined and fighting for the much-needed elbow room, keeping the legs from cramping beneath seats in front of them, and willing time to pass quickly so that their feet can touch land rather than worry themselves with being in the air for more than twenty-three hours.

"Long-Vanh, come on." Uncle Ngô insists.

People continue to go around me. Uncle Ngô sets the luggage down and passes through the metal detectors. Because he didn't empty his pockets, Uncle Ngô sets off everything.

Mr. Gouché
Asia Minor, Los Angeles, 1979

After eight years of sewing dresses and saving most of her money, coupled with the money Uncle Handsome Harlemite saved from all the overtime and double shifts he worked, he and Aunt Pham Thi have been shopping for a house. They found one, or rather, Mother and Aunt Pham Thi spotted one during their evening walk: a three bedroom house which sits high atop Vernango Street with only two front patios on both sides of the steps. Each patio is above a garage, no narrow strip of dirt, just a sidewalk.

After months of going to banks to get the best rates, Aunt Pham Thi and Uncle Handsome Harlemite settled on Bank of America on the outskirts of Hollywood. The rate was just as high as the others, but what made them decide on this one was a bank employee named Mr. Gouché, a white man who speaks Vietnamese, and that it wouldn't be any trouble for him to come over after work and discuss the details.

Aunt Pham Thi comes home two hours early to meet Mr. Gouché. Mother decides she should meet him as well so that she can explain the details to Aunt Pham Thi although Uncle Handsome Harlemite and Dad wrote down all the questions for her.

They come home at three-thirty to put together the evening's meal from the ingredients Phượng and I prepared since this morning. After they cook and wrap everything, they go around the apartment and clean up as I make the *nước mam*. The sugar slowly dissolves as it grates between spoon and bowl. Mother hasn't spoken a word to me all weekend, not even to let me know when lunch and dinner were ready. Ever since the incident, I've been staying in my room doing homework the teacher gave me for the three days I am suspended. I'd come out of my bedroom only to find my meals on the table. She didn't even leave them where I normally sat. Just placed them at the edge of the table as if to let me decide where I wanted to sit.

Aunt Pham Thi moves about the living room, straightening framed pictures, making sure books do not lean on the shelves, rearranging the porcelain figurines, and dusting. From time to time I taste the *nước mam* but it is too salty, so I add more sugar.

There is a loud knock and everyone stops and looks in the direction of the door as though expecting the person to enter. Aunt Pham Thi opens the door and steps back, surprised to see a tall white man with a full head of large, blond curls.

"Mr. Gouché?" her voice rises sharply. "Come in, come in," she motions with her hand. "You not get lost?"

"Oh no. I actually know this neighborhood. I've helped others buy their first home."

"Vu-An, this is Mr. Gouché."

"Rất vui được gặp bạn." He bows.

"I hope you are hungry. We make—"

"—spring rolls," Mr. Gouché walks past Aunt Pham Thi to the dinner table, drawn by the pyramid of stacked spring rolls. "*Nước mam*." He points to one of the five bowls of fish sauce.

"Then you hungry?"

Mr. Gouché turns to her and smiles. "I never pass up spring rolls or phở. Or Vietnamese food for that matter. I love it all."

"We also have bitter melon soup," Mother adds.

The smile quickly disappears, and his eyes droop. "I haven't had that since I was in Vietnam. None of the restaurants here in L.A. make that. None. You didn't have to go through all this trouble."

Mr. Gouché slips off his jacket and drapes it over one of the chairs. He draws the chair away from the table and sits down. We all join him at the table, and he's sitting there with hands clasped in front of him, waiting.

"Please, please, help yourself," Aunt Pham Thi urges him.

Mr. Gouché smooths down his tie before reaching across the table to pick up a spring roll, dips it in the *nước mam* and takes a big bite. His eyes close and his shoulders slump as he lets out a moan.

"You like?" Aunt Pham Thi asks. The women lean in their seats, waiting for him to answer.

He sits there with eyes closed as he chews his food. Without opening his eyes he nods, and it's like watching him move in his sleep.

·······

Every station is covering the latest on the Iran Hostage Crisis. President Carter sent eight military helicopters in to rescue the hostages, but three of them got destroyed in a sandstorm, so they aborted the mission. Carter is holding a press conference, fielding questions, shaking his head apologetically, and sending his sympathies to the families whose sons died in the sandstorm, and to those who are still hostages.

Mother and Aunt Pham Thi remain at the dinner table held captive by Mr. Gouché, and I hate him for speaking to them in their language. It's not only the language, but the way he speaks to them, like he's known them since Vietnam, as though he had visited their actual homes for dinner, and this was some kind of reunion. The mothers sit forward with one hand on their cheek like children listening to tales. All throughout dinner they catered to him, pushing dishes in front of him, insisting, "Eat, eat. More, more." They even poured his drink. And when I wanted more, Mother told me to help myself.

Right now he is more Vietnamese than I can ever be. The mothers' grins grow wider when his voice rises as he strikes the air before him the way the deaf speak. When his voice falls to a lull, his hands glide in front of him as the women sit, stunned at this American whose voice knows the emphasis of pitch, the stress of syllables, and what they mean.

Grace

Tuesday morning we go to the bank—Aunt Pham Thi, Phượng, Mother, and I. For a Tuesday morning it is busy. Customers stand in a long line between velvet ropes, jotting figures on pieces of paper or softly mumbling calculations to themselves like prayers. Some stare hard at the tellers, willing them to hurry. They blow air from their mouths to be heard, and their shoulders droop.

"God. And I thought the lines to the gas pumps were long," a man in a pinstriped suit says. The others in line chuckle.

Mr. Gouché waves for Aunt Pham Thi to come to his desk.

"You want me to go with you?" Mother asks.

"No. I sign papers only."

She heads over to Mr. Gouché, and we remain seated on the couches next to the line of desks for loans and new accounts. Mother sits facing the double glass doors while Phượng and I sit on the other side. The big black block between us serves as a table containing pamphlets for mutual funds, home loans, and car financing. The people at their desks are cradling phones between their shoulders and necks, nodding and punching numbers on the plastic keypads of calculators, or they're jotting down numbers on yellow legal pads.

All along the wall are framed paintings of lilies and roses, bowls of fruits, and polo players on horseback swinging water color mallets. Aunt Pham Thi sits forward in her chair with elbows resting on Mr. Gouché's desk, her eyes following the movement of his pen across the pages he flips over for her. At times she looks up at him to nod, then continues scanning the section he taps with his pen.

Mother frowns at the words she reads from the pamphlet she holds close to her face. When she is done, she folds it back up, sets it down, and takes up the next one.

The customers in line shift the weight of their stance from one leg to the other. They pluck lint from their pleated slacks and from off the sleeves of their blazers. The women make sure the buttons to their satin blouses match while men straighten their ties and check to make sure the narrow end isn't longer than the wider. Always, there is a person who mistakes the function of the velvet ropes when he leans his hand on it, and the metal base wobbles on the tiled floor, disrupting everyone's calculations. Mother looks over at Aunt Pham Thi who is signing whatever paper Mr. Gouché puts in front of her. She hesitates each time, pen poised in hand, and Mr. Gouché gestures with his right hand, assuring her of what she is signing. She nods her head and leans forward with both elbows on the desk and signs.

Mother continues reading the pamphlet. Her eyes move over the pages as she slips in and out of whispering what she reads. She closes the pamphlet and stares straight at me. The lines over her forehead deepen, and her lips widen.

"What?" I stutter. I turn to Phượng, but she is staring at the line of customers.

"Oh my God," Mother mumbles. Her bottom lip quivers and so does her voice when she repeats, "Oh my God."

"What?" I say again and turn to the customers who look about wildly at the tellers and at each other. Those working behind desks stand up at the same time, and they all hold pens or telephone receivers in hands. The customers step backwards, catch the person's feet behind them as they fumble with the cash and checks they try to pocket. Mother bolts from the sofa and runs around the block-shaped table and grabs a hold of my wrist and yanks.

"Come. On." She grunts.

Mother pulls until I'm on my feet. She reaches over, takes a hold of Phượng's wrist and says, "Let's go."

Mother drags us across the lobby. Four men in black clothes and ski masks aim guns from one person to the other, taking count as they move forward. Mother keeps running with a hand around our wrists, and Phượng and I try to keep up with her. We run past the four men, and I hear one of them yell, "Don't let them out! Stop them! Stop them!"

"Stop them who?" the other one asks.

Mother flings open the doors. We run down the block past people who step aside and watch. We run against red lights, and cars skid to complete stops or swerve. And still we run, kicking up our knees despite our legs tightening up with each stride. We run even though we are wet with sweat and we breathe through and exhale from our mouths. And still we run with our pulses beating in Mother's hands. Mother suddenly stops, and we all stand in the middle of the sidewalk, in the middle of everyone staring while we catch our breath.

Before we turn around to look down the streets we just ran, before Mother can even say it, Phượng mumbles,

"Mom."

Phượng and Mother look at each other and tears begin to well up.

Mother holds Phượng. Together they cry. Their hands
move over each other to sooth the trembling. People slow
down to watch them, and I stand staring at them as well. I
just listen to their sobbing and keep my distance.

"Is everything all right?"

I turn to see an old woman at my side.

"No," I say. "Can you call the police? Please. Someone
is robbing the bank. Down there," I point.

The woman gasps as she clutches her chest.

"Her mother," I point to Phượng, "is still in the bank.
Please. Call the police."

From afar I hear sirens, and it isn't long before the
squad cars arrive. There are a dozen more speeding down
the street in a line, riding each other's tail. They pass us
and head for the bank.

I turn to the old woman and state the obvious. "They're
here."

········

Had we gone during lunch break, had Aunt Pham
Thi fought Mother's insistence that the papers be signed
immediately, we would have been home getting ready for
dinner. Had we not come, we would have missed all of
this, watched it on the television in our own living room
and considered the idea that it could have been us. We
could have been sitting at home hoping Mr. Gouché was
all right. Had this not happened, the whites would have
been driving through Asia Minor to beat the rush hour

traffic. The Japanese and Koreans wearing sun hats would probably wander about their gardens, picking leaves and pruning branches and wondering why the whites weren't driving through the neighborhood and not have given it another thought. Mother would have been telling Aunt Pham Thi of her hopes of getting Lý Loc into the United States. But this is not the case. Mother shakes her head from time to time as she stands in direct line of the double glass doors trying to spot Aunt Pham Thi.

We are all across the street standing behind the black and white striped barricades the police set up. Everyone came down, including Yên. Dad wanted to take me home, but I wouldn't budge. When he told me to get inside the car, I told him he had to beat me first, and then I walked away and stood by Mother.

Uncle Handsome Harlemite left work as soon as he heard. He is still in uniform and the police had stripped him of his gun belt when they found out his wife was in there. Said they didn't want him to take matters into his own hands and accidentally shoot someone, especially his own wife.

Uncle Handsome Harlemite asked to negotiate a trade: to take his wife's place, but the policemen didn't want to rile the gunmen. Besides, they would only get suspicious if they sent in a man wearing a Forest Lawn Mortuary security guard uniform. They'd think he was a cop all the same, gun or no gun, black uniform or blue.

So far no one knows who they are. They haven't said what they wanted, although it's clear even to me that they want money. And that's all I understand: that they want money, and they have enough hostages to make the police meet any demands.

Crouched on the rooftops of neighboring stores, the
S.W.A.T. team waits. With black baseball caps worn backwards, they aim and stare through the telescope of their
rifles from time to time. The police are behind their cars
with guns drawn. They speak into walkie-talkies, and helicopters circle like dragonflies. Television news crews are
here. Their vans are parked a ways from the crowd. The
big antennas are angled to receive better transmission, and
the satellite dishes are turned to cup the day's dying rays.

Uncle Ngô stands behind Yên. He rubs her shoulders
as he rests his chin atop her head. Every time I look up at
him he is peering through the glass doors.

"I hope he is not in there," Yên says. She's been saying it ever since she arrived. Those were her first words. "I
hope he is not in there," and Uncle Ngô keeps reassuring
her that he is probably out collecting cans and bottles.

He leans his mouth close to Yên's ear and whispers,
"I'll be right back," when he sees me staring at them. Uncle
Ngô takes me by the shoulder and we squeeze between
people until we are far enough away from her. We stand
facing each other, and before he speaks he looks back at
Yên.

"Did you see him?"

"I'm sure it's him. It sounded like him."

Tú Đức is a given. I tell Uncle Ngô the others must
be China Dog, Fat Chan, and the pimpled one. I tell him
all of this, and he stands close with wrinkled brows and
pursed lips. He asks me if I'm sure, and I nod my head
before mentioning the odor of piss, and how when we ran
past them I nearly gagged. And there is the chip-faced

Buddha he wears around his neck.

When I am through telling him all I know, he straightens back up. He opens his eyes, places a hand on my shoulder, and squeezes it. He turns and looks in the direction of the crowd. Above everyone and in between them Yên stares straight at us, and we know she knows. She can see it in the way Uncle Ngô and I stand close together, creating a wall for our words.

Uncle Ngô makes his way over to her, and by the time he reaches her she is trembling as she begins to cry. Uncle Ngô slips an arm around her waist, draws her near, takes his other hand, and holds the back of her head to steady it against his shoulder.

....

Connie Chung of Channel 2 News stands next to her cameraman as she shuffles through 3-by-5 note cards. A woman wearing a vest with different sized pockets swarms around her, applying blush on her nose and cheeks. Then she takes a small soft black brush from one of the pockets and dusts Connie's face as she shifts through the cards. As she mouths words to herself the woman sprays and brushes her hair, and parts the bangs from her forehead.

"Do you see her?"

I look straight ahead at the double glass doors. The sun's rays make it hard for me to see past the glare coming off the glass.

"Do you see her?" Mother asks again. She moves her head from side to side as she shields her eyes with one hand.

"No," Uncle Handsome Harlemite says. "I don't see

her."

His hands are in his pockets. The light blue shirt is untucked, and he has taken off the tie and stuffed it in his back pocket. The thin end hangs out, and I want to tuck it in for him. Dad stands with arms crossed in front of him, and at times he glares at me, and I think to myself, *I'm not listening to someone who left us for some woman.*

Uncle Ngô is still holding Yên from behind. Her crying has stopped; the wrinkles underneath her eyes have formed, and she looks tired. The crowd has grown, and the police have set up more barriers to keep them back.

"Someone is coming," Mother says, and she says it too loud because the police officers cock their guns and point them toward the door. The only sound now is the helicopters circling high above the bank's rooftop. The locks to the double glass doors turn, and someone waves a white handkerchief. He sticks his head outside and squints behind his glasses.

"Don't shoot," he waves the handkerchief furiously, "don't shoot."

The man steps away from the door with hands out before him like he's walking around in a dark room. The door swings shut behind him, and he continues to move forward. He steps off the sidewalk, knees bent, hands out in front of him, handkerchief pinched between two fingers. When he gets to the center of the street where he is surrounded by guns and the crowd, he straightens up and lowers his hands.

"I am Mr. Yi. I work here."

One of the policemen steps from behind the squad car and places his gun in his holster.

"What's going on?"

Mr. Yi brings one hand up to shield his eyes. "They have demands. I tell you, and you do. You do, and you get one hostage."

"What are the demands?"

"One million dollars. The bank does not have one million dollars. You get one million and I take it to them. They get it, you get one hostage."

"Is that all?"

"No."

The crowd remains quiet to hear him. The cameramen are in front of the crowd, filming him, and Connie Chung is standing beside one of them, microphone in hand.

"They will let you know. Later. For now they want one million in one hour. No million dollars, they will kill one of us."

"Who are they?" the officer asks.

"They are Vietnamese Nationalists. There are four. One million dollars, one hour."

The police officer and Mr. Yi stare at one another for a long moment. Mr. Yi trembles. His shoulders are hunched up, tensed, and he looks like he's shrinking the longer he stands in front of the drawn guns, beneath the fading sun. The S.W.A.T. members squint through the telescopes of their rifles.

Finally the police officer asks, "Is everyone all right?"

Mr. Yi opens his mouth to speak, but he nods his head instead.

"Are you sure everyone is OK? No one has been harmed? Not in any way?"

Mr. Yi shakes his head. "No one has been harmed. Everyone is okay."

"Okay. Go back inside. Tell them we'll work on the million. We'll have it here as soon as possible."

"One hour," Mr. Yi shouts over his shoulders. "One hour or one dead."

"What kind of weapons do they have? Do you know?"

Mr. Yi turns around and narrows his eyes behind his thick glasses. The sharpness in his voice surprises us.

"I don't know. The kinds that kill. That's all I know."

He stands there a while longer, glaring at the officer before heading back to the double doors. One of the doors swings open, and Mr. Yi enters. The door closes behind him, and he is swallowed up by the glare off the glass doors. The moment the lock slides into place two shots go off. Everyone jumps or ducks from the loud, sudden noises and it takes me a long time to realize what just happened, that they shot Mr. Yi and that the second loud bang wasn't a gunshot at all, but his head striking the glass.

········

"Now will you go home?" Dad asks.

I'm vomiting in front of an antique store with a potbellied stove in the window, cups placed on saucers arranged around the stove's short legs. Although I have my back to Dad, it's no use. He knows I can't control my terror, and so he keeps insisting that I go home or at least stay in the car.

"Well, are you?" Dad's voice grows rougher.

I shake my head no.

"You're damn stubborn you know that?"

I stand back up and just look at him. I wish for someone big enough to beat Dad for not being home those couple of days he was with Sharon, those days he wasn't my father. Here he is trying to tell me what to do, like he's been with us all along.

Yên is crying again, and Uncle Ngô holds her close. Mother stares at the doors with her arms crossed in front of her. Phượng and Mia haven't said much. They stand together ducking and weaving their heads to get a view of their mother, but they haven't said if they've seen her.

They took Mr. Yi's body away after two customers from the bank dragged him out onto the sidewalk. The two customers went back inside knowing a rifle was pointed at them. Stapled to Mr. Yi's lapel was a note: *Because he took too long outside, I shot him.* Unsigned. The note was as brief as their demand: one million dollar, one hostage. And it was as brief as the consequences: no million, one dead.

Two police officers placed Mr. Yi in a black plastic bag and zipped him shut. They hauled his body inside the back of an ambulance, shut the doors, and drove off without turning on the siren.

There are more people, just as there is an increase in police force since Mr. Yi walked back inside the bank only to have the back of his head blown against the glass door. But what is fresh in my mind is not the loudness of the gun blast, or the quick head jerk from the shot, but how his feet slid from under him, slow and controlled, and the back of his head, like a mop, smeared a broad stroke of blood down the center of the door.

The blood is still there. It takes away the glare of the sun, and we can see the gunmen clearer now. Three of them point rifles at the customers while one directs the men and women to stand with arms linked in front of the door. The hour is nearly up when a black Ford crawls through the crowd, past the police cars and the black and white striped barricades. The man parks the car in front of the bank, gets out and opens the trunk. He has to bend his knees when lifting two white bags out of the trunk. The man in the plain black suit sets the two bags on the sidewalk and walks back to the trunk for two more bags. After setting them on the sidewalk along with the others, he shuts the trunk and gets back in the car. The Ford makes a u-turn and heads back to where it came.

Another person is sent to unlock the door. A hand appears, waving a white handkerchief spotted with blood, and it is Mr. Gouché. He stands tall and straight as he makes his way to the bags in the middle of the sidewalk. Without saying a word, he pockets the red-spotted handkerchief and stoops down to pick up two bags. He carries them to the door where one of the gunmen waits. Mr. Gouché gets the other two bags and disappears inside the bank. The door barely closes before it opens again, and I can hear Connie Chung whisper into her microphone, "Wait, he's coming back out."

Mr. Gouché raises his hands as he makes his way to the edge of the curb.

"They have a second demand."

The same officer, the negotiator, cocks his head to the side.

"They want bulletproof vests. For each vest, you get a hostage."

"No," the negotiator shakes his head.

"What the fuck you say no for!" Uncle Handsome

Harlemite yells.

The negotiator continues shaking his head. "No way. I haven't received my one hostage for the million dollars. Where's my hostage?"

Mr. Gouché looks over his shoulders at the double glass doors, the streak of blood running down one of them. He opens his mouth to speak, but he can't. Instead he shakes his head. It is at that moment, a man stumbles out of the bank with his hands in the air, and he moves toward the street in jerking, hesitant motions while side-stepping like a crab to watch the gunmen behind the bank doors, and I believe he is afraid if he were to turn his back to them, he is going to be shot. But once in the street, he runs toward the officers who immediately grab him and he is swallowed in a crowd of black and tin badges and polished buttons and belts. We turn to the bank, and Mr. Gouché is gone.

·········

It is night now, and we can see the people clearer. They remain linked at the arms in front of the double doors and the plate glass windows. Their heads lean to the sides or dangle forward. Some hold hands. The gunmen stand behind them, but one of them paces back and forth gesturing with one hand while he holds the gun at his side. Mr. Gouché is behind the manmade fence as well, offering his palms to the one gunman as he shakes his head and shrugs.

The gunman points to the door. Mr. Gouché shrugs and shakes his head for so long that the gunman points his weapon at Mr. Gouché, prompting him to put up his hands as if to catch the bullets. The gunman motions him over to the door with the barrel of his weapon, and Mr. Gouché breaks through the chain of people to unlock the door and comes out without a handkerchief.

"Because you have not agreed to a hostage for a vest, they have changed their minds. They will offer any hostage who wants to leave in exchange for a bulletproof vest. But," Mr. Gouché holds up a finger, "that person has to walk out with a bullet in the leg."

"What?" the negotiator says.

"Any hostage may leave if he or she wishes to be shot in the leg." Mr. Gouché repeats.

"No, no." The negotiator waves his hand. "Tell them we'll give them a vest for each hostage."

"They will. But that hostage has to be shot."

"That's not necessary."

"It's too late they said." Mr. Gouché points his finger at the negotiator. "Because you did not agree in the first place, four people will have to suffer if they want to be released. Four."

"You fucked up," Uncle Handsome Harlemite says.

The negotiator ignores him. After everyone finishes mumbling, as soon as everyone quiets down and the only noises are the helicopters circling the night above, the officer asks, "Are there any hostages who would be willing to do it?"

"They haven't asked, but I wouldn't be surprised if they all volunteered."

"Shit," Uncle Handsome Harlemite mutters under his breath. "You want *me* to negotiate. I'd do a better job than you."

The negotiator swats his hand in Uncle Handsome Harlemite's direction. Mother covers her face with her hands. Uncle Ngô wraps his arms tighter around Yên, and Phượng holds herself about the stomach.

"Look, just tell them we'll give them what they want. Just give up hostages."

"They'll give up hostages, but they'll be wounded hostages. They want to show you they're serious. So have the vests ready."

Before he turns to go back inside, Mr. Gouché spots Mother and he says, "Cô ấy khỏe."

Mother nods and Phượng straightens up, and it is the first time I see her take in a deep breath. The negotiator turns to one of his men and says, "Have medic ready. Have them ready to run up and grab them."

The lead gunman paces behind the line of customers, only now he has a handgun; Uncle Handsome Harlemite thinks it's a .9 millimeter. The lead gunman jabs the air with it as he speaks, and his head jerks from hollering, though we cannot hear a word. He stops all of a sudden, gun pointed at the floor. Only his head moves from left to right. One man dressed in a three-piece, wide pinstriped suit lets go of the hands of the people beside him and steps back. The two people in line look down at their empty hands, and to fill in what is missing they take a hold of each other's hand.

Behind the line, the gunman observes the man who broke the link. As he paces back and forth, he is looking at the man's wide pinstriped legs, and once, the gunman even looks at the .9 millimeter in his hand. He gives the gun to the second man, who is chubby in size, and he shakes his head. The main gunman holds it out to him and yells at him to take it until finally he does. The second man holds the gun away from his body. He has to lean forward to cock the gun and the moment he aims at the back of the man's calf, a quick burst of light blasts from the gun. We all jump away from the barricades, from the ringing sound, from the man who screams when he drops to the floor and grabs his calf with both hands. As he curls up into a ball and cries, eyes shut tight, mouth open wide enough to let out the size of his scream, the gunman shakes and clenches his hand before bending down to pick up the gun from off the floor. The wounded man curls himself tighter until his forehead touches his knee.

Mr. Gouché runs to unlock the door and holds it open. He waits for the man as he claws at the linoleum tiles toward the door. Dragging the weight of the bloody leg behind him, he begins to choke, and I can't bear to hear him. His grunts come low and rise until he has to breathe again, and I want him to let it all out or shut up.

He finally makes his way to the door and grabs a hold of Mr. Gouché's leg who actually shakes his leg free of the man's grasp and urges him on, telling him, "Go. Go. Please get out."

The man crawls outside and stops at the sidewalk where he bares his teeth as he breathes quickly and squints at the crowd, at the policemen aiming their guns. And he holds out a hand, but he is not out far enough for Mr. Gouché to close the door.

"Go. Please," Mr. Gouché tells him, even nudging him with his foot.

The line of hostages stares wide-eyed and trembling.

Some can only take so much as they shut their eyes and turn away. Those who watch the blood-streaked trail wonder if they can stand to bleed that much and be lame for the rest of their lives.

The man crawls forward a little more until he is at the curb, and we are crawling with him. We are weighed down in place by his dead and bloodied leg. Hands claw at the ground until he is taken up into the awaiting arms of men dressed in pressed uniforms, whose job it is to mend and heal. After he is placed in the back of the ambulance, there is nothing for us to see but Mr. Gouché holding the door wide open.

"Give me the vest." He holds out his hand to the negotiator who already has one.

The negotiator turns to the officer standing behind him who is holding three. The negotiator places his in the officer's hands and tells him to take all four to Mr. Gouché. That he doesn't want to see anyone else getting shot. That one wounded and one dead are enough to know they are serious.

Mr. Gouché takes them and locks the door. We watch as he breaks through the line of people and gives the vest to the second gunman. He holds it in his hand and studies it, feels its weight. The whole time he's staring at it and lifting his hand up and down, he's probably wondering if he bartered well, if giving a man a limp he will forever remember for the rest of his life was a fair trade. He drops the vest to the floor and runs to the back of the bank, but he only gets to the counter of DEPOSIT and WITH-DRAWAL slips before he pulls up his ski mask, drops to his knees, and vomits.

• • • • • • • •

As promised, they gave up three more hostages wounded in the leg for three vests. But it wasn't as bad as the first man. They collapsed to the floor upon being shot, but none of them stayed down long enough to yell and curl up into a ball. It's like they took lessons in what not to do. They immediately balanced themselves with hands on the floor like a sprinter just before jumping at the gun; they lifted themselves up on their one good leg and hopped toward the door, and once outside they even used their bad leg to run into the arms of awaiting paramedics, into the comfort of a crowd, the warmth of the night, the sound of the whirling blades from the helicopters, the stars, the moon.

• • • • • • • •

It has been twelve hours since Mother, Aunt Pham Thi, Phượng, and I went to the bank. Twelve hours since we last had a meal, went to the bathroom, felt the sun go down. Twelve hours since we ran from the bank the moment we saw the four men enter the place with guns that seemed bigger than us, bigger than the men who pointed them at customers and bank tellers. It feels longer than the Iran hostage situation. At times I wonder if this lasts as long as what's going on in Iran, can I be here through the whole thing.

I picture it lasting just as long. We'd have to go back to school, of course. Phượng and I would go straight to the bank after school only to find the same negotiator taking a battery-operated shaver to his chin and cheeks while standing in the middle of the street memorizing food orders for the hostages and the gunmen. As long as it took, traffic would be detoured, though they had considered reopening the street, just let the drivers gawk at the hostages linked at the arms facing them the way the whites beat traffic through Asia Minor.

One night when people turn on their televisions to watch the evening news, they'll discover that this hostage situation takes headline news over Iran, over Carter debating Reagan during the presidential election. I picture us sleeping in the streets with only blankets covering us with our pillows against the curb, people setting up lawn chairs, unrolling sleeping bags, pitching tents, and eating meals packed in Igloos or red ice chests which require two people to carry, and Connie Chung getting a haircut while she sits in one of those fold-out director's chairs. I picture the negotiator getting scruffier even though he had shaved during the afternoon, and thinning from staying up for twenty-four hours to trade hostages for demands. I imagine the people around us growing restless as they burn the red Communist Vietnamese flag, the large gold star in the middle consumed in flames. And there will be Vietnamese people bowing before the bank in prayer for the four men. Yet a separate group of Vietnamese will be here to protest what they are doing, to plead with the men not to ruin it for them, that what they have in America is good, and they should be grateful. The Ayatollah Khomeini will watch this from his living room or in some tent in the desert, and think how weak the gunmen are for giving up hostages. And he'll even make a phone call to China Dog,

Tú Đức, Fat Chan, and the pimply boy and tell them, "You are going about this the wrong way. No more negotiations. Resist all they throw at you, even pizza and hamburgers. And Twinkies and Ho-Cakes. Forget Coca-Cola and Fresca. Take what you demand, and give the Americans nothing in return."

It is the twelfth hour, and the men and women are still linked at the arms. They shake their legs loose of tightened muscles, dry their hands against their skirt or blazers, and mouth prayers to themselves.

Uncle Ngô offers to buy us pastrami sandwiches at a deli just a couple of blocks away. He doesn't want to burden anyone by having them move from their spots, knows they'd rather starve than eat. But I am hungry after vomiting hours ago from Mr. Yi's getting shot in the head. Phượng and I follow Uncle Ngô and Yến through the thick crowd to where the streets are empty. Lights in the buildings and stores are still on, but the SORRY WE'RE CLOSED signs show. We get to an intersection where there are people and cars driving about, and we feel we're back to normal again. We cross the street and enter Art's Deli. The counter is crowded with men leaning forward on their elbows as they stare up at the television fastened to the wall in the corner. It is set on Channel 2 and Connie Chung is holding the microphone to her mouth while scanning her notes. The bank is in the background, and we can see the line of customers linked at the arms. In the bottom right-hand corner of the screen are the words CHANNEL 2 LIVE.

"The hostage situation has just reached its twelfth hour," Connie Chung says, "and so far two demands have been met. The first demand was for a million dollars delivered at this location in four sacks at approximately 5:05 p.m. The second demand was for four bulletproof vests. However, it came with a price."

The screen cuts to a man crawling on his hands and legs. Watching the man crawl on television isn't the same. It's like watching some cops and robbers movie, and I was on a set watching them film; only there wasn't take after take, but one chance to get it right. In the bottom right-hand corner it reads RECORDED EARLIER.

"Damn!" Some of the men in the deli exclaim.

Again the screen cuts to the other three men who hobble outside the bank and rush into the arms of paramedics. The men at the counter shake their heads and sit back. Uncle Ngô approaches the far end of the counter, but Art is too busy watching the screen, so Uncle Ngô has to clear his throat to get his attention. Art comes away from the television, walks down the length of the counter and leans forward with forearms resting on the top.

"What can I get for you?" he asks, glancing back at the television several times.

"I need two hamburgers and two pest-tram-ee sandwiches. Four cokes. We're over there," Uncle Ngô points to us sitting at one of the many available booths.

"Sure thing. Be about ten minutes. Hey Darla," he calls to the far end of the bar, and a woman turns away from the television. "Four Cokes for table five."

Connie Chung is on again.

"We've just learned that the four young men are Vietnamese, and they've just delivered their third demand. They want a plane to take them back to Vietnam. Now the question is, why are they doing this?"

The screen cuts to Mr. Gouché standing in the middle of the street, surrounded by policemen, the crowd, and cameras. The Channel 2 News camera zooms in for a close-up.

"Their goal is to save grace. Their fathers all served in the South Vietnamese Army. Their fathers lost the war, of course; these four men want to execute this heist in order to return home and tell everyone what they did. They want to be the heroes their father never became."

Mr. Gouché turns around and walks back to the bank's doors despite the questions shouted at him from police officers and reporters.

"We have just learned that one of the hostages is actually Vietnamese as well, and there were some speculations that she might be in on the robbery, but that is not the case. Her husband is out here worried and concerned about her safety, naturally, and he has made it clear that she is in no way tied to the robbery. She was here solely to sign the papers for a loan on a new home for them and their two daughters.

"Aside from that, there are more hostages than what you see behind me. These hostages are made to stand as a shield. The other hostages are kept behind the counter. On occasions I have seen one of the gunmen make his way behind the counter and this leads me to believe that is where they are kept. This is Connie Chung reporting live from Los Angeles where I will have more on the standoff. Back to you, Jim."

········

I didn't think I'd be able to eat, but after I was done with my sandwich, I wanted more, but I knew we weren't going back to the deli. Besides, we had missed so much while we were gone that we had to learn about it on television, and it just wasn't the same as being there. I felt removed from everything, like I didn't have any control over what was happening, but to see everything unfold made me feel like I did. It seemed I could determine how much pain the hostages were allowed to feel, or willed them to stand for hours on their feet and not feel wobbly, or make their palms sweat.

The policemen gather around in a tight circle. The negotiator talks and makes eye contact with each one. They all watch him without so much as a glance to the sides. After a couple of minutes, they break the circle and get back to surrounding the bank from all angles.

The negotiator speaks into the walkie-talkie. After he is done, he clips it to his belt and looks about him, at the crowd, at the officers, the S.W.A.T. team on the rooftops, the cameramen, Connie Chung, and up at the helicopters, circling.

He steps from behind the barricade and enters the center of the street and stands in front of the bank with his hands out to the sides. The gunman points his weapon at Mr. Gouché and motions him through the line to unlock the door. He opens it wide enough for him to stick his head outside.

"We have news," the negotiator says.

Mr. Gouché steps outside. The door swings closed.

"Tell them we have a van arriving soon. It will take them to the airport where there's a plane waiting to fly them home. Tell them they can take as many hostages in the car as they want. And just to let them know we're not going to do anything foolish, the driver will be an officer, unarmed. Nothing on him but his uniform. We'll even send him in so they can pat him down if they like," the negotiator holds up his hands. "We want this to go well. We don't want anyone else getting hurt. If they want to leave the country, then we'll let them. Just tell them not to hurt anyone else."

"OK," Mr. Gouché nods before heading back inside. The other three draw around him, heads thrust forward. The gunmen look at each other before nodding in agreement. They break from the circle, and from behind the line of hostages, Mr. Gouché faces the double doors and nods his head.

"OK, bring him through." The negotiator yells over the squad cars and the crowd.

The crowd parts to let the van through. Murmurs rise from the crowd and the police slide the barricades aside and the driver parks the van along the curb and gets out. Dressed only in uniform as the negotiator promised—not even a cap or badge—he walks around the car and heads straight for the double doors and stands there. Mr. Gouché unlocks the door and lets him in. The officer steps inside, and the hostages sigh from the sight of someone else besides themselves stuck in the bank. They let him through, and immediately the gunman waves his gun at him. The officer proceeds to the counter where he leans against it with legs spread. With the rifle aimed at him, the second man pats the officer's legs, chest, belly, and back.

The gunman orders the officer to take up the sacks of

money, and he obediently picks up one in each hand. Mr. Gouché holds the door open for the officer as he leaves the bank. He sets the sacks of money on the street to open the van's back doors. After hoisting them inside, he goes back inside to get the rest, and as he leaves the bank the second time with the last two bags, that is when it all happens.

An object is launched from the direction of one of the squad cars and Mr. Gouché watches it sail towards him. When he blinks he realizes what it is and before he can move, it hits him in the neck with such force that he's thrown off his feet and lands flat on his back. Smoke gushes from the can and swirls about the hostages' feet. Big clouds swallow them. Before the door shuts, another smoke bomb launches inside the bank and hits a woman on the arm. She grabs the spot, doubles over, and the other hostages cover their mouths and noses coughing. The smoke grows in size, turning the place white. Officers wearing gas masks run for the front doors with shotguns aimed.

The moment they enter, shots are fired and most of us run away or take cover behind the squad cars. Uncle Handsome Harlemite and Dad drop to the ground. Uncle Ngô pulls me and Yên to the ground and I realize those who stayed are lying on their stomachs watching the front doors. From the thick wall of white smoke, men and women appear; their eyes are closed as they feel the air with their hands. Women hack and cough and stumble in high heels. They bump into one another, and one man even swings at random and hits a woman in the head. Police officers run in and grab the men and women by the arms and hustle the hostages into the backs of ambulances, or sit them down on the running boards of fire trucks and strap oxygen masks over their faces. Shots thunder within the bank.

"That's not supposed to happen," I say.

"Shhh," Uncle Ngô draws me nearer. He pushes my head to the ground, and I have to squirm in order to watch the front doors. "Keep your head down."

"But that's not supposed to happen. Everything is supposed to go well," I cry.

The double doors close, shutting in all the smoke and the place grows whiter. The bank's fluorescent lights only make it harder to see through. But I can still make out the shapes staggering close to the windows and doors and they are coughing and hacking. Blood splatters against one window at the same time a gun goes off, and I watch it for a long time, watch it run down the window in thick streams. Another woman's screams are cut short as a gun goes off and a much larger splash of blood explodes against the glass.

A bullet hits the glass and it cracks into tiny fragments. A second hit collapses the whole thing. Smoke drifts outside and makes its way toward us. Because the glass wall is gone, people get up from off the street and from behind ambulances, fire trucks, and squad cars, and begin running around the corners of neighboring buildings. The cameraman is low to the ground while filming. Connie Chung squats behind a car, plugging her fingers in her ears, the microphone clutched in one hand.

Uncle Handsome Harlemite and Dad stay where they are. The billowing smoke covers the sidewalk and car like a low-lying fog, and like ghosts the hostages stumble out through where the window used to be, their hands out-stretched before them to feel something familiar. Bullets whizz over us and deaden into the brick buildings behind us, shattering windows and boring holes into doors.

"Just stay down," Uncle Ngô says. "Just stay down."

More policemen run up to snatch blinded hostages away from the front of the bank, but one woman emerges from the smoke, and it seems as soon as she realizes she's outside she starts to run, but it isn't before long she trips, and as she falls forward, her hands make no movement to break her fall. She lands face first, and her head bounces off the sidewalk once.

Uncle Handsome Harlemite gets up from off the ground and calls out his wife's name as he makes his way towards the bank.

"What the hell are you doing?" The negotiator yells. "Get out of there!"

He waits until there are no shots before he comes from behind the car, wraps an arm around Uncle Handsome Harlemite's neck and drags him back behind the car. Dad crawls over and helps the negotiator contain Uncle Handsome Harlemite.

One of the gunmen walks outside, gun pointed at the ground. When he struggles to lift the ski mask from his face, the police officers close in on him, ordering him to put down the weapon. But he continues to struggle with his mask. He gives up and the moment he raises the other hand to take off the mask, the cops shoot him.

"He's dead," I say. "They shot Tú Đức."

Uncle Ngô stares at the body lying on the sidewalk. He shakes me by the shoulder and tells me to keep my head down.

"They just killed him Uncle Ngô."

More officers wearing gas masks walk out with hostages. They escort them to the paramedics who sit them on the curb and check them for injuries. When the shooting stops, Uncle Handsome Harlemite flings the negotiator's arm away and stands up.

"Pham," he yells. Uncle Handsome Harlemite runs toward the bank, checks the hostages sitting on the curb. Other officers walk past him and enter the bank to survey the loss.

"Pham," he yells again, his voice hoarse.

Uncle Ngô sits up and draws me near so that I'm pressed against his chest. He covers my other ear so that I can't hear Uncle Handsome Harlemite cry out for her. But even over the static and squawks of the walkie-talkies, the loud chatter from what remains of the crowd, the police officers conferring with each other, the paramedics shouting for oxygen and bandages, I can hear Uncle Handsome Harlemite yelling for her as he enters the bank. And I begin to cry again, knowing she is dead. I know this as the sheets are being placed over the bodies. If she were alive, even hurt, she'd respond to his calls. She'd get up from off the floor just to see us again. If she were alive, she'd do that. The smoke clears and I want it to linger for a while longer so that I don't see what I know.

Inside the bank, Uncle Handsome Harlemite stands over several bodies. He looks down at those about his feet, and for a long time he doesn't move.

"Come here Long-Vanh." It is Mother standing in front of an antique shop along with Mia, Phượng, and

Yên. "We'll wait for Pham right here."

I want to tell her it is not possible. If she were alive, she'd get up from off the floor, feel her daughters' arms around her.

The paramedics make their way inside the bank with stretchers and gurneys. They wheel out the wounded with oxygen masks affixed to their faces and carry out the dead on stretchers covered with white sheets.

"Where are you, Pham?" Uncle Handsome Harlemite cries out from within the bank. "Where are you?"

I can hear someone insist for him to calm down. "He's not allowed in here; now get him out, dammit!"

They load the wounded and dead into the ambulances, shut the doors, turn on their sirens as they drive off, and more officers enter the bank to survey the damages. The officers busy themselves sending away the crowd. Though it is still filmy inside, and all the bodies have been taken away, the officers are in the bank counting and identifying shells on the bloodstained floor.

Aftermath

When they carried out the dead, they had covered them with white sheets. The living had oxygen masks, or they simply lay unconscious on the gurneys with a blanket drawn up to their chest. Aunt Pham Thi was not one of them.

Mother holed herself inside the house for weeks. Dad continued to go to work. When he came home, he found Mother curled up on the couch or in the bedroom. He never said a word to her, not even a "Good evening" or "Good bye" or "Good morning." He simply came home, fixed dinner, and watched a little television before going to sleep. Some mornings I'd find him on the couch, sleeping in an upright position, and when he finally woke up, took a shower, he still looked like no amount of sleep could erase the sluggish way he carried himself off to school and work. Even when he studied he didn't seem interested as he calculated numbers, always sighing and erasing mistakes only to start over.

For two weeks, Mother wore the same clothes after showering and brushing her teeth. The jeans and T-shirt she wore were wrinkled to the point where the creases gave the appearance that she was fading. She didn't say a word and I didn't try getting her to speak.

I woke up every day and went to school as usual. It was funny. When I was there, I didn't think about the bank, Mr. Gouché and Mr. Yi, Uncle Handsome Harlemite enraged, his daughters crying, all the blood, Connie

Chung. I participated in class and received all the attention from my teachers; they were amazed at how quickly
I learned my multiplications and fractions and divisions
with all their remainders. Fat Chan was dead.

We later learned that he was one of the gunmen, but
I went to class each day never thinking about him, never
worrying about spitballs in my afro or looking over my
shoulders after school.

Only when I walked home did I think about that evening and what was lost because my walk home took me by
Hernandez's Sew Yourself. I couldn't help but look inside
hoping to see Mother sitting at the Singer in front of the
shop, away from the Mexican women and their children,
but mainly to see Aunt Pham Thi sticking yellow safety
pins to the hems of dresses she just finished. No matter
how many times I reminded myself she was dead, I still
looked inside the way the tongue automatically felt for a
tooth only to discover there was only a gap where it should
be.

I walked over the little hill and every Monday I expected to see Tú Đức deep inside a trash can, emptying it
of its contents, seeking its worth. Uncle Ngô told me that
he had to go and identify his body in the morgue since Yên
was scared to do so. He told me it was Tú Đức, though a
part of his skull had been chipped away and there was this
big gash, he said, a wide gaping hole staring at him. He
could see the inside where a large portion of the brain was
gone. And his mouth, Uncle Ngô told me, was open, the
corners stretched at the sides as though he were about to
scream, but that part of the brain that allowed him to do
so was already gone and so he couldn't complete what he

wanted to yell. He did take the laughing Buddha with its chipped corner from around Tú Đức's neck and gave it to Yên. She did not want it, so he gave it to the mortician to be buried with him.

Every day on the way home I also passed by the apartment. Most days I'd see Uncle Handsome Harlemite's car parked in the dirt lot, but I never went up to see them, except today.

I climb the steps to their apartment and just as I raise a fist to knock on the door, I stop myself and realize not only where I am but the possibilities of what may happen. I turn away and quietly walk back down the steps, hoping no one heard me, but when I make it to the bottom, I stop and look up to where I stood. Before I can think it over, I climb the steps two at a time and knock.

A chair scrapes the kitchen floor and Phượng says, "Don't worry, I'll get it."

The door opens just a crack, and Phượng's eyes grow larger.

"Hi," I say, trying to smile.

She opens her mouth to speak. Instead she squeezes through the tight space she allows for herself and closes the door behind her.

"What are you doing here?" she insists.

My lips twitch, and I feel ridiculous for smiling. "I just came by to see how you are doing. How are you?"

Phượng crosses her arms in front of her and looks at the doormat.

"You shouldn't be here," she whispers. "Dad is…" She looks up.

"What?"

"You shouldn't be here," she raises her head. "He's drinking right now. He starts when he wakes up and he just keeps drinking until he goes to sleep in the afternoon. Then he wakes up and begins again." She unfolds her arms. "Mia stays away most of the time. I don't blame her because he tells her she looks like a slut. Then the next minute he tells her how much she looks like mommy and he begins to cry."

I watch her the whole time she speaks, and when she finishes, I look down.

"He cusses at your mom and dad and Uncle Ngô, and the police officers." Phượng's face scrunches up like she doesn't know what to say next. "He calls up your dad late at night and cusses him out, too. Did you know that?"

"No," I say, and look away, remembering I overheard Dad telling someone on the phone to calm down. But Dad never hung up the phone. He stayed on however long it took to get the person off the phone so that he could go back to sleep.

We stand there looking at our tennis shoes. I listen for the sound of Uncle Handsome Harlemite's footsteps approaching the door but it is quiet inside.

"No one comes to visit us. Not Yên, your mother or father. Uncle Ngô did once. He came over and stayed for a short time. He brought us *simoi*. Dad sat at the dinner table. He paid no attention to Uncle Ngô. He just sat there, and Uncle Ngô kept talking to us, and you could tell he didn't feel like being here, so he left."

"Do you want to spend the night at my place? A couple of nights, even?" I ask.

"Can I?"

"Of course. You need to get anything?"

She shakes her head and begins walking downstairs. I follow her and wonder if Mother will mind her staying with us, or if she'll actually speak now that someone else is staying over. When we climb the steps to my house, I know Uncle Ngô is home because above us comes the crank of the socket wrench tightening a bolt. Phượng says hello, and Uncle Ngô does a double-take. The motorcycle is on blocks. The chrome parts shine so bright that I squint. Before standing up he sets the wrench on the ground and wipes his hands with a rag.

"Hi Phượng," he says.

"She's staying for a couple of days," I tell him. "She's going to stay in my room," I add.

"Good. Very good."

"The bike looks good," Phượng says.

After wiping his hands he goes on to wipe each finger and says thank you. Phượng and I go inside and it is no surprise to find Mother sleeping on the couch.

"Just like your Dad: she stays home and does nothing."

"She drinks?"

"No. Maybe she should. Maybe it'll get her to talk at least."

"No," Phượng shakes her head. "It will only make her worse."

········

Because I have a twin size bed, I am on the floor talking up to Phượng. The geckos cling to the window screen. They dart about for the mosquitoes and gnats, and Phượng lets out a *humph* once in a while.

"They do this every night. Uncle Ngô says they are my ancestors here to protect me from bad dreams. I guess they're your ancestors as well."

"Does it work?"

I nod before answering yes. "The nights they are not around, I have nightmares. Sometimes I wake up scared. Each insect they eat means they're getting rid of bad dreams."

"*Humph.* Then I should have a good night's sleep."

We remain quiet for some time watching the geckos feed off the screen. Mother is at the dinner table writing a letter to Lý Loê. I have heard her tear the sheet from the pad and crumple it, sigh, then begin again. A couple of times, there comes the crumpling of paper a short time after starting and I know she's trying to pick the right words. Dad is getting only four hours of sleep before he has to work at eleven p.m. But then the phone rings and before the second ring finishes, Dad answers it.

There is silence for a while before Dad even speaks, and Phượng sits up in bed and says, "It's my dad."

"You're in no condition Harlemite. Yes she's here. She's sleeping. It's no one's fault. I need to get to sleep."

I can hear the bed creak from his sitting up, and then he shifts his weight when sitting at the edge.

"It's no one's fault. You need sleep."

Phượng gets out of bed and closes the door to what she has heard every night in her own home.

The Land South of the Clouds

Mother walks out the front door and heads to the mailbox. She lowers the door, squints inside, reaches a hand in, and pulls out a bundle of mail. As she goes through each piece of mail, Mother mouths the name or company on each envelope before tossing it to the ground. She goes through the bundle quickly and reaches inside for the next stack. Bills and letters pile all around her feet, and still she pulls out more, mouthing one name after another so that they become one continuous word.

She reaches in and shovels out all the letters, and she doesn't pause until she comes across a clutter of envelopes with blue stripes along the edges. But she continues, reaching inside and sweeping them all onto the patio. The letters cascade down the steps and onto the street below.

She cleans out the last of the letters before peering inside the mailbox. Mother reaches in with her right hand. The box swallows her arm whole. Her armpit is butted up against the edge. She cranes her head back and shuts her eyes against the sun, and grunts. Sweat forms over her brows, and her neck is beginning to glisten. She pulls but only manages to keep her armpit from touching the mailbox. Her body curves taut from her pulling.

Still, she strains with the box. Her arms shake. Her legs tremble so much that more than once they buckle from under her, but she catches herself each time. The blouse is wet against her body. Streaks of sweat fall along the sides of her temples and collect at her chin. Mother bares her teeth as she pulls, and her elbow is now exposed. She stops for a moment and pants. Before continuing, Mother breathes in through her nose and blows air from her mouth in quick spurts. Her grunting gets louder.

"Long-Vanh. Help. Me."

I wrap my arms around Mother's waist.

"Pull," she forces the word.

I tighten my hold around Mother and together we pull. Her stomach tightens, and I feel it fill up and deflate with each breath. We go at it for some time until she says, "Okay. Let go."

I stand aside to watch. Mother relaxes her whole body, takes in a couple of deep breaths, fixes her hold on the object inside the box and takes in one last breath. Leaning away from the mailbox, she yanks and out comes what she has been reaching for all these years. Mother ends up on the ground with her back against the patio's ledge, catching her breath. Her eyes shut to slits and the lids waver as she struggles to keep them open. An old man stands before us. His clothes are wrinkled like the flesh around his neck.

He stands doubled over from old age. His hair is as white as the dress shirt he wears. The sleeves are long; the cuffs cover his knuckles. He straightens up like a flower at dawn. His eyes are closed. He stretches the tendons in his neck, and his balled fists open. I can see the outline of his ribs against his shirt. They stick out at places: poorly mended bones that stretch the skin around the area.

He lifts his head and I see that his eyes are shut tight. He pries them open against the sun's brightness, blinking repeatedly before he is able to keep them open. The muscles beneath his eyes twitch as he squints at the tall skyscrapers in downtown Los Angeles. The freeways are knotted up by traffic and the tops of buildings choke from the brown smog. The man's shoulders slacken.

"Long-Vanh." Mother calls from the patio floor. "This is your grandfather, Lý Loĉ."

·········

Because it has been years since he last slept in a bed, I have to share mine with Lý Loĉ. We lie facing the window. Moonlight comes through and casts the geckos' shadows against the walls. The geckos are out in large numbers, and we watch as they wait and catch insects. Lý Loĉ places both hands behind his head and lets out a sigh.

"They remind me of my wives," he says. "They wait and take."

I turn my head to look at him. I can barely make out his words. They come out warbled, come from a mouth filled with crudely healed cuts and the broken jaw that never realigned right. When he speaks, a corner of his mouth stretches downward from the weight of syllables.

"That plump one there," he brings one hand from behind his head and points at a gecko in the middle of the window screen. "That is Thành. She was always greedy. It was hard to keep her because she wanted everything: jewelry, gambling money, jade, and opium. I kept her for as long as I did because she was my first wife. At least she was faithful."

The bed slightly moves when he shakes his head. Thành, the plump gecko, scrambles for a moth; she is always moving. At times, she crawls over another gecko to snatch at the moths.

"But that one there," he points at the lower corner of the

screen. "You see her?—the little one?"

Among the geckos a small one stays in one place as those around her dart here and there.

"That is Yên, my youngest wife. So obedient is she. Very small and quiet. She never asked much from me. Be careful of the shy ones Long-Vanh. They play timid, but they are not, especially in bed. Her sexual appetite is insatiable. She wanted me all the time. Sometimes I had to hide from her. Sometimes I had to beg her no more. She always wanted to go again even when I wasn't erect. I am old. I was old then. But she would pout and beg, and she didn't care about jewelry or money or opium."

Lý Loĉ sighs. I turn my head to watch his profile. His eyes are half closed from dreaming.

"Her breasts were small, her nipples always perky. They were so hard that I thought if I suckled them long enough they would erupt ripe with the sweetness of figs, thick and syrupy."

"Lý Loĉ," I say.

Lý Loĉ's eyes open wide and he blinks several times before turning in my direction.

"Yes?"

"I'm only ten."

He stares at me for a long time before he says, "Oh."

········

It is not the sun coming in through the window that wakes me up, but someone's breath warming my face. Lý Loĉ sits beside me in bed. He is dressed in the clothes he wore yesterday afternoon when Mother pulled him from the mailbox.

"I need your help," he says. "I cannot do this alone."

Lý Loc leads me out onto the patio, and the first thing I see are big green mountains, a green lush in color, a green daily drenched with water. These are not the ones I am used to—brown and faded in appearance—but mountains that seem to be alive, breathing.

"I need your help," he says again, the corner of his mouth stretching and closing to complete the p *sound.*

The door to the mailbox is open, and there are clumps of red clay and blades of grass pasted around the edges. Lý Loc reaches in with one hand and his whole arm is swallowed up by the box.

"Come, Long-Vanh. Take a hold of me."

I wrap my arms around him and I can feel his ribs and how they stretch his skin. The way they protrude in places sickens me.

"Hold tighter," he says.

He leans away from the mailbox, and I pull, afraid we will go over the ledge if what he is tugging on suddenly gives. The mailbox begins to tremble. Lý Loc grunts as he grits his teeth. He slackens a bit before yanking, and dense green water gushes from the mailbox. The stream is so strong that it shoots over us, over Montana Avenue down below, over the houses across the street. The currents snake their way to downtown; they uproot trees and swallow houses whole and carry off cars. The green body of water curves around the newly planted mountains. The currents slow down as the water level settles.

I stand beside Lý Loc, silent and unblinking.

"The Mekong Delta," he motions with his hand.

• • • • • • • •

We take a junk to get to the mountains. The man work-ing the oars is wearing a sun hat to hide his face. His black pajama shirt is buttoned to the neck though the sleeves are rolled up to his elbows. His forearms flex with each rotation of the oars, and a crop of veins surface thick and permanent from beneath the landscape of muscles and skin.

The weather is no longer what it used to be. The air is heavy with water. Our shirts cling to our wet bodies, and we lean over the side of the junk to wring sweat from our clothes.

"Maybe I should have left the weather behind," he smiles as he takes up a portion of the hem in both hands.

I can see his ribs where they have cracked and the spaces between the breaks. Purple markings point out where these breaks occurred.

"But if I had, you would not get mountains as green as these," he points toward the horizon.

Drifting by our junk are what are left of trees. Tables and chairs, bottles and aluminum cans, clothes and chil-dren, men and women stay afloat and roll with the strong currents. Other Vietnamese people in boats cast out fishing nets to catch the debris floating by and haul them in. Their sons and daughters untangle the debris, keeping what is use-ful.

We make our way beneath freeway underpasses, and we have to lie low because the water is too high. Cars are still on the exposed backs of freeways, stuck and waiting, useless and ridiculous. The man rows the boat between the twin towers of the Atlantic Richfield Company. Men in undone three-piece suits and women in lace-collared dresses bang on the tinted windows as we pass by. The rower gets us past the skyscrapers and out into the open where the air is heavier. I have to take off my shirt and twist it, but when I look up, I catch Lý Loc staring at my chest and ribs. He sees how thin I am, how the skin stretches tight over my ribs and how each one is spaced equally apart from one another. I put my shirt back on.

········

The rower ties his junk to the pillar of a wooden pier. Lý Loc gets out first and he helps me up. We walk hand in hand toward the other fishermen carrying baskets of catfish and buckets of eels from the boats to the backs of awaiting trucks. The ground is wet and littered with fish guts. Gulls and blackbirds waddle around feeding off the ground.

"Where are we going?" I ask.

"Home," Lý Loc says.

As we walk away from the river, away from the stench of fish and salt, I turn to look behind me. The skyscrapers of downtown Los Angeles stand in water, and the houses and apartments have long drowned and died and are now homes for eels and fish and stray octopuses, squids, and sharks who mistook the salt of the Mekong for the ocean. The air is brown over there, brown and thick, and Dad is entangled in sleep.

········

We ride in the back of a motorized rickshaw. The driver winds through a shaded road lined with tall mai trees in full bloom. Their petals catch the light of the sun, and as we *speed by, the trees are ablaze. Mother is smiling the whole time. I don't know when she appeared. The wind loosens her hair she keeps in a bun. Thin strands wrap about her face and neck, and across her lips and teeth, but Mother doesn't clear her mouth of them.*

We leave the tree-lined road and pull out into the open where stretched on either side are rice paddies. The stalks are tall and each blade is stiff and golden in the sunlight. From above the tops of stalks, I can see the backs of men and women stooped over, planting. Their heads come up for a quick moment when they walk forward, only to stoop again.

We pass up other men and women walking alongside the roads with bamboo poles shouldered behind their necks. Hanging at each end is a basket filled with eggs, mangoes, freshly picked lychees, bunches of bok-choy, water cress, eels, and catfish. We leave trails of dust, which veil the people we pass, but they keep walking with heads up, hands gripping each end of the bamboo shoots for balance.

The motorized rickshaw pulls into a small village of bungalows and two-story villas with porches. Lý Loĉ gets out first and helps Mother out. He reaches for my hand, but I am already climbing out on the other side. The rickshaw drives around in a circle and heads back in the direction of the rice fields.

Lý Loĉ and Mother climb up the wooden steps and enter a home whose double French doors are already opened.

"But what about Dad?" I ask as I follow right behind them.

Mother turns around and her lips quiver.

"But we're home," Mother says.

The corners turn up again, and her eyes widen. She

turns away from me and walks inside the house.

· · · · · · · ·

It is the afternoon, siesta time, and for someone who is bent, broken, and scarred, Lý Loĉ walks well ahead of me. His hands part the branches, clear away the vines from his face. Although the mai *trees are ablaze with yellow flowers, the jungle is dark the farther we walk. In a small clearing a hammock stretches between two tall banyan trees. Lý Loĉ climbs inside. It is big enough for both of us. He helps me inside, and the hammock sways from my effort.*

"Remember this?" he smiles as he settles back into the meshing. "I used to take you here for a siesta. Remember?"

I lie next to him.

"Yes. I remember."

Lý Loĉ bridges his hands behind his head and sighs.

"Some afternoons you were awakened by the sound of bombings in the distance."

Just then there is a rumbling far off in the distance like pent up anger. The hammock still swings and I cannot tell if the Earth is moving.

"You were afraid. Do you remember what I told you?"

I frown and shake my head.

"No?" His eyes become round. "I told you, 'Do not worry. It is only the dead playing in heaven's field.' Remember?" He smiles. "'The land south of the clouds is heaven's playing field.'"

I erase the frown from my face and say, "Yes. Now I remember."

"And you would stare up into the trees and try to see them in the sky. You would always ask, 'Where? I don't see

them. Where are they?' And I told you, you could not see them, but you could hear them. You fell back asleep trying to see them."

Another rumbling comes. This time it is closer. I stare up and I can barely make out the blue sky through the trees' leaves and thick branches, branches so huge they hold up the sky.

....

"Stir. Keep stirring," Mother commands.

The stove is too high and I'm standing on a stool in order to look inside the pot to see what I'm stirring. The broth, thick and dark, parts from the ladle I grip with both hands.

Mother is in the living room, surrounded by Lý Lộc's wives all standing still as flowers atop foot stools. Tape measure dangling from her shoulders, a red pencil tucked behind one ear, she moves from one to the other, inserting pins in frayed hems, measuring arm lengths, cutting patterns from different fabrics, fitting sleeves, tucking cuffs to expose their thin white wrists, measuring seams, drawing lines down the length of the gowns, cutting away excess material, darning buttons, stitching clasps and hooks, and all this she manages to do without tripping over the floor strewn with unfurled rolls of satin, silk, and muslin, tomato-shaped pin cushions, and spools of thread.

"Stir," Mother says again. "Just stir."

I keep stirring. My arms tire from the thickening broth. In one rotation of the ladle, a fish tail surfaces and sinks, the severed head comes up, the puckered lips swallow broth, and the eyeballs stare up at me before disappearing.

. . . .

Evening, and everyone is gathered at the dinner table: Mother, myself, Lý Loĉ, and his seven wives. The wives are dressed in their new áo dàis, their tunics buttoned. With chopsticks in hand, Thành lashes at the food in the center of the long table, never failing to pick up marinated sliced pork, slices of cucumber, clumps of rice, strands of fried noodles, or snatching a piece already in the grasps of another's chopsticks. Yên sits there with her bowl of rice cupped in her palm, waiting to take after the melee is over.

I ask, "When are we going back? I miss Dad. I miss home."

Mother and Lý Loĉ look at each other from across the table. Mother opens her mouth wide to speak, but Lý Loĉ intervenes and says, "Tomorrow. We go back tomorrow. We have two homes. It is only fair."

Vu-An dips into the tureen and plucks an eyeball from beneath the dark broth.

. . . .

The noises of Lý Loĉ and his wives wake me up. Their hands smooth over each other's skin, reshape bones, and arms and legs twine like rope, like vines. Their disjointed hushed breaths fuse into hisses and finally there is one breath rising and falling, one breath that fills the room. In the dark, they start off as eight; they twine and become one swathed in sweat, saliva, semen, and sheets.

I go to the kitchen for a ladle of water from the bucket. In the dim, Mother is at the large chopping table, cleaver in hand. A child's clothes are on the floor. She wipes the sweat from her forehead with the back of her hand before turning the child onto his back and begins. Blood covers the whole table and drips onto the floor, collecting in large pools. She sees me. Mother stares at me for a long time while she tries to catch her breath.

"He always bothered me. He was a bad child," she explains.

She grips the boy's wrist, holds up his arm so that she can get a clean swing at his elbow. She hacks at it several times before it gives. Still holding the forearm by the wrist, she turns it over in her hand, observing the meat. Tossing the forearm into a cauldron, Mother takes the stump at the elbow and chops at the boy's shoulder.

·········

Home, and we share a bed again. The moonlight shines through my window and the geckos are swollen from eating so much. Lý Loĉ and I sit facing each other with our legs tucked underneath us, he has his hands on his knees to support the weight of his voice carrying him forward. I lean just the same to see him in the dark and to hear him whisper.

"We ate sugarcane out on the porch. When you were three, we'd eat them out on the porch. Remember?"

I think of sucking the sweet thin strands from between my teeth. Before I can answer him, he continues.

"Of course you remember. Remember the marketplace?—the buckets crammed with eels, crabs, fish, and sea urchins?"

The words pass from his lips, contorted to accommodate syllables and inflections of a language he just learned, and always his lips yield to the limits of what his crudely healed scars will allow him to manage. His voice grows harsher with excitement, and spit collects at the corners.

"No," I cut him off. "No. No, I don't remember doing such things. I am not allowed to. Mother told me never to dream of you. She told me I was too young to remember you, so I don't dream of you."

Lý Lôc's eyes remain wide open as he sits up. His mouth is open. He leans forward again insisting I remember them. Words spout from his mouth so fast that the spit at the corners of his lips begins to drip on his shirt, and I want to wipe them. Instead I shake my head.

He begins to wilt and turn pale. His shoulders slump within his pajama shirt and his head lowers until he falls over onto his side and curls up. Both knees come up until they touch his chest and his arms wrap around his ankles.

⋯⋯⋯

Mother screams, "They're here! They're here!"

Lý Lôc and I join Mother out on the front patio. Down below on Silver Lake Avenue men in black pajamas and pith helmets tote machine guns. They march down the center of the street, stop in front of a house and go inside. There are shots before men, women, and children come out with hands behind their backs. And I recognize them— Koreans, Chinese, Japanese, and Vietnamese people we pass on our way to work. They continue down the streets rounding up everyone. Still, shots are fired but no bodies lie in the streets.

Coppola stands beside a cameraman, directing him as to where to point the lens. He cups his hands around his mouth and shouts down to them, "Don't look at the camera! Keep moving! Keep moving! Don't look at the camera, goddammit!"

"When you brought Vietnam, you brought them also."
Mother says. She slumps to her knees and cries in her hands.

The men in black pajamas continue to run down the
streets and trample through gardens, break windows with
the butts of their machine guns, and burst through front
doors. They come out with more people surrendering their
hands to the air. Black smoke escapes from the windows of a
few houses before blazes eat them from the inside out.

"Lý Loê," Mother looks up at him from the patio ground.
"Make them go away. Make them go away."

Lý Loê turns away from the ledge and stares at the black
mailbox. He walks to it and pulls down the door. Bending
over to look inside, Lý Loê reaches in and feels around, head
turned up to the sun. But he reaches in farther and puts his
head inside. He wiggles his body until he is swallowed whole
by the mailbox.

The men in black pajamas run up Montana Avenue.
Their arms barely swing as they hug their machine guns
to their chests. Mother stands up and wipes her eyes as the
men jog up the steps.

"That's it, that's it. Keep moving," Coppola yells. "Keep
moving, but don't look at the camera."

Without stopping, they run to the mailbox. Like smoke
sucked through a vent, they funnel into the mailbox. With
them follows the Mekong snaking its way up Montana Av-
enue. The mountains melt into the rice fields, and with the
low clouds, they drift across downtown Los Angeles and pass
through the mailbox. Even Coppola, the man who claims he
is Vietnam, passes through.

Everything. Everything Lý Loê brought from Vietnam is

gone, and there is only downtown Los Angeles: the Bonaven-
ture Hotel, the Sheraton, the twin towers of the Atlantic
Richfield Company, First Interstate Bank, other mirrored
skyscrapers, the Hollywood sign now muddy and brown, the
knotted freeways and a sea of cars. Mother is not standing
next to me, crying. She is gone.

Saving Grace

If there is one saving grace about the trip aside from seeing Mother and knowing she is alive, it is staying up late with Mother the night before Uncle Ngô and I drove back to Hồ Chí Minh City. Mother made tea and I did most of the talking. I told her everything: the simple wedding Phượng and I had on the patio and our honeymoon in San Francisco, Uncle Handsome Harlemite, about Dad's misunderstanding that night when Uncle Ngô told him to leave, and collecting all those articles over the years in hopes of locating her. She just listened.

I tell Uncle Ngô all of this during our layover in Bangkok while we sit and wait for those to get off and for others to board. He asks me if that is all; did she say anything else? I tell him that was it. I talked, she listened.

Uncle Ngô blows air from his mouth and looks down at his hands. He rubs them together, blows air noisily from his nose, and bites down on his bottom lip. He says he has kept it from me all these years because he didn't know how to tell me or when. He apologizes, says he should have told me before the trip, but he had hoped Mother would tell me.

"I guess your mother, she forget what she promise me when she leave."

Uncle Ngô took Mother to the airport some time after midnight seventeen years ago. She came to him while he was sleeping, and when he looked at her, he knew what she wanted. He refused at first, telling her he didn't want

327

a hand in her leaving, and so she went upstairs and called a taxi. Only when she waited outside with nothing but the clothes she wore, her green card, and passport, he waited with her. He told her not to go, but she kept quiet. When the taxi finally arrived, Uncle Ngô sent the driver off with a ten-dollar bill and told Mother to get into his car instead. He paid for her plane ticket to Bangkok and from there she would have to manage her way into Vietnam. But he took her and together they sat and waited for boarding call. The whole time they waited she explained her reasons for leaving. Aside from wanting to see Lý Lộc and to take care of him, it was because of Phạm's death. She blamed herself. She could not live in Los Angeles and face Phượng, Mia, and Uncle Handsome Harlemite. She placed all the guilt on herself.

"That day, she did two things wrong," Uncle Ngô says.

The two things Mother did wrong were that she did not think to get Phạm out of the bank. When she saw the gunmen, she only thought of herself, Phượng, and me. Worst of all, she ran for blocks never thinking of Phạm until she came to a stop.

"I try and tell her she was scared. It normal to be scared," Uncle Ngô says. "But she kept shaking her head. She think she should have stayed."

That was the second mistake. She didn't stay. Rather than running, she should have called out to Phạm, tell her to run, or try to get her out of there, past the gunmen, then they would stay together. That whole time Mother stood in front of the doors waiting for the outcome of the ordeal, she had wanted to go back inside to take her place, especially when the gunmen requested passage back to Vietnam. That would have been her way out had everything gone as planned.

But things did not turn out the way she wanted them to, and so the two mistakes she made equally bothered her. Because of this she went into a deep depression. Those couple of weeks she moped around the house not saying a word to anyone, she thought about two things: Pham's death was her fault, and she had to return to deliver the news in person.

"She could not face Pham's family. That day Phượng come to sleep oh-ver-night, she decide to leave."

When Uncle Ngô is through, things begin to fall into place. It explains why I felt dizzy that day Phượng and I waited outside the coroner's office. It was the way Uncle Ngô carried himself, the lack of emotions he showed toward Uncle Handsome Harlemite's death. Uncle Ngô was so distracted by what he had done that he forgot to take off his gloves. The whole time he was in the coroner's office, he decided then as he stared into the gaping hole in Uncle Handsome Harlemite's head that he would keep Mother's promise a secret. If anything bothered him about Uncle Handsome Harlemite's death, it was that when he returned from the airport that morning, he drove by the apartment on his way home. He said he slowed down since the sun hadn't risen yet, and he saw Uncle Handsome Harlemite's silhouette in the window. He was pacing. Those were the two things that kept him silent that day: that he had driven Mother to the airport so she could disappear from our lives, and that he had seen Uncle Handsome Harlemite alive just hours before he shot himself. But most of all, he was thinking whether or not he did the right thing in driving Mother to the airport and if he would ever be able to keep it to himself. For seventeen years he carried this knowledge, and during that whole time he had hoped to find the right moment to tell me, and I think of Uncle Ngô going to bed every night, weighed down, not by dreams, not by a promise, but the weight of a Samsonite he doesn't even know existed.

He thought that day would come when Mother called me in Los Angeles to have us come out. We sit there and Uncle Ngô looks up at the air nozzle and I know he wants to reach up, even though it is open, and fiddle with it.

"At least you took her to the airport," I finally manage. "It was good she had you take her. She had someone to see her off. At least she wasn't alone."

Uncle Ngô nods. People begin to board the plane. They take long glances in my direction as they look for their assigned seats and when they stow their carry-on bags in the overhead compartments.

"She was never embarrass of you, Long-Vanh. It was never you."

• • • • • • • •

I've been in the lavatory since they turned off the seatbelt sign. I just sit here, picturing Uncle Ngô driving Mother to the airport, and I feel small and alone again like the day I realized she had left. Even smaller because she had help from someone else other than me. The first day I acted as though I didn't care, glad even that she was gone. But it hit me the next night when Dad and Uncle Ngô took Mia and Phượng out for pizza, and rather than go with them, I stayed home and watched television after doing homework. Although the television and lights were on, the house was quiet.

A particular commercial came on, one I had seen so many times. Someone placed a suitcase in a cage, and the gorilla walked around it, observing it for some time before pushing it over on its side. It grabbed the handle and began dragging the suitcase around the cage, even beating it against the bars while holding onto the suitcase. The gorilla threw the suitcase on the ground and stomped on it, beating it with both fists, trying to crack it open. The commercial ended with the name brand in large letters: Samsonite.

The realization that she was gone made me tremble. I went into my bedroom and opened my closet door and found the Samsonite where I had left it the night I brought it back inside. I dragged the suitcase from the closet, set it in the middle of the room, laid it flat on the floor, and undid the locks. I took one of the *áo dàis* and felt the material, sniffed it and thought I smelled Mother in the satin fibers of the dress. I set it aside, and as I brought out the others, a bundle of letters fell from between one of the dresses. I undid the rubber band and took the first one from its envelope, unfolded the pages, and the letters dressed in accent marks stared at me, taunting me to understand their meaning, and I wondered if I would ever learn Mother's language. I continued going through Mother's things and came across a manila envelope containing photographs, and one of them was the Labor Day picnic in which Mother put her arm around me and smiled. I went through all the photos and came across an 8 x 10 black and white photo of Lý Loc. The dress shirt he wore buttoned up to

the neck was as white as his hair, and the cuffs covering
his knuckles made him appear young like a child waiting
to grow into clothes two sizes too big. His jaw line was
narrow, chin pointed. Lý Loĉ's stern expression gave me
the impression he could command the camera when to
snap, not the photographer. I sat in the middle of the floor
among Mother's *áo dàis*, pictures, and letters staring at Lý
Loĉ.

Knowing she left everything behind made me cry.
Aside from the money, she took only her passport and
green card. Leaving me, Father, and Uncle Ngô, the dresses, the snapshots, and the letters was her way of saying
she didn't need any of us, none of the items around me, so
long as she went with her father in mind.

········

We arrive at LAX at 6:30 in the morning, go to customs to present our claims sheets of all the items we
brought back from our trip, and then leave the airport and
search the parking lot, and it's a nice sight to see Uncle
Ngô's Monte Carlo he's had for seventeen years, the same
car he said he would paint, but the restoration of the Harley consumed his time.

And I know he feels the same way, the way something
familiar is comforting even if you've seen it every day of
your life, but being away from it, whatever it is, and for
however long, it's comforting because you rely on it. It's
there and it won't leave you unless you part with it. Before
climbing inside the car after loading our suitcases inside
the trunk, he smooths his hand over the top of the car,
even smiles. And that is the same way I feel when we come

home from the back end of Montana Avenue so that Uncle Ngô can park the car facing downhill for when he gets up in two days to return to the shop.

"I sleep for long time. Maybe twen-tee-for hours. Maybe more. How-eh-ver long, you and Phượng not make much noise. Okay?"

I turn to him wondering if he actually thinks Phượng and I will do anything tonight. I want to tell him it's doubtful, but just as we're coming down Montana Avenue, I see Phượng pulling away from the curb and I realize it's 7:30, the time she leaves for work at a bank in Chinatown.

I want to tell Uncle Ngô to get out and go up to the house, let me take the car, or at least have him park immediately so I can climb into mine and follow Phượng, follow her down Montana Avenue, stop behind her at every sign, at every red light before crossing intersections, and then enter the on-ramp where I wait behind her, wait for the green light to allow us to enter onto the freeway and merge into traffic. But I want her to see me behind her, see that I've returned and that I'll be home when she gets off from work, waiting.

But her car is gone and Uncle Ngô parks in front of the garage.

....

I wake up at four in the afternoon, and I can hear Uncle Ngô snoring. After getting dressed, I go to the kitchen and grab three kitchen trash bags and leave the house for the garage. With the door wide open, there is enough sunlight for me to leave the overhead light off, and I begin removing the lids off shoeboxes and start dumping the contents into the trash bag.

After filling up two bags and knowing a third won't do, I head upstairs and take two more. Phượng is parking the car across the street by the time I get down there, and she does a double-take before she turns off the ignition. She gets out of the car, drapes her cardigan sweater over one arm, and slips the thin strap of her purse over one shoulder. She crosses the street and never blinks. I set the Hefty bag on the ground to meet her.

"Hi," she smiles and wraps one arm around me and kisses me.

When I feel her pull away, I wrap my arms tighter around her and breathe her in until she slips her other arm around me.

"I've missed you, Phượng."

I feel her go slack in my arms when she lets out air, and she says, "I've missed you, too."

When we finally part, she looks down to adjust the cardigan over her arm.

"So how was it? Seeing her?"

"It was all right," I sigh. "It was what I expected."

We look at our shoes, at the boxes and lampshades and chairs all around us, and I wonder how Uncle Ngô lived in such a small place all those years. Even with all the boxes and other junk removed, the place is only small enough for one car.

"Uncle Ngô?"

"Sleeping. He's been sleeping ever since we got back, so don't make too much noise."

"What are you doing?" she asks as she taps the Hefty bag with her foot.

"Cleaning." I reach down and grab the Hefty bag by the sides and open it.

Headlines and covers of magazines and pictures face up at us, and there comes an intake of breath from Phượng.

"You don't have to do that," she says after a while.

"No. I need to. I got to see her, Phượng. I got to spend time with her, speak to her. I know all there is to know. There's no point in keeping any of this. It's over."

"And how is she?"

"She's fine. She's where she wants to be. I'm fine too."

"Okay," her eyes become moist, and not wanting to cry, she moves in and hugs me. "Did you take out anything for dinner?" she asks.

"I woke up an hour ago. We can go out if you like."

"Sure. Let me change out of these clothes."

Phượng heads upstairs, and I continue emptying the contents of the shoeboxes into the trash bag. When I come to the next box, I lift its lid; I stop for a moment and stare at the photographs. I lift each one out of the box, and they are the photos Dad took of the Labor Day picnic at Griffith Park. And there are several where Mother is smiling, especially in the one where she has her arm around me. I replace the lid on the shoebox and set it on the shelf next to the Buddha just above where Uncle Ngô's bed used to be, and there are only the bundles of letters left, the ones I showed Mother when I visited her. She didn't want them, so I took them back, unsure what to do with them.

I slip one letter from the envelope and unfold it, and I am met with words whose consonants and vowels are joined together by accent marks that hang off them, crescents and dots house them. The accent marks surrounding the consonants and vowels seem to beautify Ly Loč's time in the reeducation camp, to lessen the beatings and starvation, but the adornments are deceptive. There are accent marks that spear consonants through their mid sections while others pierce vowels diagonally or horizontally. I stare at the configurations and know that the markings dressing the words are signals and cues that dictated to the reader how they should be read, that if you want to know what is going on, you'll have to understand their marks. They will guide you in when to lower your tone or raise your voice. It's all in the syllable commanded by each marking, and if you can do that, then you'll understand the news.

But I just blink at the letters, at the words with their markings and I can't even begin to know how to pronounce them correctly. Mother understood them, understood how the accent marks mapped the years of Ly Loč's break and ruin before his release. Understood how to form the proper pitch according to the markings, understood the words would wall off her own son from knowing, and it was the reason why she denied teaching me how to speak her language when, as a little kid, I asked her.

"No," she said. And when I asked why not, she said, "If you mess up the pitch, you will make no sense. You always want to make sense."

The paper is worn to where I can see the words written on the backside, to where over time I'm sure the letters have taken on new meanings when the sides blend. I even step outside of the garage and hold up the single page to the blue cloudless sky and the sun is bright and blinding against the white. I try to distinguish the words, but the

faint blue ink grows fainter to where I can't tell if I'm reading the words on the front page forward.

The front door slams, and I hear the jingling of keys
as Phượng locks up. I quickly fold the letter, place it in
the envelope and slide it back with the others, wiggling
it underneath the rubber band. I stand there staring at
the bundle of letters in my hand, and Phượng makes her
way down, the keys sounding out the rhythm of her descent. Her shadow stretches across the sidewalk before she
comes into view, and she finds me standing in the garage.

"Ready?" she asks.

"Yeah, I'm ready," I say as I take the bundle and throw
it in the garbage bag. I take the other bundle and throw it
in the bag.

Phượng looks at her shadow, even moves one leg and
then the other to see her other self move as I tie the bag,
carry it out to the garbage can and place the lid over it. As
I lock the double doors to the garage, Phượng studies the
bamboo shoots that have grown thick and close together.

"So where do you want to go?" she asks as she looks
up at one of the tall shoots, even tugs on one of the leaves.

"I thought maybe we could walk down to Hoover
Street and have Thai or Mexican."

"Walk?" she looks at me.

"Yeah, walk." She looks down the sidewalk, down
Montana Avenue knowing that there is a steep descent after the Casa de Maria Apartments. And she's most likely
thinking about the climb after being full from a meal. "We
used to walk," I say.

"Yeah, but we were kids."

"I'll even hold your hand on the way down," I say.

She tosses her head back when laughing.

"We're still kids, Phượng. Come on."

She pockets the keys and I take her hand and we begin walking past the Casa de Maria Apartments. Already we're leaning back, careful not to turn our ankles from forcing our feet down too hard, and for a moment I think about Lý Loễ's letters in the trash can and wonder if I should get them out when we return from dinner. For a moment I regret having thrown them away, and I want to tell Phượng to wait just a second, to sit on the ledge of one of the houses, and run back and get them. But I remind myself the letters belong to Mother. They were never mine to keep.

I grip Phượng's hand tighter to where her head slightly turns to me. She looks straight ahead, even wiggles her fingers to get a better hold. With heads down, shoulders back, we continue to descend upon a place we've known since we were children.

Acknowledgments

In the spring of 1990, while attending California State University, Northridge, I work-shopped my first short story about growing up in Vietnam. I received some good criticism, but the one major critique I received was that I put too much into the eighteen-page story. Afterwards, a fellow classmate told me out in the hallway that I had good material, but that I shouldn't cram everything into so short a space and I should consider writing a collection of short stories or even a novel. Thank you, Harlan Hammack, for your advice.

I would like to thank Neil Connelly who, in 1996, spent a whole evening listening to me talk about my upbringing and background; to playwright, poet, and novelist Kenneth Robbins for believing I can be bigger than I imagined myself to be; Dorothy Robbins who has always been a keen reader and critic of all my work; Pulitzer prize winning writer Robert Olen Butler for being my first mentor in fiction and teaching me the importance of yearning, and Louisiana poet laureate Darrell Bourque for being my latter mentor and friend. You have been a godsend to the state of Louisiana and the arts. To your grandson, Bill Turley, who has supplied yet another great painting for my book cover.

I especially want to thank my mom, who left more than her father and family behind, but a whole country for what America could promise us, and what saddens me most is that you never returned to what is beautiful, and that is why in June/July of 2002, I made the trip back for both of us.

To my daughters, Layla and Naomi, and my wife, Robyn: one day, God willing, I will take you there.

Thanks to the following editors who included chapters in their journals: Lawrence-Minh Bui Davis, *Asian American Literary Review*; Paul Lai, *Kartika Review;* my former professor Mona Houghton, *Northridge Review;* Janet Hill, *Gumbo: Stories by Black Writers*; Jack Heflin, *turnrow*; and Russell Leong, *Amerasia Journal.*

And of course, to Mary Karnath Duhé, James D. Wilson, Michael Martin, and Melissa and Matthew Teutsch at UL Press for working with me once again to see that an important part of me came to fruition. I cannot thank you all enough.

Publication history for
The Land South of the Clouds:

"Chapter 5, Tuesday: Kill the Children." *Asian American Literary Review* 3 (2012): 246-49.

"Chapter 4: The Bone Orchard." *Kartika Review 2011 Anthology: Asian Pacific Islander American Literature.* Eds. Paul Lai et al. San Francisco: Kartika, 2011. 69-71.

"Chapter 4: The Bone Orchard." *Kartika Review* 11 (2011): 26-27.

"Chapter 3: Night: Lessons in Translations." *Northridge Review* (Fall 2011): 36-39.

"Chapter 25: August 15, 1979 Friday." *Northridge Review* (Spring 2008): 66-69.

"Chapter 34: The Land South of the Clouds." *Northridge Review* (Fall 2003): 50-59.

"Chapter 12: Tan Son Nhut Airport, Ho Chi Minh City, 1997." *Gumbo: Stories by Black Writers.* Eds. E. Lynn Harris and Marita Golden. New York: Doubleday/Broadway, 2002.

"Chapter 2: Monday." *turnrow* 2.1 (2002): 169-74.

"Chapter 1: Asia Minor, Los Angeles June 1979." *Amerasia Journal* 26.3 (2001): 133-36.